For a Wonderful lady.

7.

MW01105876

PRISONER OF HOPE

HELEN HARRIS

WESTBOW
PRESS®
A DIVISION OF THOMAS NELSON
& ZONDERVAN

WestBow Press books may be ordered through booksellers or by contacting:

WestBow Press
A Division of Thomas Nelson & Zondervan
1663 Liberty Drive
Bloomington, IN 47403
www.westbowpress.com
1 (866) 928-1240

ISBN: 978-1-9736-1138-7 (sc)
ISBN: 978-1-9736-1137-0 (hc)
ISBN: 978-1-9736-1139-4 (e)

Library of Congress Control Number: 2017918979

Print information available on the last page.

WestBow Press rev. date: 12/14/2017

This book is dedicated to my son, Jeffrey,
triumphant in life and in death.

FOREWORD

WHEN HELEN TOLD me she wanted me to write the foreword to *Prisoner of Hope*, I was honored. The writer's group, Living Stone, that we both belong to helped birth the book. I remember the first time Helen brought us a story from this book to our group. She fascinated us with a story about Jay William running away from his "prison" of abuse. After hearing this story, we knew knew there had to be more and we encouraged her to write them down and bring them to writer's group.

She then told us she wanted to put it all together cohesively and write a book because she promised her dad she would write his life story. We encouraged her to write it. In our group, however, we just got bits and pieces of his incredible life. The book you hold in your hands is the final result.

Helen is an intregal part of our writer's group, and her kind spirit encourages us each time we meet. She tells this story without blame or recrimination. She simply lays out the facts the way she understands them.

You will know what I mean when you read these pages. Jay William endures some horrendous abuse, but he never loses hope. His story is an inspiration to anyone going through tough times because his struggles only increase his faith.

Savor this book like a good cup of hot tea on a cool afternoon.

Patricia Robert
Orchids in the Cornfield 2005
Guild Song 2017

ACKNOWLEDGMENTS

MANY PEOPLE GAVE me support and encouragement as I worked on this book, and I am most grateful to them.

I thank my son-in-law, Jim Roy, for showing me how to take advantage of technology like my personal computer. Without his expertise, I don't know how I would have completed this project.

I thank my daughter, Lisa Roy, for spending countless hours editing my book.

I thank my husband, Joe, for giving me the freedom to write day and night. He never complained about the time I took to work on my project.

The words of encouragement I received from my children and grandchildren often kept me going when I became weary.

My cousins the Craigs were helpful and supportive, providing important family information.

Rachel, my illustrator, was only fifteen years old when she enthusiastically did the drawings for this book based only on email from me. I thank her for enhancing my book with her talent.

My sister, Velma, was a great source of information, and I appreciate her contributions.

I am grateful to the Living Stone Writers for words of wisdom and encouragement, especially when my inspiration failed.

Thanks to Jay William for entrusting me to write his story.

Most of all I thank my Lord and Savior for his help, and I pray that I honor him in this book. I pray that readers will see how he can turn tragedy into triumph.

—Helen Harris

CHAPTER 1

MARJORIE HAWKINS CLEANED her small two-bedroom home early that morning. The date was March 13, 1913, and her older children—Jerome, Wanda, and Loretta—were outdoors helping their stepfather, Red, water the family's early spring garden. They lived in a sharecropper house for free, but they were obligated to help their landlord with the crops. In the fall they harvested the cotton.

All of them would work in the fields from sunup to sundown, picking the cotton from the prickly open bolls. They would place it in the long sacks they wore on their backs. When a sack was full it was weighed and thrown into a wagon. The landlord would take the cotton to a gin where the tiny seeds were removed. The family could hope to make up to 50 percent of the money received for the raw cotton. In many cases, this was the sharecroppers' only income for the year.

They chopped the weeds out of the cotton in the late spring and summer months to assure a good crop. This too was a sunup-to-sundown job. They often received a small sum of money for the work—maybe a dollar a day.

Like most neighboring youngsters, Marjorie's children did not attend school regularly. She did her best to teach them the simple life skills like reading, writing, and arithmetic. The girls were in charge of labeling and counting the jars of canned food; they also kept a written inventory of the jars. They could read the mail that occasionally came to their home.

On this March morning, Marjorie hand-washed and ironed the family's clothes. She did this chore almost every day. *Just because we live in a sharecropper house doesn't mean my family has to look worn too,* Marjorie thought. She was proud of her family and of her simple life in Tipton County, Tennessee.

In the afternoon, Marjorie cooked a pot of beef stew, baked biscuits, and made a huge blackberry cobbler for her family. She was sure everyone would be hungry after working outdoors all afternoon and picking up the enticing aroma of dinner. A gentle breeze from the Mississippi River wafted through the windows.

Marjorie was feeling especially energetic this day. Her baby was due soon. This encouraged her to spend extra time with her youngest daughter, Catherine, who was two years old. Catherine's curly red hair and deep dimples brought a bright smile to her mother's face. Marjorie sang an old song she had heard picking cotton as a child.

> "I love to tell the story of unseen things above, of
> Jesus and his glory, of Jesus and his love. I love
> to tell the story because it is true."

"Someday I am going to learn the rest of the words to that song," she told Catherine. "Wouldn't it be nice to sing the song to Daddy? I wish I could remember the name of the family I heard sing the song. They were the friendliest and nicest people I ever met. Yes, we are going to find the rest of the words to that song. I know your daddy would be pleased if you sang it to him."

William Shamus Hawkins was known as Red by most of his family and friends. A short time back, he had wrestled under the name of the Red Irishman. He had curly, bright-red hair, a gift from his Irish mother. An amateur wrestler beginning at thirteen, he was quick and light on his feet. He was usually favored to win the matches held at the Lyceum Theatre on Second and Jefferson streets in downtown Memphis; the place hosted both amateur and professional wrestling.

In the summer of 1909, Red was scheduled to wrestle another amateur, who was from Chicago. The promotors considered them evenly matched. The event was widely advertised, and the Mississippi River steamboats brought in a large crowd. All tickets were sold, and people waited outside the building that afternoon, hoping to get inside.

Fired up and determined to win, Red tried a move he had been practicing for weeks but had not attempted in the ring. He sprang from the top rope and flew through the air toward his opponent but landed on his head and was knocked unconscious, losing the match. Worse yet, the severe injury ended his wrestling career.

Red could find no lasting relief from the headaches that troubled him. Having spent much of their savings trying to help him recover, his parents could no longer afford to live in Memphis. The family traveled to rural Randolph and moved into a vacant sharecropper home. The three of them helped with the cotton crop and were permitted to plant large vegetable gardens and to sell a portion of their crops in Memphis.

Marjorie never got tired of hearing how Red and his parents ended up in Randolph. She smiled at the thought that this almost-famous young wrestler was now her husband. She was a widow with three children when they married. Now twenty-eight, she was no less pretty—but my, oh my, did she feel contractions?

"Uh-oh, Catherine, I think it's time to ring the bell for your daddy to come to the house." Marjorie felt the familiar labor pains and winced as she rang the dinner bell to get her husband's attention.

Red heard the clanging and stopped what he was doing. "Something is up, Jerome!" he told the boy at his side. "Momma would not ring the bell unless there was a problem. Let's climb into the wagon and get up to the house quickly! Jerome, you drive please!"

As soon as Red set foot in the house, he knew it was time for the midwife. "Jerome, keep the wagon hitched because I want you to go and fetch Miss Pansy from the shantytown."

Pansy Jones was known to treat the poor and had delivered most of the babies in the Tipton County area, including Catherine. Pansy was a tall, stoutly built black woman who always wore a clean scarf on her head and a dress with a printed apron made from a flour sack. She had several children whom she ruled with a loud voice and a caring heart. Though she was busy with her own family, she always dropped everything to help women deliver their babies.

Jerome hurried the horses as fast as he could, but the deep ruts in the old dirt road slowed his pace. When he reached the shantytown, he had to ask for directions to Miss Pansy's place. He finally arrived at her home and told her why he was there. Miss Pansy instantly grabbed her worn shawl and the pair headed for the Hawkins home.

Meanwhile, Red was barking orders to Wanda and Loretta, the two older girls. "Tear up those old sheets while I build a fire in the kettle outside and boil the water," he told them.

They quickly finished ripping the sheets and piled them on the table for Miss Pansy. Then they went to Marjorie's room and asked if they could do anything else for her. Marjorie told them to check on little Catherine in the girls' room. They found her sound asleep. The two began laughing and making fun of their stepfather.

"Oh, I can see it now, Loretta," Wanda said. "He will make us fix pretty little Catherine's hair with a ribbon matching her pretty little dress. He is always buying Momma pretty fabric to make dresses for her and Catherine. I think he gave up on you and me dressing like ladies."

"If we did what he wanted us to do, we would be like the

Carter sisters," Loretta replied. "We would wear pretty dresses and we would go to church on Sundays. No way. I'll wear my overalls."

"I have a great idea!" Wanda said. "When Momma has her baby, we will volunteer to take precious Catherine for a walk and lose her in the woods. Can't you just hear her screaming and see her red hair all tangled and full of cocker burrs?" The girls were laughing so hard they woke up Catherine.

Marjorie heard the child crying and called for her two older daughters. "Momma, do you need us?" Loretta asked as they entered the room.

"Yes, did I hear Catherine crying? Is she okay now? Girls, please listen to me closely. I am going to need a lot of help caring for Catherine until I am strong again. Red is good to me, and I am asking you to be fair to him. I know your brother is not, but I expect better behavior from my girls, okay?"

"Yes, Momma, we will be the best girls in the entire countryside," Wanda said.

The two noted Red's smile and wink at this reply.

Suddenly they heard the wagon and Miss Pansy's loud voice. "Miss Hawkins, don't you worry. Miss Pansy is here to help you deliver your baby!"

The girls greeted her on the front porch. "Right this way, Miss Pansy," Wanda said.

"Girls," she snorted, "I know where Miss Hawkins's room is at. Why, I was here only a few years ago. Now get out of my way. I have a job to do. Mr. Red, you are going to have to join your boy on the porch. This is a woman's job."

"Miss Pansy, I will be out of your way soon," Red said with a smile. "I want just a minute with my wife and I will leave peacefully."

Miss Pansy returned in a huff five minutes later. "Out now!" she scolded, shooing him with her big apron like he was a housefly. "I will let you know when the baby is born."

A half-hour later, the baby arrived with a loud cry. "Mr. Red," Miss Pansy shouted, "you have yourself a healthy young man with curly dark-brown hair like his momma. You can see him just as soon as he is cleaned up." She let the girls help her do that. Then they dressed the baby in the clothes his mother had made for the occasion.

Wanda and Loretta were fascinated with the new baby boy.

"Loretta, isn't he the cutest thing you've ever seen?" Wanda said. "Hey, young man, you are going to be so loved. You are one handsome little boy."

Red and Jerome walked into the room to greet the new baby. Red sat in a chair by Marjorie's bed, and Miss Pansy put the baby in his arms. "Thank you, darling," Red told his wife, giving her a quick kiss. "You knew I wanted a boy with your hair color. He is so handsome and favors you."

Catherine heard all the voices and waddled into the room. She was surprised to see a baby in her daddy's arms. Red put his arm around her, and she looked at him with questioning eyes. "Catherine, this is your new baby brother. Come and say hi to him."

Her eyes got large and she asked, "Jay? Jay?"

Marjorie smiled and said, "Yes, that is his name, honey. His name is Jay William Hawkins."

"And that is a good name," Red said. "Jay William Hawkins. I love his name."

With that, Miss Pansy said, "I must be getting home to my own children."

Red stood up and told Jerome to give Miss Pansy two of the frying chickens from the yard. Jerome got two, tied their legs together, and carried them to the wagon.

Miss Pansy gave the chickens an admiring grin and said, "They are nice-size fryers!" She climbed into the wagon, rejecting Jerome's help. The two then headed back for the shantytown.

Wanda, Loretta, and Catherine crawled into their bed. Tired from such a busy day, they fell asleep immediately.

As Jerome drove back to his house in the dark, his mind was filled with many thoughts. He put the horses in the barn as he had always done. He stood outside for a while thinking about his life. He thought about his own daddy, who had taught him by example everything he needed to know about taking care of the women in their family.

Jerome entered the house and slowly pulled out the rollaway bed from behind the stove in the living room. He pulled off his shoes, socks, and pants and crawled into bed. Pulling the covers up to his waist, he tried to sleep but could not stop the thoughts flooding his mind.

There had been too much excitement this day. Jerome had been trying to figure out how to get Red to leave so he could regain his position as man of the house.

This baby boy really messes things up, Jerome thought. *I saw how Loretta and Wanda looked at him with pride and listened to their silly comments about him. I am not going to let this son of Red's ruin my life by making Red my momma's favorite. Momma will give all her time to Jay William, and Red will be right there at her side. Then where will I be? Left to take care of the fields and the horses and everything else, that's where!*

I don't think Red deserves my respect; he broke my trust by marrying my momma and keeping it a secret from me. They didn't tell me for almost a year. I'll have to come up with another plan to make Red leave. I will get Wanda and Loretta's support somehow.

The thought put a smile on Jerome's face and he fell asleep.

CHAPTER 2

SUMMER NIGHTS WERE special at the Hawkins house. Though the porch was hot and dusty, it was the family's gathering place. This night was no different. Jay William was now five months old and a delight to his parents and his sisters.

Catherine was forever at his side playing with him, and Wanda and Loretta were surprised that they didn't mind caring for him. Sometimes they resented the responsibility of watching over Catherine while Momma attended to Jay William, but he was such a good baby that it was hard to hold a grudge against him. Tickling his toes or blowing raspberries on his tummy made the girls laugh almost as much as it did Jay William. Sadly, Jerome spent as little time as possible with his baby brother and for the most part ignored him. He stayed busy around the place, keeping the barn cleaned and the horses fed while brooding over his low place in life.

Marjorie had completed most of the canning of the vegetables and had even canned fish that the family had caught over the summer. This part of the evening was a time to relax and to rest up for the next day's chores.

As on many other nights, Wanda and Loretta sat on the front steps of the porch watching their momma and Red play with Catherine and Jay William. Loretta took a piece of string out of her pocket, and the two girls played cat's cradle. Jay William rested on his daddy's chest, and Catherine sat between her momma and daddy. Red's rich baritone voice soothed everyone who heard him sing. He cleared his throat and sang a lullaby to Jay William.

"Hang your head over and hear the wind blow.
On the wings of the wind over dark rolling deep,
Angels are coming to watch o'er thy sleep.
Angels are coming to watch over thee.
Hang your head over and hear the wind blow."

Catherine pulled on Red's sleeve and said, "Daddy, I want to sing to my baby brother too. Can you please teach me the words?" Red sang a simple lullaby to her, and after hearing it twice, she joined in, singing,

"I see the moon and the moon sees me.
God bless the moon and God bless me.
There is grace in the cottage and grace in the hall.
And God's grace is over us all."

Marjorie breathed in a rare moment of happiness. She did not deserve such joy in her life. After all, her older children were still not happy with her choice of Red as their stepfather, and their selfish ways troubled her. She did not dare bring up the subject because she did not want to break the special bond between her and Red and her little ones. *Best to let sleeping dogs lie*, she thought as Loretta and Wanda took off for the barn to tease Jerome into catching fireflies with them. She and Red sat for a little while on the swing with the two sleeping children.

"Marjorie," Red whispered, "let's put these two sleeping angels in the house before the girls come back and wake them up."

Marjorie rose and gathered Catherine in her arms. She and Red tiptoed into the house, and after placing gentle kisses on the children's foreheads, they returned quietly to the porch swing to enjoy some special time together. They sat in the moonlight, listening to the gentle creak of the swing's ropes, neither one saying a word to disturb the peacefulness. Marjorie broke the silence by saying, "Red, I am so happy with you, but I worry about the older children. I know they give you a hard time."

"I have difficulty with their attitude in the field," Red replied. "Jerome has often told me that he wants me to leave and never to return. I know he can't think of me as his stepfather, and his attitude seems to be rubbing off on Wanda and Loretta. I'm trying my best to be a good husband and father. I think we should present a united front to the kids. I also think putting God in our home would help all of us."

Marjorie shifted nervously on hearing the phrase "God in our home."

"Please do not mention God to me right now," she said stiffly. "He has never helped us before, and I told the three older ones he is not to be a part of our family."

Hearing this, Red's heart softened toward Marjorie. He took her hand, pressed it to his lips, and said, "I believe in God, and I believe he brought me here. I could have gotten angry at God when my dream of being a professional wrestler was shattered in a second, but I knew he had another plan for my life. I was sad to lose my dream, but I did not get mad at God. My Irish grandmother was the one who taught me about him and his mercy."

Out of the corner of his eye, Red saw Jerome chasing the girls out of the barn. Red shook his head as if to clear away cobwebs and then turned his full attention back to his wife.

"I met Jerome when I first moved here. He told me he was fifteen years old. He was six feet tall and very muscular; I was surprised when Mr. Watson, your neighbor, said Jerome was not quite twelve. I learned that after we were married. Anyway, he heard I had been a wrestler, and he wanted some tips on wrestling. I was happy to offer them. He caught on quickly, and I thought he had great potential.

"I helped him do his afternoon chores so we could spend more time together. I enjoyed his enthusiasm for the sport. I thought perhaps I could be a mentor to him, and maybe he could become what I did not—a professional wrestler. He loved the way you and the girls sat on the front porch and cheered him on when we wrestled in the evening, and when the neighbors cheered for him, he felt special.

"Jerome told me he had never heard his momma laugh so much. He said, 'Don't you think my momma is pretty when she laughs?' I believe it was shortly after that I began my endless proposals to you," Red said with a chuckle, gently poking Marjorie in the ribs.

Marjorie laughed, remembering how special Red's attention had made her feel.

Off in the distance Wanda and Loretta were busy scooping fireflies out of the air and putting them in each other's hair. A slight breeze stirred the air, and a lonely cricket began his nightly serenade.

"It was a mistake that I did not tell the children of my intention to marry you. I do wish I had asked Jerome for his blessing. Maybe that's why he shows so much anger toward me. He challenges me whenever I ask him for help with anything. He will never accept me as the man of this house, Marjorie," Red said with regret.

"I just want Jerome to accept me as your husband and as the father of Catherine and Jay William," he added, a hint of determination in his voice. "If my old granny were still alive, she would say to us, 'You cannot change the past, but you can learn from it and plan a better future.'"

They sat in silence a bit longer, reflecting on how far they had come and on the changes needed to make their lives more enjoyable. Without another word, they stood up and headed for the front door hand in hand, realizing there was work to be done in the morning.

CHAPTER 3

JAY WILLIAM WAS now nineteen months old. He enjoyed running and playing in the yard with Catherine. He was well behaved, and neighbors marveled at his ability to keep up with his sister. He was a chatterbox, speaking in complete sentences, and people were surprised at his large vocabulary. Jerome would go with his family to the field, pick a little cotton, and put it in a flour sack. He and Catherine often got tired and played near Red and Marjorie while their parents continued to pick cotton. The crop was now almost entirely harvested, with only a few green bolls remaining; they would open later and be pulled.

On a cool October evening, Red and Marjorie sat on the front-porch swing. It was rare for them to have time alone together. Catherine and Jay William were snuggled in their beds, and the three older children were on a hayride sponsored by the neighboring Watson family. Since most of the cotton had been harvested, everything seemed quiet and peaceful.

"Let me tell you a little about my life before you came to this area," Marjorie said. "I was only ten years old when my sister, Sophie, married and left me to care for two sickly parents. They died on the same day four years later. She refused to come to the funeral or to help with the expenses. I have not seen her since."

Red looked at Marjorie with surprise because she had not talked about this before. When she hesitated, Red said gently, "Please go on." He took her hand and listened.

12

"Andrew McCardy, a twenty-nine-year-old gentleman I hardly knew, paid the funeral expenses, and I felt obligated to marry him for his generosity and kindness. He was good to me and is the father of Jerome, Wanda, and Loretta. We started a savings account at the bank shortly after we married, and we dreamed of owning a farm.

"Jerome was born the first year of our marriage and looked like his daddy. He was the joy of Andrew's life. The two were inseparable. Loretta was born twelve months later. I gave birth to Wanda eighteen months after Loretta's birth." Marjorie looked out into the field as she gathered her thoughts.

"I would help Andrew in the fields. He made a special strap that fit around my waist and was attached to a folded quilt. The girls played on it together. Jerome stayed right with his daddy. He loved kicking the dirt and watching it fly. It was good for the kids to have so much time with him.

"Our youngest baby, Rosemary, arrived when Jerome was nine years old. We decided I should be home with the children. Poor man, he worked from five in the morning until it was too dark to see. Andrew would come to the house for forty-five minutes sometime between 11 a.m. and 3 p.m. to share a meal with us. Sometimes he would take Jerome to the field for a while. We were happy and talked about how close we were to being able to purchase a piece of land for our own place.

"Then, during a lightning storm one evening, Andrew's favorite horse, Mr. Willie, kicked him to death." Marjorie shuddered as she recalled that night. "It was such a shock to me because he was always so careful. Jerome witnessed part of that tragedy and will probably always remember it.

"Life became really tough after Andrew's death. I had enough money to last for a while, but then another tragedy struck: Rosemary died three months later from scarlet fever." A shadow seemed to fall over Marjorie's face as she continued. "That event changed me. I no longer wanted to live. I was so angry, frightened, and worried about what would happen next. Most days I stayed in bed and would not eat until Loretta began to force-feed me.

"Three weeks after Rosemary's death, a widow woman, Mrs. Grady, who lived about a half-mile down the road, came to our house and bluntly told me it was time to get out of bed and to be a mother to my children. She said that God had never given her children and that she wanted to help me with mine. Every morning for the next few weeks, I would hear her talking with my children and helping out in any way she could. One morning, she made me get up and fix breakfast. Eventually I was able to get things done, but my heart was not in it.

"Jerome milked the cow and did other chores his father had taught him to do. Loretta and Wanda gathered eggs and brought them to the kitchen. Eggs were a big part of our meals. Mrs. Grady was generous with her encouragement, but I was not always appreciative or kind to her," Marjorie said with regret in her voice.

"Mrs. Grady planted our garden that year and taught my girls things I should have been teaching them, such as how to sew and to cook. They loved her and she loved them. Helping them seemed to fill the void she felt over being childless.

"Then another tragedy struck: Mrs. Grady died suddenly. The girls were heartbroken. They asked who was going to love and help them; I said nothing. I should have said, 'I will love you and always be there for you,' but I had nothing left to give. I knew I had to feed and care for them, but I could not love them as I should have.

"At that point a group of ladies from Grace Methodist came to our house bringing food and clothing for the children. They told me they were concerned because I was not taking care of my children's needs. They told me if I gave my life to God and trusted him, he would help me. I told them to take their God back to their church, and I forbid my children to attend church. I told these ladies their God had caused the deaths of the children's daddy

14

and sister and now the wonderful Mrs. Grady." Marjorie spoke with contempt.

"I was like a dead woman, walking around confused and angry. I sat my children down and told them that there was no kind and loving God and that there was no room for such nonsense in our family. 'Don't be fooled by those who invite you to church,' I said. 'Preachers are the worst and you cannot trust them.' I did not send them to school anymore, and I made friends with no one.

"I am a terrible mother," Marjorie said, and she began to weep uncontrollably. Red took her in his arms and held her until the crying stopped.

"Honey, that is all in the past," Red told her. "You are a very good mother to Catherine and Jay William. Let's make this an evening to remember."

Red cleared his throat and sang Marjorie a love song. She snuggled close to him, reminded again how good he was to her and the children. She asked him if he thought the family could be united and the animosity between him and the children ended.

"I believe God is the answer to that," Red replied.

Marjorie became angry. "I thought I had made myself clear," she said. "I don't want God's help; if he exists he does nothing but cause me harm. I don't want him in this home!"

Red gently took her hand and asked, "Just how much do you love me?"

Smiling mischievously, Marjorie replied, "More than enough!"

Red produced a sack from behind his back and said, "Here is a little something I got for you in town."

Marjorie opened the sack and found fabric in three beautiful designs.

"What am I supposed to do with this?" she asked with a laugh.

"Make something pretty for you and the girls," Red replied.

"I want my wonderful wife and girls to look good when we go to Memphis next month."

"We have never been there before," Marjorie said. "Why should we go now?"

"I think you will enjoy this trip," Red replied. "We'll make special memories for our children. I have made plans to go to the Memphis Zoo and to the Lyceum Theatre, where I almost became famous, and then to look up some old friends in the city. I want to eat at my favorite restaurant. This will be a fun adventure, and perhaps it will bring us closer to being a family."

"Can we afford to do this, Red?"

"Yes," he said with a smile. "I have money saved from my wrestling days that we can use for this trip. What do you say, Mrs. Hawkins? Are you ready for the city lights?"

"I hope the kids will like it," Marjorie said. "I hear laughter and loud voices down the road. I think they are heading home. Tell them about the trip in the morning. Why don't you go to bed while I talk to them?"

The kids were happy and excited when they returned home. Loretta and Wanda snuggled against their momma on the swing, and Jerome stood leaning against a post. After some small talk, Marjorie said, "I want you all to show more respect for Red, and I would also like you to spend a little more time with Catherine and Jay William." The three children listened politely. Her speech finished, she joined her husband in the house.

"Poor Red. He had to send a woman to speak for him," Jerome said snidely. "I don't like him or respect him, and I won't be happy until he's gone."

The girls made no reply and went into the house to get ready for bed.

Red proposed the Memphis trip to the children the next day. He was enthused about his announcement and made a special effort to include Jerome.

"I can't wait for our family to see Memphis. Jerome, I believe you will enjoy this story. Preparations for the zoo began in 1904 when Colonel Robert Galloway asked for funds to build a home for a black bear named Natch, the mascot of the Memphis Turtles baseball team. He had been chained to a tree. The city built a home for him and for other exotic animals in the next few years." Red turned toward the younger children and did not see Jerome roll his eyes.

"Will we see the animals and can we get some?" Catherine asked.

"I want one too," Jay William said.

"Please hold your questions until we finish telling you about the trip," Marjorie said. "Jerome, I think this will interest you. Red is taking us to the place where he wrestled, and perhaps you can speak with some of the wrestlers there."

"Red is a has-been wrestler," Jerome replied. "I'm not interested. I doubt if any of them would remember Red anyway. May I be excused? The animals need to be fed. I'll stay at home and do my job. A real man doesn't have time for such nonsense."

Silence filled the room. Red did not overreact. He simply gave Jerome permission to leave.

"I'm taking Catherine and Jay William outside to talk with them about the trip," Red said. "They seem interested in the zoo." With that, he took their hands and led them out of the house.

Marjorie spoke to Wanda and Loretta about the trip. She showed them the new fabric and told them they could choose what they wanted her to sew for them. An awkward silence followed.

"Momma, we'll tell you later whether we want to go on the Memphis trip," Loretta said. Then the girls went to the kitchen to start their morning chores.

Marjorie was disappointed about their lack of interest in the trip. She joined Red and the younger children outside. She and Red spoke to them about the zoo and about other points of interest.

Jay William pretended he was a black bear. Making the

17

growling sounds Red had taught him, he chased Catherine around the yard.

Loretta and Wanda soon joined Jerome in deciding to skip the trip. Marjorie asked Jerome if he would take her, Red, and the two younger children to Mumford to catch the train that would bring them to Memphis, and he agreed to do it.

Early on a Sunday morning, Marjorie, Red, Catherine, and Jay William boarded the train for Memphis. They arrived at nine, ate breakfast in the train station café, and decided that their first stop would be to the Memphis Zoo.

The toddlers were disappointed that due to a cold spell, Natch and the other bears had gone into hibernation. Red got pamphlets with pictures of the bears for the two to take home. They found plenty of other animals to enjoy, especially the monkeys. They also liked feeding the baby goats.

Jay William and Catherine begged not to leave the zoo, but after being there for three hours, Red wanted to go downtown so Marjorie could do some window shopping. He hoped to show her new fashions. Marjorie had a pencil and paper and sketched pictures of several dresses. Then they walked to the Lyceum Theatre at Second and Broadway but found no wrestlers. Red was visibly disappointed.

He led Marjorie and the kids to a park where they had ice cream. Then they walked to the place where Red had lived with his parents before the family moved to Randolph. The landlady, Mrs. Williams, saw them coming and opened the door and invited them in. She told the youngsters how much she had liked having their daddy living in the flat next door and invited the family to spend the night at her place.

Red and Marjorie talked it over and decided the kids would be better off in a place with just the immediate family. After a meal of sandwiches and soup plus cookies and ice cream, Red told Mrs. Williams they would have to decline her offer but were delighted to have spent time with her; he thanked her for the delicious meal.

When Red asked Mrs. Williams to recommend a good place to stay overnight, she said, "Red, I have an empty flat that is ready to rent, but no one has looked at it yet. Why don't you take your family there? I would be honored to give it to you for the night."

"Okay," Red said, "but I want to pay for the cleaning after we leave. Is two dollars enough?" Mrs. Williams said that was more than enough.

Red and Marjorie took the kids to the flat and gave them a bath in the tub. They were excited to see how the water vanished down the drain. Jay William found the toilet even more exciting and begged to flush it for everyone who used it. This was the first time Marjorie and the children had seen indoor plumbing.

The next morning they walked back downtown for more shopping. Marjorie wandered around and got more ideas for using the new fabric. Red purchased a fedora for Jay William and a pretty hat for Catherine. He asked what he should buy for Wanda, Loretta, and Jerome. Marjorie decided he should get a box of fancy handkerchiefs for each girl and a nice shirt for Jerome. Red wanted to buy his wife a new hat, but she refused the offer.

The four of them were tired but happy when they boarded the train that afternoon for Mumford. Marjorie thought they had had a wonderful time in Memphis, but she yearned to return to her home in Randolph. She decided that she desired the country life, but she thought Red seemed more at ease in the city.

Jerome was waiting for them at the station. He helped them into the wagon, and they headed home. The girls were all smiles when they saw Catherine and Jay William and heard them talk about all they had done. They helped the toddlers into bed and smiled when they saw Jay William still holding on to his pamphlet about the black bears.

The following morning at breakfast, Marjorie and Red presented the gifts they had purchased in Memphis. "We talked a lot while you were gone," Jerome said, "and we all want to be more cooperative and spend more time with Jay William and

Catherine. So with your permission, I would like to let my friends see my little brother in his Memphis fedora after we finish work today."

Red thought this sounded too good to be true and was suspicious of the request, but Marjorie said, "We must trust him and let him introduce his brother to his friends. You should be happy that he is finally showing an interest in Jay William." Against his better judgment, Red agreed, hoping to appease her.

Wanda and Loretta wanted to take Catherine for a walk in her new hat. Red was leery of this sudden change in attitude, but he saw that the idea pleased his wife greatly. Besides, Marjorie and Red needed time to relax and to reflect on their trip, and this plan worked for them.

Jerome seemed to like taking his brother to the Watsons' home where other young people gathered. At first Jay William wanted to go with him, but soon he went reluctantly. When he began to stutter, Red mentioned the problem to Marjorie. She said that Red was too protective and that he didn't like or trust Jerome. In any event, she said, Jay William would outgrow the stuttering.

When the stuttering became worse, Red took a walk down to the Watsons' home to see what was upsetting his son. He listened from a distance as Jerome used vile words and ordered Jay William to repeat them. Jerome made his demand over and over. Jay William shook his head and with a stutter said, "I don't want to say it."

The crowd chanted, "Do it! Do it! Say it, stuttering little preacher boy!" The young men's laughter grew louder and louder. "Do it! Do it!"

Jay William began to cry. Red strode into the yard and picked up his son. He looked at Jerome and said, "I am ashamed of you, Jerome, for treating your brother like that." He turned to the others and said, "You guys have had your fun; I'm taking my son home to his mother. Next time pick on someone your own size."

Red comforted Jay William, telling him what a good boy he

was. Returning home, Red placed the boy in Marjorie's arms, where he felt protected and safe. "Now we know why he was stuttering," Red said after recounting what had happened. "What do you think about your precious son Jerome now?"

"It was a cruel thing to do to Jay William," Marjorie said. "I'm sure Jerome didn't intend to hurt his brother. He was probably trying to impress the others. He has always had trouble getting along with others his age. I will speak to him immediately when he gets home."

"You have to defend him, don't you?" Red replied. With that, he took his son into the house and played with him before placing him in bed.

Meanwhile, Catherine was enjoying the attention of her sisters' older friends. They told her what pretty hair she had and made her feel special. Wanda and Loretta were much kinder to the little ones than Jerome was. Catherine looked forward to her walks with her sisters.

Jerome slept in the barn that night. He was furious at Red for embarrassing him. He had no remorse for what he had been doing to Jay William. *Red is going to leave, and soon,* he told himself.

Marjorie did not mention Jerome's conduct when she saw him the next morning. The girls brought Jerome breakfast while Red was playing with Jay William and was distracted.

Jerome asked them to take Jay William on a walk with Catherine and to bring the two children to the Watsons' place. The girls agreed to his request. After all, they were teens and liked boys. They did this a few times and never said a word about the taunting of Jay William. They warned Catherine not to be a tattletale.

Jerome was determined to find a way to force Red to leave, but he did not realize that Red's love for his children was stronger than their hatred for him. With God's help, he dug in his heels and refused to let them run him off.

Loud arguments grew frequent, and that troubled Jay William

and Catherine very much. Jerome did not have a kind word for either of the small children. He took every opportunity to pick on Jay William, calling him Momma and Daddy's pet. "I will get you sometime, and don't you forget it," Jerome said. "You better not tattle on me, or I will hurt you. And that goes for you too, Catherine."

"You must put boundaries on your teenage children before they destroy these innocent children of ours," Red told Marjorie. "I am not going to stand by and watch it happen." Red was so upset that he began to lose weight and his migraine headaches increased in severity and frequency. He had no money for medicine, and a cool, dark place was the only relief he could find.

The doctors in Memphis had told Red stress would trigger a migraine headache; they recommended he rest in a cool, dark room to prevent muscle spasms. A migraine results from blood vessels in the head dilating and constricting rapidly, leading to muscle spasms that increase pain; it is a hard cycle to break. Red got no help from Marjorie, and his parents had moved to Dyer County.

Red prayed, asking God to show him what he should do. He did not want to leave his children, and he could not take them with him. He had been taught that a child needs a mother more than anything else.

The older children told Marjorie he was lazy and slept in the barn all day while they did all the work. The girls followed Jerome's advice and tied horseshoes to a bucket that they swung over Red's head while he was resting in the barn. He was so sick that he stumbled in the house after vomiting several times in the backyard. He didn't know where to turn for comfort.

With a cold cloth on his head, Red curled up beside Jay William, who was napping, and fell asleep. Marjorie knew he had a headache and closed the door so he could rest.

She made supper and allowed him to sleep. Red woke up when he heard Jay William crying. Jerome was calling him a stuttering preacher boy. Marjorie did nothing to stop Jerome. Red got up and took Jay William to the bedroom. He played with him for a while and then sang him a lullaby until he fell asleep.

The next morning, Red woke up early and went to the field to pull cotton bolls. Picking cotton required pulling the soft cotton with seed out of the open bolls, which were sharp and cut the fingers. People could pick as much as they were able and were paid by the pound.

Picking cotton was hard work, but pulling bolls was harder. Bolls that were not open during the fall harvest had to be left behind. The bolls that opened after the cotton was harvested were not as good a grade but were worth something. The whole boll would be pulled off the stalk and sent to the cotton gin. Because this cotton was of a lesser quality than the handpicked cotton, it fetched a fraction of the price.

Red worked until dark, not stopping to eat. The result was a full-blown migraine headache. He went to the barn and lay down on the straw, using his nine-foot cotton sack for a cover. When he awakened the sun was up. His headache was finally gone. Red trudged toward the house still upset that no one had come to the field to help him pull the cotton bolls off the stalks.

When he stepped onto the porch, he heard Marjorie's older kids telling her how they had let him complete the cotton boll removal. He heard them laughing and that threw him into a rage. He opened the door with such force that he pulled the hinges from the frame.

"Marjorie, I have had enough of your ungrateful brats. They are disrespectful and downright mean to me. Your girls tied horseshoes to a bucket and swung it over my head while I was suffering with a migraine. Only a warped brain would think of doing something so cruel. They wanted to increase my suffering.

"And one more thing: the teasing of Jay William has to stop. He is a smart, well-mannered child. I am shocked that you allow your kids to hurt him like that. I want it stopped now!" Red's voice grew louder. "I want some respect from you too. Your brats lied about me, and you did not even stand up for your husband. I will not tolerate much more of this nonsense."

Jay William began to cry because he had never seen his father this angry. Red left and got paid for his previous day's labor. Then he walked to town and purchased Christmas gifts for his children and food for Christmas, which was the next day.

Six months later, Red was awakened in the middle of the night when Jerome began beating him on the head. "I'll stop if you'll leave quietly," Jerome told him.

"I have had enough of you and your sisters," Red said. "I'm out of here." He took his clothes and walked off into the night, not knowing or caring where his angry footsteps would lead him.

Marjorie said nothing when she heard Red had left. Jay William and Catherine screamed and cried for their daddy, who always made them feel safe and loved. After listening to them for a few minutes, Marjorie told Loretta, "Take those crying children out of my room. You and your sister keep a close watch on them. They may run away looking for their daddy. I want you girls to help me take care of them. Now I'm going to bed. I can't take this anymore; I just want peace and quiet."

CHAPTER 4

ANGRY AND EMBARRASSED, Marjorie again withdrew from life. Jay William missed his daddy, and his stuttering became worse. He began to regress. His older sisters were concerned. Catherine could seldom get him to play with her. Jay William wanted to hide from Jerome, who called him a crybaby whenever no one else was around. "Where is your daddy, little boy?" he would say to Jay William. The boy would close his eyes and bang his head on the floor. Jerome found this funny. Loretta saw this happen and told Marjorie about it.

Marjorie had compassion for Jay William when she heard what had happened. She asked him why he was afraid of Jerome, and the boy replied, "He doesn't like me and he doesn't like my daddy. I need my daddy now."

"I know," Marjorie told him, "but your daddy is not coming back. Don't think about your daddy and it won't hurt so much. You go with Loretta now and she will feed you." Jay William clung to his mother, and Loretta had to pry him from Marjorie's neck.

Loretta tried to get him to talk about his trip to the zoo, the train ride, and other things he had done in Memphis, but Jay William would just cry and call for his daddy.

The neighbors missed seeing Jay William outside with Catherine in the yard. Some of them asked Jerome what had happened to the boy. Jerome said that the child's daddy had left and that Jay William might as well have left too because he was acting weird. Jerome said he didn't care about Jay William.

Mr. Watson, a widower who lived one house down the road from the Hawkins family, became very concerned about Jay William's welfare. He brought over his son and a couple of other neighborhood children and tried to get Jay William to join them in play. Jay William just watched from the front porch as Catherine played tag with the other kids. She was happy to have playmates.

Mr. Watson brought the group over frequently to encourage Jay William to socialize again, but the boy just watched the other children play from his safe place on the porch. One day Mr. Watson came by with his wagon and horses to see if Catherine and Jay William wanted to go for a ride into town. He asked Marjorie if that would be okay.

She asked if Loretta and Wanda could ride along to keep an eye on Jay William. "I'm afraid he might try to run away to find his daddy," Marjorie said.

Mr. Watson had no problem with taking the two girls, and Wanda and Loretta were excited to get away. Loretta found the fedora that Red had purchased for Jay William in Memphis. Marjorie had kept it out of sight after Red left, because Jay William had insisted on sleeping in it.

Loretta set the fedora on Jay William's head. A big grin appeared on his face and he said, "My daddy bought this for me. I want my daddy."

"I know you do, honey," Wanda said, "but he's not coming back. Daddy was sick and he had bad headaches. Maybe a doctor is helping him. Don't you worry; we will take care of you now."

Catherine took his hand, and he started singing a song about the moon that they used to sing with Red. Catherine sang it more loudly, and Jay William increased the volume. Soon Mr. Watson said, "For goodness' sake, don't you kids know a quieter song?"

"I have to sing loud, Mr. Watson, because Jay William can't sing very well," Catherine said.

"Catherine, I can run faster than you," Jay William said. "Daddy told me that."

"Now, Jay William, you know Momma said we can't talk about Daddy anymore."

"I know that, but you are not going to tattle on me, are you?" Jay William asked with a frightened look on his face.

"No," Catherine said, "but you know Jerome will hit you if he hears you talk about Daddy."

"I'm afraid of Jerome," Jay William said. "I saw him hit Daddy when Daddy was sleeping with me."

"We must not talk about it, because Momma said so. Hey, let's play zip. I see two white horses over there. See?" She pointed to the pasture.

Zip was an old game that children in the South played while traveling. They received ten points for each zip or white horse they saw if they called out zip first. By the time they got to town, Jay William was winning by thirty points, and he liked that.

Mr. Watson took the four of them to a general store where he bought five ice cream cones. They sat on a bench outside and ate them. A puppy came up wagging its tail, and Jay William let the dog have a lick from his cone. Loretta told him to throw away the cone, but he refused.

"It won't hurt him to eat the cone, because the part the dog licked has melted," Mr. Watson said. "Let him figure out some things for himself, okay? I know you girls are taking care of the younger ones now, and that is a pretty big task. Most girls your age are out with beaus. Are you really doing okay helping out with the young kids? I have a word of advice for you regarding Jay William. Don't tell him no so much, because he is a smart little boy and he must explore without being afraid."

"We just want to make Momma's job easier since she is so embarrassed about Red leaving the little ones," Wanda said. "She doesn't want to do anything but stay in bed all day. Jerome runs everything and everybody at our place since Red is gone. He is so mean to Jay William. I don't know what was better—Red and Jerome at odds all the time or Jerome being man of the house. Momma would be upset if she knew we talked to you about this."

Mr. Watson said he was not prying but cared about them and the difficulties the family was experiencing. He came up with an idea he thought would help the girls and might interest their momma in socializing again. He said he would order a catalog from Sears, Roebuck & Company and they could make wishes based on things they found in this thick book.

He said his wife had often found enjoyment in looking at the things she wanted but couldn't afford and would copy ideas from the wish book. "You girls are growing up fast and will be getting married someday," Mr. Watson said. "You need to start making wish lists now for your homes. Let's go order that wish book now." As luck would have it, the store clerk gave them her copy.

They purchased a few items in town and headed for home. Mr. Watson asked Jay William to sit by him, and the boy happily did so. Mr. Watson taught him a new song: "I went to the animal fair. The birds and the beasts were there. The big baboon was combing his auburn hair by the light of the moon. The monkey bumped into a skunk and fell onto the elephant's trunk. The elephant sneezed and fell on his knees, and that was the end of the monk, the monk, the monk."

By the time they returned home, Jay William's appearance and behavior had completely changed. He was animated, smiling, and talking almost nonstop. Marjorie was surprised and questioned the sudden change.

"Momma, I had so much fun and I'm not afraid anymore," Jay William said. "Mr. Watson is a nice man, and he made me feel happy and safe. Please may we go to town in his wagon again soon?"

Marjorie did not know what to say, but she managed a weak smile and told him, "Perhaps, little man." She then spotted the large book in Loretta's hands. "Where did you get that?" she asked.

"I got it at the store where Mr. Watson took us. He said his wife and his daughters often look at it. They even designed their dresses to look like the ones in the catalog."

Suddenly, Marjorie felt a little inferior, a feeling she had not had before. *Perhaps I should talk to Mr. Watson and see what he did to make Jay William change his attitude so quickly. Tomorrow I will do just that; I will speak to Mr. Watson,* she thought.

Jay William went to bed without crying for his daddy, and he wanted to talk to his momma about the trip to the zoo. For the first time in a long time, Marjorie put him to bed herself.

The next morning, Jerome again said hurtful things to Jay William. "Hey, did you find your daddy in town yesterday? No, because he doesn't want to be found. Go ahead. Cry for him again, you crybaby!"

Jay William paid him little mind, and Jerome left in a huff. *I'll have to find something else to say to him to make him cry,* he thought, muttering "little brat."

Catherine and Jay William played in the yard that day. They put chairs two in a row and pretended they were going to town. Jay William made himself the driver. Catherine wanted to be the driver, and the two began to argue. Loretta took them for a short walk and they calmed down.

CHAPTER 5

JAY WILLIAM WAS now five years old and was adjusting to life without his daddy. Jerome was still taunting him, but he had gotten better at handling the abuse. It was nearly Christmas and he wanted a red wagon for a gift. That was next to impossible because the family didn't have money for pricey toys.

He suddenly remembered hearing about God and about answered prayer. His daddy had always prayed when he was with them, so Jay William secretly prayed that he would get a red wagon and that Catherine would get a doll.

Jay William realized that if the others knew he was praying he would be in big trouble because Marjorie preached to them that there was no God.

One morning in early December the temperature was a record eighty-two degrees, and Jay William felt lucky to be outdoors playing in the sunshine. He heard a commotion and a man's voice calling his name. He looked down the street and saw a white horse galloping toward the house.

The rider was wearing a three-piece suit, and his red hair glistened in the sun. He also called out to Catherine. The rider got off the horse and raced toward the pair at an unbelievable speed. He had a red wagon and a doll and handed the gifts to the kids.

Suddenly, Marjorie emerged from the house with a rolling pin. Jerome was on her heels. "Just who do you think you are, Mr. Hawkins, riding a white horse to our house like you live here?"

Marjorie demanded. She took the wagon from Jay William and the doll from Catherine and threw the toys at Red. "Take these back with you. My kids don't need these things from you. Get out of here now before I turn Jerome loose on you."

By this time it seemed everyone from the countryside had come to see the excitement. One of the men told Red he should leave while he was in one piece. Red never had a chance to hug his kids. It was a sad day for Jay William, and he would repeat this story to his children for years to come. He and Catherine were heartbroken and confused.

Mr. Watson became a hero to Jay William and Catherine when he sat on the porch with them. "I know how sad you must be feeling, because you wanted those toys very much," he said. "You must understand that your daddy has not been around for a long time, and his sudden appearance wasn't welcome here. Your life has been really good without all the fighting between him and Jerome.

"Your daddy appears to be doing well for himself. He was wearing an expensive suit that guys around here can't afford. He was riding a very nice horse too. Your momma was angry because she has been struggling to support this family without a man's help. She cannot afford to buy gifts like the ones your daddy brought you. Your daddy didn't do a smart thing by riding in like he owned the place. It just wasn't right for him to do that."

Putting an arm around each of them, Mr. Watson said, "Now let's dry up those tears and see what we can do to make Christmas fun for you."

Jay William asked if he could share a secret. Mr. Watson took him for a short walk and asked, "Okay, what is your secret, boy?"

"Sir, I guess this is my fault because I broke a rule by praying," Jay William said. "Momma says I am not supposed to pray. She says there is no God, and if there is such a thing, he sure is not welcome here. I asked for a red wagon for me and a doll for Catherine. I thought it would be nice if we could have those things to play with. Am I in deep trouble now?" He asked this question with such solemnity that Mr. Watson tried hard not to laugh.

"Jay William, I will not tell your secret to anyone," Mr. Watson said. "You meant well. Many people pray, but you must do what your momma tells you. Now I will talk with your momma, and we will try to find toys for you two at Christmas. You want to race back to the others now? I bet I can run faster than you can."

Mr. Watson allowed Jay William to win the race, putting a big smile on his face. While Jay William and Catherine played tag in the yard, Mr. Watson spoke with Marjorie about toys for the two youngsters. Marjorie had been shaken by Red's appearance that afternoon.

"Marjorie," Mr. Watson said, "will you listen to me without getting all upset about your young children?" She shook her head yes, so he continued. "Those kids are doing without things they need to help them later in life."

Marjorie began to sob. "How can you say that? You see how hard I try. I cook their meals and they have clothes on their backs. What more can I do as a single woman who has been scorned and then embarrassed by her ex-husband?"

"First of all, quit feeling sorry for yourself," Mr. Watson said. "We have all tried to help you out with them, and yet you don't listen to them when they talk to you. Can you tell me what they want for Christmas?"

"We don't talk about stuff like that," Marjorie replied. "I didn't even know that they knew Christmas is coming soon. We do not have money for toys."

"Ever since our last trip to town where there are Christmas displays in all the stores, that is all they talk about with me," Mr. Watson.

"Look, Mr. Watson," Marjorie said curtly, "we just cannot afford a Christmas tree and gifts. I will cook a decent meal, and that will be our Christmas around here."

"Marjorie, what harm is there in allowing those little ones to have hopes and dreams? You should want your children to have a life better than you have had. I tell you what. I will help you plan a Christmas for those two little ones without it costing you an arm and a leg. Give me a couple of days to think about it, and I will get back to you." He took hold of her hands and said, "Please. Will you do that for them?"

"Okay, Mr. Watson. If you can do this without asking anything of me, I guess I can't say no," Marjorie replied.

"I said without costing you much, but you do need to make a little effort. Tell you what. I will sleep on this and take you to town tomorrow to get some ideas. Is that a deal?"

"I guess," Marjorie said. With that, Mr. Watson said his good-byes to everyone and left.

Marjorie tried to sleep that night, but her mind was racing. What a day it had been. Seeing Red had upset her. She had been terribly embarrassed when he left, and then he had returned like some kind of rich man. Now Mr. Watson wanted to have a fancy Christmas for her and Red's kids. *What shall I do about all this?* Marjorie wondered. *I am too tired to figure it out; perhaps tomorrow I will be able to do that.* She closed her eyes and fell asleep.

CHAPTER 6

BRIGHT AND EARLY the next morning, Mr. Watson hitched his horses to the wagon and headed for Marjorie's house where the family was just finishing breakfast.

"Good morning to all of you!" he bellowed.

His enthusiasm was more than Marjorie could take at that hour. "Lower your voice," she told him. "You're loud enough to wake the dead."

"Catherine and Jay William, I need you two to stay at home with Loretta and Wanda today while I take your momma to town with me."

"We want to go, too," the pair whined in unison. "We want to see the pretty Christmas trees."

"Today I need you to stay at home and cut out some ornaments to place on the Christmas tree that we will get for you. Can I depend on the two of you doing that?"

"You mean we will have our own Christmas tree here in our house?" Jay William asked.

"Yes," Mr. Watson replied, "if you stay on your best behavior. Loretta and Wanda will help you choose the right things to put on the tree."

Within the hour, Marjorie had on her best clothes and was sitting in the wagon. As they headed into town, Marjorie was apprehensive about whether people would accept her traveling alone with Mr. Watson, and she raised the issue with him.

"Marjorie, get your mind off yourself and keep it fixed on those little ones of yours," he said. "I have decided to make Jay William a toy wagon with the help of my sons, Ted and Fred, and perhaps Jerome. Last night I couldn't sleep well, so I got up and started making plans for the wagon. I used my coffee saucer to trace an outline for the wheels. The big boys will have to cut out the wheels with a saw and sand them to help them roll smoothly. I'll build the frame with wood from my old chicken house. I'll build the tongue of the wagon in a T-shape so Jay William can pull it. I have red paint left over from the barn. It will not be a fancy wagon like the one Red brought him, but it will serve the purpose. Your job is to make a doll for Catherine."

"Me, make a doll?" Marjorie cried. "I don't know how to do that."

"You will learn," Mr. Watson said. "I will take you to a lady who will show you how to do that. You will meet her in just a few minutes."

Arriving in town, they tied the horses to a hitching post near the general store. Then they walked to the post office where Mr. Watson asked if Miss Franklin was available. A lady with a big smile soon appeared from a side room. "How are you, Mr. Watson, and you, ma'am?" she asked. "I have a few minutes before my shift begins. How can I help you?"

"This is my neighbor, Marjorie Hawkins," Mr. Watson said. "The two of us are planning a Christmas surprise for her five-year-old boy and her seven-year-old girl. I know you have made cloth dolls for little girls for charities. Is there any way you can help us out?"

"It's nice to meet you, Marjorie. My name is Susan Franklin. I don't have any dolls available now. The ones I have made are all spoken for, but perhaps I can help you make one for the little girl. When could you get together with me? I have plenty of fabric for one doll. Perhaps we can make two changes of clothing for the doll. Little girls love to dress and redress their baby dolls."

Marjorie sat with a blank look on her face. Mr. Watson came to her rescue. "What works best for you, Miss Franklin?" he asked. "I can bring Marjorie into town whenever it's convenient for you."

"I can help you tomorrow before my shift begins," Miss Franklin said. "I begin at 9 a.m. Can you be here at eight?"

"I will have her here at eight," Mr. Watson said. "Does she need to bring anything with her?"

"Perhaps a needle and a thimble and any special fabric you would like for the baby doll's clothes," Miss Franklin said. "I have all the other supplies."

"I can bring those things," Marjorie said with a smile.

"Thank you for taking the time to do this for us," Mr. Watson said.

"My pleasure," Miss Franklin said. "I'll see you at eight tomorrow morning. Now I must get to work. Good-bye for now."

The two left and went for a walk down the street. Marjorie viewed all the Christmas trees and decorations in the store windows, looking closely at the tree ornaments.

"Mr. Watson, if we could get another catalog, we could make ornaments out of the pictures in it. We could cut them out and paste them onto cardboard cut to match. I could cut a slit on top of each ornament and slide it onto the tree."

"Do you think that would work? Wouldn't you need to buy glue?" he asked.

"We can make glue out of flour and water. Oh look," she said, pointing at a tree in a window. "They have red berries on the Christmas tree. We can pick berries from the woods and put them on a string. I save the string from flour sacks, and I have a big supply of it."

Mr. Watson smiled at seeing Marjorie excited and happy. *How pretty she looks right now*, he thought. He grabbed her hand and said, "Let's go see if they have an extra book for you in the store."

Sure enough, the clerk handed Marjorie one with a smile. "If you want your gifts by Christmas, you have to order within the next three days," the clerk said.

Marjorie thanked the clerk and went off to look at the Christmas trees in the store. She borrowed a pencil and paper and made notes. She realized she needed a bigger needle to turn the berry strands into garlands. She saw a tree with popcorn strands and made a note of that. It was a very productive day.

When they returned to Marjorie's home, Jay William was surprised to see the smile on his momma's face. "Momma, did you see the Christmas decorations?" he asked. "Did you like the Christmas trees? May we have one as pretty as the store has?"

Marjorie nodded her head yes but said she would need help from everyone. She shared her plans for the tree with the older girls so they could help and instructed Jay William and Catherine on what they could do.

No one admitted it, but Red's attempt to make Christmas nice for the little ones had given everyone an incentive to brighten the holiday for Jay William and Catherine.

Mr. Watson got four teenage boys to cut out and sand one wheel each for the wagon, promising a prize to the boy who did the best work. They did not usually get an opportunity to compete like that, so each took the job seriously.

The next morning, Mr. Watson was at the house early. Marjorie had her fabric and needle and thread ready for the doll making session with Miss Franklin. Marjorie told Wanda and Loretta to take Jay William and Catherine to the woods to gather red berries for the Christmas tree. Jay William was excited about helping the big girls pick berries. They got two buckets full along with red-stained hands.

Mr. Watson left Marjorie at the post office to meet with Miss Franklin. She led Marjorie into a side room where she saw a finished doll. Miss Franklin had another doll cut out from unbleached muslin and partially stuffed with straw. She instructed Marjorie on how to finish it. The hair was to be made from yarn, which came in yellow and red. Marjorie chose red. The hair would complete the doll's head. Miss Franklin provided patterns for Marjorie to cut out the doll's clothes. The hour went by quickly for the two ladies. Marjorie placed the doll and the clothes to be sewn into a cloth bag and thanked Miss Franklin for her time and supplies.

"It was nice meeting you, Marjorie," Miss Franklin said. "I hope that your little girl will love her beautiful baby doll and that you will have a wonderful Christmas with your family."

Marjorie thanked her and said, "I have never experienced anything like today. I have never taken time to do something fun for my children before."

Mr. Watson was waiting for Marjorie in the wagon. He brought her home and hurried off. He had to work on the little wagon for Jay William and to see how the boys were doing with the wheels. He was feeling good about the project.

Marjorie showed the older girls how to string the berries with a needle. Jay William watched with great enthusiasm. Jerome was out in the barn working to make his wheel the best for the wagon Mr. Watson was building.

Marjorie looked at the items the little ones had cut out of the catalog. When she saw that Jay William had cut out pictures of animals from his prized zoo brochure, she wanted to cry at his sacrifice. She glued them onto cardboard and cut slits on the tops of the ornaments so they could be stuck on the tree. For the first time in her life, she was having fun. When Wanda and Loretta had finished stringing the berries, Marjorie hung up the garlands to dry behind the kitchen stove.

She took out the doll after the younger ones had gone to sleep. It was completed except for the hair. Loretta wanted to do that for Catherine. Wanda wanted to sew the cut-out dresses together. All were enjoying the excitement of planning Christmas in their home.

Marjorie told the girls about the strung popcorn, and they

wanted to do that as well. Jerome came in from the barn to show off his wheel. He had worked on it all day, and it was smooth. He used soap to make the wheel slick. "I hope Jay William appreciates the work going into this wagon. The little fellow can be okay sometimes, but he is mostly a pain like his old man," Jerome said.

"I hope you will not say that ever again," Marjorie told Jerome. "We all know you did not like Red, but don't take it out on Jay William anymore."

Surprised that his mother had stood up to him, Jerome could only say, "Okay."

The four of them sat down and finished planning the Christmas Day festival. They decided to include the Watson family in the holiday event.

The day before Christmas, Jerome cut down a cedar tree and nailed it to boards to help keep it up. Then he put the tree in a pan of water. After placing the berry and popcorn strands on the tree, the older girls helped Catherine and Jay William add the paper ornaments.

Christmas Day was like no other in the Hawkins home. A six-foot tree decorated with paper ornaments and strings of popcorn and red berries stood in the living room. It was very pretty indeed. A ham and chicken with dressing were cooking in the oven. Mr. Watson and his twin boys were there along with Loretta's beau, Charles Lawson.

Everyone was anxious for the little ones to see their gifts. They were sent outside to see how the tree looked in the window. When they returned, there were gifts under the tree. Catherine immediately spied the baby doll with red hair.

"Oh my goodness, is that mine?" Momma shook her head yes. "Oh how beautiful. Look, Jay William, she has another change of clothes." Jay William was happy for her but was looking for something he wanted, a red wagon. Suddenly Jerome came out of the bedroom, pulling something behind him.

"That is my red wagon," Jay William exclaimed, "and it is

wooden just like yours, Mr. Watson! Oh thank you, thank you, Jerome."

Jerome blushed and said, "Buddy, I can't take credit for anything but the left front wheel."

"You made the wheel, Jerome?"

Then Jay William did something that surprised everyone. He hugged Jerome's neck. "Thank you, Jerome!"

Jay William filled the wagon with whatever he could find and pulled it throughout the house as everyone applauded.

"Mr. Watson, who gets the prize for the best-made wheel?" Jerome asked.

"Well, it was a tough decision because all four are nice and smooth, but we decided on yours," Mr. Watson said. He gave Jerome a new pocketknife.

It was a good day and everyone had fun, especially Jay William and Catherine, who went to sleep with their Christmas toys.

CHAPTER 7

THE FOLLOWING YEAR, 1920, brought many changes in the Hawkins house. Loretta eloped and became the wife of Charles Lawson. Mr. Watson spent a lot of time at the house. He was often there in the mornings when Jay William woke up.

Mr. Watson spent more time with Marjorie than with the children. Jay William heard his momma and Mr. Watson talking about sending him and Catherine to school. Momma said that was not necessary, but Mr. Watson disagreed.

"Those children must go to school," he said. "They need an education to succeed in the future. Jay William is so smart, and it would be a terrible mistake not to educate him."

Mr. Watson called Jay William and asked him, "Son, do you want to attend school and learn how to read, do arithmetic problems, and write? Your momma and I have been discussing it. I would like your opinion."

"You mean go to the school where Johnny Moore goes? Can Catherine go too? I don't want her to be at home without me. Momma, please can we both go to school?"

"We will see after your sixth birthday," Marjorie said. "You have to be six years old to attend."

"Momma, my birthday is next week. Can I go then?"

"I'm not sure," she said. "We'll have to talk to the school people about that. You may have to wait until the next school year begins."

"Momma, I don't want to wait until then. Please, Mr. Watson, can you talk to them and see if I can start next week after I'm six years old? You know about me more than anyone else."

Mr. Watson looked at Marjorie. "What do you say, Momma? Can we go to the school and see if this smart little boy can start this year?"

"You are the one who wants Jay William to do this. Why do I have to go with you?" Marjorie asked.

"Marjorie, it would be good if you did," Mr. Watson said. "The school needs to know you will support and help him. Yes, I think you should go too."

The next morning Mr. Watson, Marjorie, Jay William, and Catherine went to the one-room schoolhouse to see if the children could attend following Jay William's sixth birthday. Miss Armstrong, the teacher, asked how they would get to school each day. She wanted to talk with the children before she decided.

She spoke with Catherine, who was now eight years old, and asked if she would like to stay for class and learn. Catherine was excited and wanted to stay but only if Jay William could stay too. The children were invited to listen and to watch the other children do their lessons.

The first class was arithmetic. Jay William caught on immediately. He knew his numbers well and could add quickly. He watched the other children raise their hands to answer questions, and he suddenly raised his hand when an addition problem was presented. Miss Armstrong asked why his hand was up, and Jay William said, "I know the answer. It's sixteen." He was correct and Miss Armstrong was impressed.

She asked Jay William to go to the blackboard and write his numbers. "I'm sorry. I don't know how to do that yet," he said, "but I can try if you'll help me." He copied the numbers up to twenty-five, but his writing was clumsy and hard to read. It made some of the children laugh.

"Okay, children, let's not laugh at Jay William. Let's try to help him," Miss Armstrong said. "He really wants to learn. How about it? Who would like to stay in at recess and help him with his writing?" Three hands went up.

Miss Armstrong chose Shelby Young, a nine-year-old. Jay William learned quickly and Shelby loved helping him. Mr. Watson and Marjorie returned at noon as Miss Armstrong had asked them to do.

"These children need to be in school now," Miss Armstrong told them. "Since I have only ten students this year it's possible for them to start but only if they get practice at home with you. Jay William is most anxious to learn, and Shelby is willing to help him. Now we must get a volunteer for Catherine. I need to tell you the school rules so you know what is expected. I will try fitting the children in the class if you will make sure they are here daily. Is that possible?"

Marjorie was surprised that her children wanted to go and were permitted to start right away. She looked at Mr. Watson for an answer. He agreed that the children would be at school.

Jay William and Catherine were admitted to school on March 7, 1920. It was a good thing Mr. Watson had taught the children the alphabet on their many trips with him to town. He had also taught them how to read signs and food labels. This gave them a rudimentary basis for learning.

The following morning Jay William was up early and fed the barn animals while everyone else was still asleep. He then went to the front yard and wrote his letters and numbers in the dirt. He wrote his name several times.

Marjorie scolded him for getting up so early. "You are going to be tired before school is over," she said. "You cannot be doing schoolwork all the time."

"You should be smart like me and learn to do farmwork," Jerome said. "Someday I will be a landlord without having to be a sissy schoolboy. If you need more work to do, I can give you more."

"Jerome, please don't tease him," Marjorie said. "You have been doing so well. Jay William is not like you, and you cannot make him that way."

"Oh, I forgot," Jerome said. "Red is his father and that explains it, doesn't it? Jay William, you still have to feed the barn animals before you go to school."

"I did it already!" Jay William replied.

Mr. Watson entered the kitchen. "The young ones will need a lunch for school today. Do you have it made?" he asked Marjorie.

"What should I fix them?" she asked. "I've fried some apple fritters. Is that okay?"

"Yes, if we add these sausage biscuits I have made. Add a pint of milk and that should be good enough. Are you youngsters ready to go to school? I can take you in the wagon today, but tomorrow we will walk you there. It's a little more than a mile. Marjorie, are you going to town with me?"

"I wasn't planning on it," she said, "but if you give me time to get ready, I'll go with you."

"Put a move on, lady. We can't allow the schoolchildren to be late. They will get in trouble if they are."

"Why will we be in trouble, Mr. Watson?" Catherine asked.

"It's called being tardy, and that is not allowed. You will probably have to line up after the teacher rings the bell. Just watch the other children or ask someone what the bell means. A bell is used for many reasons, so watch and be ready to move, okay?"

Jay William ran to sit beside Mr. Watson in the wagon. "No, schoolchildren sit in the back seat," Mr. Watson said. "You must make many changes now that you are a student."

Catherine was quiet on the way to school while Jay William chattered all the way there.

When they arrived they gave their lunch to Miss Armstrong to put away. "Let me show where to put it," she said. "It belongs on a shelf in the entry room."

44

They followed her into the room and saw a water bucket with a dipper on another shelf. There was also a washbasin, a bar of homemade soap, and a cotton towel so students could wash their hands after recess. On the wall above the washbasin were nails for hanging caps and jackets.

In a short time Miss Armstrong rang the bell and the children lined up. Girls were on one side and boys were on the other. Jay William followed the other boys, but Catherine began to cry. "I don't know what I'm supposed to do, and I'm not as smart as Jay William," she said. Miss Armstrong took her hand and led her into the room.

Miss Armstrong asked Catherine if she was afraid of school. "Yes," she said, "but I want to be here, even though I don't know how to add numbers like Jay William does."

"You will learn soon," Miss Armstrong said. "Now tell the class your full name and what you enjoy doing."

"I like to play with my baby doll, whose name is Marie Ann Hawkins," Catherine said. "I am her mother. I am a good mother and she loves me. I like to dress her every day and brush her red hair."

Catherine then took a seat along with the other girls in the first-, second- and third-grade section of the room. Jay William was in the section with the boys.

At recess, the other girls showed Catherine how to jump rope. She relaxed and enjoyed playing with her classmates.

Jay William did very well at arithmetic and was asked to go to the fourth- and fifth-grade section for that class. He did not want to take time to play at recess but wanted to do more math problems.

Miss Armstrong made him go out and watch the other boys fly their kites. This was a good opportunity for Jay William to make more friends. He knew Johnny Moore because they lived near one another. Johnny showed him how to fly a kite and said he would see if his uncle would make Jay William one.

Mr. Watson picked them up at the end of the school day. Jay William and Catherine were pretty quiet on the way home. They were excited but tired after the long day in class.

Jay William completed his afternoon chores in record time. He wanted to review his school day. He begged Catherine to bring her baby doll, Marie Ann, and come to his front-porch school. First he went over the attendance roll, listening as Catherine said "present" for Marie Ann and herself.

Next on the agenda was a review of the alphabet followed by a spelling quiz. Catherine wanted her turn at being teacher, and she gave Jay William arithmetic problems to solve.

Jerome interrupted the class by calling them to dinner. He hissed at Jay William on the way and called him sissy schoolboy. Jay William hardly reacted to him.

By the third week of class Jay William had proven to be quite the scholar, especially in arithmetic. He loved having the teacher give him multiple sets of numbers to add in his head. He could not get enough of it. When Miss Armstrong gave him the last set, he answered without hesitation.

Multiplication was next, and Jay William learned a rhyme that he and the others recited. "Twice times one is two. This book is nearly new. Twice times two is four. Lay it on the floor. Twice times three is six. We are always playing tricks. Twice times four is eight. The books are always late. Twice time five is ten. Let's do it all again."

The children learned through memorization, and this method worked well for Jay William. The first poem he memorized was this: "A big black bear stood on a ball. I was afraid he would fall. But no, he rolled it all around. I had a ball and I stood on it and fell to the ground."

Jay William and Catherine loved the opportunity to be with other children. This had been something missing from their lives.

Mr. Watson continued making frequent visits to their home. He had opened up opportunities for all of them. Marjorie was more active in her children's lives. Jay William came home from school one day and discovered she had ordered a three-piece suit for him plus a new hat.

"Please try it on and let me see my preacher boy in it," she said.

He did as she asked and his mother began to cry. "Why are you crying, Momma?" Jay William asked.

"Because you look so handsome," she said, snuffling. "Now let me see what you look like with your new hat on."

Jay William put on the hat, but he didn't want to give up the fedora his daddy had bought him in Memphis. His old hat made him happy when he wore it.

"It's too small for you to wear now," his mother objected. "Keep it but wear your new one now." Jay William agreed and wore the new suit the rest of the day.

Jerome teased him about it. "Hey, preacher boy," he said, "where are you preaching tonight? Are you going to use those new words you learned at school?"

Jay William said nothing because he knew Jerome wanted to make him cry.

"Jerome, must you always try to upset your little brother?" Momma scolded. "You have to get over Red and act like a man if you want more respect from all of us."

Jerome stormed out of the kitchen and headed for the barn.

Jay William did not understand his big brother at all. He went to the next room and recited the lesson he had learned that day for Catherine. She always liked the review he insisted on doing at home.

CHAPTER 8

JAY WILLIAM WAS now eight years old, and life was constantly full of surprises. Jerome seemed to be mad at him and at everyone else. He moved out of the house and into the barn.

Jay William was now sleeping in the living room on the rollaway bed, which had to be folded up and put behind the stove daily. He still was responsible for feeding the animals in the barn. He was always afraid his big brother would be in a bad mood out there. Sometimes Jerome hit him just because he could. That's what he told Jay William.

School was Jay William's only escape, but he could not go every day anymore because the family always seemed to have odd jobs for him to do. He still went every chance he could. He was now in eighth-grade arithmetic and still surprised others with his ability to work problems so quickly in his head. But Jay William was having difficulty with reading. Miss Armstrong encouraged him and gave him a book to take home to practice, but Mr. Watson was the only one who could help him with his reading, and he was busier than usual lately.

Jay William wished his family was not so angry and would stop hollering at each other. Mr. Watson was still at their house daily but seemed more interested in Marjorie than in Jay William and Catherine.

Catherine did not miss school as much as Jay William did, but it seemed she preferred to be with Wanda rather than with him.

Jay William often went to the woods to think. He wondered if there was a God. His momma said there was not, but his daddy had told him there was a God who loved him.

Many of the children at school went to church, but his momma never permitted him or Catherine to join them when they were invited. The school had a Christmas program, but they were not allowed to go because their momma said people would talk about God there.

Someday I will find out for myself, Jay William thought.

One morning he woke up to babies crying in his mother's room. He knocked on the door and she invited him in. He saw a girl baby and a boy baby. His momma smiled and said, "Jay William, come and meet your new brother, Otto, and your baby sister, Ethel. They are twins and were born during the night."

"You slept through all the excitement," his mother said. "Would you like to hold Otto?"

"Not now," Jay William said. "I have to go feed the animals before Jerome hollers at me."

Momma has two brand-new babies; they are twins. That thought made him happy. Jay William ran to the barn as quickly as he could and was out of breath when he got there.

"Guess what, Jerome," he said. "I'm not the baby in the house anymore. There are two new babies— twins, a boy and a girl. They are so cute. Have you seen them yet?"

What happened next took Jay William by surprise. Jerome knocked him to the floor with one blow.

"Don't you ever mention those twins in my presence again," Jerome said. "They are illegitimate. It is bad enough to live in a house with a boy whose father ran away because his son stuttered. Now I have a stuttering little sissy brother plus I have to live with illegitimate twins. I am not happy about living here. Get out and stay out. You are a worthless brat, and I can't stand the sight of you."

Jay William was stunned by the force with which Jerome had

hit him. *He is stronger than ever,* Jay William thought. *How am I going to handle him now?* Jay William wished he had someone to talk with about this. Mr. Watson was not as easily available as he once was.

Jay William decided to return to the house to see the twins again. When he got to his mother's room, he was surprised to see Mr. Watson holding Otto.

"Hey, Mr. Watson. How are you, sir? Do you like my little brother and sister?"

Mr. Watson gave Marjorie a questioning look. Then she said to Jay William, "Why don't you find Catherine and read to her from your book?"

Confused by their strange looks but not wanting any more trouble, Jay William did as he was told. He found his sister outside sitting by a tree. "Catherine, I'd like to read to you from the book Miss Armstrong let me use. Is that okay with you?"

"If you want to. I don't care," Catherine replied. "First tell me what you think about having twins in our house, Jay William."

"It's okay with me, I guess," he replied. "I'm happy that I'm not the youngest in the house any longer. Jerome doesn't like it, and he got really angry at me. Look at my arm; it's still red from his fist. I think he's angry all the time now."

"Wanda says Jerome has a girlfriend and may get married soon," Catherine said. "Wanda likes Fred Watson for a boyfriend. She always dresses up nice when she knows he'll be around."

Jay William wondered if getting married would change the way Jerome treated him.

"Jay William, are you going to read to me or not?" Catherine asked with a smile. "You are smart in arithmetic, but your reading could be better. So start reading."

Jay William opened Miss Armstrong's book—a McGuffey Reader—and read a story about a boy named Jack who stole another boy's lunch because he was hungry. The other boy forgave Jack and said he would share his lunch with him the next day.

The book had a lot of stories about values such as honesty, charity, and good manners.

Catherine loved the stories and realized she and her siblings did not get a lot of teaching at home about values and character. "Jay William, why don't we play school? This time I want to be the teacher," Catherine said.

They walked to the bottom of the porch steps.

"Today I am going to teach about geography," Catherine said in her best schoolteacher voice. "I want you to tell me the capital of Missouri."

"I know," Jay William said. "It's Jefferson City."

"Jay William, how did you know that?" Catherine asked. "I didn't expect you to have the correct answer."

"I listened when Miss Armstrong told the older kids about capitals and states. I know more. Little Rock is the capital of Arkansas, Richmond is the capital of Virginia, and Springfield is the capital of Illinois. Now how about some arithmetic, teacher?"

The two played school for a little while longer, but soon Jay William started thinking about other things. "Catherine, I think we've had enough school for now," he said. "Let's go see the twins. Did you know they were coming? I didn't."

Catherine said nothing, and Jay William let the question go. Inside they found their momma feeding Ethel while Mr. Watson held Otto.

"Come here beside me, Jay William," Mr. Watson said. "I want to show you how to hold your little brother. Sit down here in the chair. Now watch how I do this. First support his head because he cannot do that yet. Now place your other arm around his body and support his back."

After two tries, Mr. Watson told Jay William he had it right. "Just don't pick him or Ethel up by yourself until we say it's okay," Mr. Watson told him. Jay William felt pretty good about himself for holding the little baby properly.

Loretta called the family to a meal of cooked navy beans, fried potatoes, stewed tomatoes, and a hot pan of cornbread.

Jerome did not join the family for supper. When Jay William asked where he was, Loretta said, "He's courting tonight."

"What is that?" Jay William asked. Everyone at the table laughed.

Finally Mr. Watson said, "Jay William, when you get to be his age, you will be doing the same thing."

"He went to have supper with Sue Johnson and her family," Catherine said. "Remember I told you he had a girlfriend?"

Jay William shrugged his shoulders and said, "May I please have some sorghum molasses for my cornbread?"

CHAPTER 9

JAY WILLIAM AND Catherine enjoyed helping care for Otto and Ethel. Mr. Watson seemed to be at their home more than his own lately. Jay William was confused about that. Mr. Watson seldom took time to converse with him except when he was helping with the twins.

Jay William did not attend school regularly, and that troubled him a great deal. He continued to read from Miss Armstrong's book but did not know many of the words and guessed at what they meant. He read to the twins whenever he could. Occasionally, Mr. Watson would monitor his reading and help him with unfamiliar words.

Some days Mr. Watson would drop him off at school on his way to town and Jay William would walk home. He liked to do that. Miss Armstrong always helped him at school and encouraged him to continue to read at home and to do multiple arithmetic problems. She knew he had no control over his poor attendance and wanted to help him in any way possible.

Jerome married Sue Johnson and left the job of milking the one cow the family had left to Jay William. He managed but was tired most days. Catherine proved to be very good in the kitchen with Wanda and could cook some meals herself. Jay William wanted more time with Catherine but appreciated any moments they had together. They occasionally managed to play school.

When the twins could sit up by themselves, Jay William and

Catherine played with them while Momma and Mr. Watson did other things together. Those were the best times for Jay William. He would sing a song and Catherine would place her hands over her ears, telling him to stop. The twins enjoyed watching their interactions.

Marjorie seemed to be on edge most of the time, and Jay William noted something was not quite the same between his momma and Mr. Watson. He would hear her crying in her bedroom late at night. One night he heard his mother say, "Please marry me so I can become a respected and honest woman, so our twins will not be scorned by society. I promise to make you the best wife you can ever imagine."

Then another voice, a calm, masculine one, responded, "Marry you?" This was followed by a laugh. The voice was unmistakably Mr. Watson's. "Now what ever made you think this was a possibility?"

Jay William's whole body reacted to the emotional pain he felt at the question. Next there were heavy footsteps casually strolling past him. Jay William pretended to be sleeping. The footsteps continued out the front door as though nothing out of the ordinary had happened.

This pattern persisted for months: tears followed by laughter, followed by careful footsteps out the door.

You just go on home to your nice house, Mr. Watson, Jay William would say to himself, *and leave my momma with her tears. You think no one hears you, but I do.*

One night, shortly after Mr. Watson left, Jay William knocked on his momma's door. When the door opened, he hugged her and said, "Why does Mr. Watson treat you so mean? I thought he liked you."

"Jay William, you shouldn't worry about this," Marjorie said. "We'll find an answer to our problem."

"What problem, Momma?" Jay William inquired.

"You are too young to know about problems," Marjorie replied.

"I don't believe so, Momma. You trust me to milk the cow, don't you? So why shouldn't I know what's bothering you and why Mr. Watson makes you cry at night?"

"I wish I could tell you, but I must think about it before I say something I'll regret later. I think you should go to bed now."

"Momma, why do you treat me like the baby Jerome always said I was? Don't I obey you?"

Marjorie shook her head. "You're a good son, Jay William. I wish I could have been a better mother to you."

"You are a good mother. I wish you would tell me the problem. Maybe I can help you fix it. Am I part of your problem?"

Marjorie started to cry. "Jay William, you are not a problem. I will tell you this much. I'm afraid you have to get up in just four hours, and I wanted to let you go to school tomorrow. I'm going to have Wanda walk you and Catherine there."

"Am I really going, Momma?" Jay William replied. "I'll go to bed now." He left her room.

The next morning he got up excited about school and thought less about the night before than his mother expected. With the children gone, Marjorie did some serious thinking about her situation. Mr. Watson had made it clear he was not going to marry her. She had made some mistakes in life that had affected her children and would not allow the twins to remain illegitimate. She did not know the answer, but she hoped to find it. She had no one to help her.

That evening Marjorie asked Wanda to go over to the Watsons' house and ask Mr. Watson if he would take her to town in the morning and drop off Jay William and Catherine at school while Wanda stayed at home with the twins. The next morning he was over at six-thirty with the wagon. He took Marjorie to the post office as she had asked and left to get supplies at the general store.

Mr. Watson picked up the children from school and they all went home. He did not stay for supper. Catherine and Jay William were excited to tell the twins all about their day at school, while Wanda and Marjorie sat at the table and talked quietly

CHAPTER 10

CATHERINE AND JAY William began to see a gentler side of their mother. She seldom raised her voice, and she taught them a song to sing to the twins. It was the same one she had sung to Catherine the day Jay William was born: "I Love to Tell the Story." She also encouraged them to sing songs they had learned at school.

At the post office Marjorie had talked with Miss Franklin and had admitted she was unable to make a home with two parents for Otto and Ethel. Marjorie said that because of the stigma attached to the label she did not want the babies to be brought up as illegitimate. She also confessed that life had been tough for Catherine and Jay William since their daddy left. She was honest with Miss Franklin about why he left and said she regretted not controlling Jerome.

Miss Franklin listened attentively and suggested she talk with her church pastor about the situation. Marjorie quietly replied, "I'm sorry but I'm not a believer in God or church."

Miss Franklin did not judge her as most did when they found out Marjorie did not believe in God. She simply said, "I'm sorry you do not know or believe in God. He loves you and believes in you, Marjorie. I'm going to pray about your situation and see if we can get some answers for you. Can you come see me in two weeks?"

Marjorie assured her she would find a way to return in two

weeks. After years of indifference and selfishness, she was sincere and honest and wanted a new life for her children. She wanted to send Jay William and Catherine to school more regularly but needed them at home. Wanda was not as dependable as she had been before Mr. Watson quit coming around. Wanda spent more time at the Watson home than Marjorie liked. She was reluctant to mention the subject, because she feared Wanda would leave the house for good.

Jay William read to the twins. Then Catherine played school with Jay William while Marjorie watched the babies. Jay William milked the cow while Catherine cooked a meal of warmed white beans, fried potatoes, and cornbread. She also made apple fritters with their home-canned apples. They sat down to eat with the twins. Jay William fed Otto while Catherine fed Ethel. The babies were very good eaters and that made Marjorie happy.

The next morning Mr. Watson brought over meat for the family and asked if he could see the twins for a little while. He was kind to Catherine and Jay William and asked if they needed a ride to school. Marjorie told them they could go and assured them she would be okay. The children left reluctantly with Mr. Watson. When they returned in the afternoon, Marjorie seemed to be okay and asked them about school. They said Miss Armstrong had complimented them on their improved reading skills. She had told them that they could take home the last two weeks of spelling words and that she would give them a grade as though they had been in class.

That evening after supper, Catherine and Jay William studied those words over and over again until they could spell them correctly. Marjorie was happy that they were studying and wished she had sent her older children to school. *Red would be pleased that his kids are getting some education,* she told herself.

Marjorie saw how Catherine and Jay William got along and remembered how Jerome always started arguments. He did not see any of them much anymore since he married Sue Johnson.

Jay William was doing a fine job of milking the cow but was too young to do heavy work.

The next morning Marjorie told Jay William to get his chores done quickly so he could be ready for school. Wanda had agreed to walk Jay William and Catherine to school, and they could return home with friends who lived down the street.

Miss Armstrong was happy to see them again and had Jay William go to the front of the room for an arithmetic test on the seventh-grade level. Jay William was nervous but solved every problem. He was so excited that he had a hard time sitting still until noon break.

Miss Armstrong asked Catherine if she was ready to compete in a spelling bee. Catherine said she wanted to know more before she agreed to take part. Miss Armstrong said she would receive a list of a hundred words to learn to spell. Not all the words would be used in the spelling bee, but the words used would be chosen from the list. Six students would compete. If one of them misspelled a word and the next person asked spelled it correctly, the one who misspelled it would be out of the competition. The last person standing would receive a prize.

That evening Catherine told Wanda and Marjorie about her opportunity to be in a spelling bee. Marjorie said she doubted anyone in the family had ever taken part in such a contest.

"I think you should do it if you want to and be the first in the family," Wanda said. Catherine smiled at the thought because she wanted to make Wanda happy.

That evening the twins were cranky because they were teething. Everyone took turns rocking them and trying to settle them down. Marjorie put sugar water on two pieces of cloth, one for each baby. They were so calmed by the sugar water that they fell asleep. The rest of the family went to bed early.

The next day Catherine and Jay William walked to school with the Moore children. Catherine could not wait to tell Miss Armstrong she had decided to compete in the spelling bee. At the end of the school day, Miss Armstrong had Jay William read the words aloud to her to make sure he could help Catherine prepare for the competition.

After washing the supper dishes and finished their other chores, Catherine and Jay William migrated to the kitchen. There Jay William called out words for Catherine to spell. Catherine had studied well and misspelled only a few of them, which he marked for her to review. Taking a break, they made a snack of cornbread and milk. They tore the cornbread into bite-size pieces, placed it in a pint-size jar, and covered it with milk. They ate this treat enthusiastically. It was their favorite snack and remains popular in that part of the country.

The following morning as Marjorie and the children sat in the kitchen, they heard a knock at the door. This was unusual and Marjorie hesitated before opening the door. There stood Mr. Watson with a box of meat.

"Marjorie, I thought you could use this. Is it okay that I brought it over?" Mr. Watson asked.

"Thank you," Marjorie said, handing Wanda the meat to store.

Mr. Watson asked if he could see the twins. Marjorie gave him permission. Once Jay William and Catherine were ready for school they went to the bedroom where the twins were playing with Mr. Watson. The children told the twins they would see them after school, and they kissed the babies' foreheads.

"Would you two like a ride to school? I'm going right by there," Mr. Watson said.

"That would be okay if you're going to town anyway," Marjorie said as she entered the room.

The children got everything they needed for school and waited for Mr. Watson to return to the kitchen. Jay William told Catherine to take her spelling list to study.

On the way to school Catherine practiced for the spelling bee and spelled all the words correctly without hesitation.

"Wow, Catherine!" Jay William said. "I bet you're going to win the competition."

"I hope so," Catherine said. "I really want to do it for Wanda."

They were smiling as they entered the classroom, and Miss Armstrong smiled back at the pair. "Well, Catherine Hawkins, are you ready for the spelling bee this afternoon?" she asked.

"I think so, Miss Armstrong, because Jay William has had me spell the words several times, and I can spell them correctly."

"That's wonderful news, Catherine. I'm happy that you and Jay William worked together on this project. Perhaps when we have an arithmetic competition, you can practice with Jay William and help him sharpen his skills for it. That will take place before too long."

CHAPTER 11

JAY WILLIAM AND Catherine had a good day at school and enjoyed walking home with the Moore children. Marjorie had news for them when they returned. She told them Otto and Ethel were going to live in a nice home in Dyersburg with a couple who could not have children and wanted to adopt them.

Catherine and Jay William were stunned by the news.

"Why can't they live with us?" cried Catherine. "We love them and they belong to us."

"We don't have enough money coming into the house to keep them," Marjorie explained. "Besides, they need a mother and father in their lives. I'm getting old, and their new parents will help them have a better life.

"I would not allow this to happen without a lot of hard thought. I know you two love Ethel and Otto. Because you love them, you should be happy that they will have a better life than we can give them. This will not take place right away. Legal work must be done before the adoption occurs.

"Spend as much time as you need to show your love to Otto and Ethel. They will leave here happy and ready to accept their new momma and daddy. I'm sorry to tell you this news. This is the problem I've been seeking an answer for, Jay William."

Jay William had no reply but asked to be excused to milk the cow. In the barn he cried and talked to the cow.

"I don't understand any of this. I don't want Ethel and Otto to leave our home. I love them so much. Why is this the answer to the problem? I'm happy that they will have both a mother and a daddy. I wish Jerome had not run my daddy off. If there is a God, will you please help me understand this whole thing? I don't like it that my baby sister and brother will be leaving us."

Jay William was withdrawn that evening. He said nothing at suppertime and ate very little. He could hardly wait until bedtime. When the rest of the family had left the living room, he pulled his bed out from behind the stove and unfolded it. As he climbed into bed and pulled up the covers, the tears flowed again.

Why does this have to happen? Jay William wondered. *Why is Mr. Watson staying away from our home? I don't understand why Momma wanted to marry him. Perhaps Miss Armstrong has the answer because she is so smart.*

The next morning Jay William milked the cow and completed his other chores early. He even gathered the eggs from the hens' nests for Catherine so they could leave for school early and arrive before the other children did. He had a plan and hoped it would work. Marjorie did not understand why he wanted to leave early but supposed it was because this was the day of the spelling bee. For the first time she permitted them to walk without a chaperone because she wanted to do all she could to help Catherine win. On the way to school, Jay William told Catherine why he wanted to get there early.

At first Catherine was upset with him.

"Our family affairs are nobody else's business," she said. "Wanda told me so."

"I don't know how that solves our problem," Jay William replied. "Otto and Ethel will be living with strangers and may cry for us. I know Miss Armstrong can help me understand the circumstances better than I do now."

They were at school before Miss Armstrong and sat on the steps for a few minutes before she arrived. She was surprised to see them there.

"Good morning. You are bright and early, are you not? Did you come early so Catherine could practice for the spelling bee in the classroom?" she asked.

"No, Miss Armstrong," Jay William said. "I want to ask you about something in our family."

Jay William and Catherine followed Miss Armstrong into the classroom.

"You see, Miss Armstrong, my momma is going to let Otto and Ethel be adopted by a couple who have no children. Momma says it's better for them to have a mother and a father to raise them. I don't understand why Mr. Watson won't marry our momma. Can you help me understand how that works?"

As Jay William spoke, tears rolled down his face and onto his shirt. Miss Armstrong wiped his tears with her handkerchief.

"I don't have the answer for you," she said, "but you must trust your mother's decision for the twins. Perhaps she cannot afford food and clothing for them without help. She must believe this couple will be happy and fulfilled when they become parents. Your mother is probably happy to know that the twins will have two parents. The past few years have been difficult for her. I can't really discuss this with you because I could lose my job if I did, but I promise to pray for peace in your heart regarding this situation. Now go and wash your face before the other children get here."

CHAPTER 12

MARJORIE MADE A special meal in honor of Catherine winning second place in the spelling bee. Wanda had made her a new dress and placed a beautiful yellow ribbon on it.

Jay William had helped his sister practice the spelling words. He had been a big part of her success, and that made him feel good. Miss Armstrong accepted an invitation to come to the Hawkins home for this special occasion. It was the first time she had been there.

Mr. Watson had asked if he could join in the celebration of Catherine's success. He got permission, but the relationship between the two families was strained at best. He was there only for dessert.

Miss Armstrong told everyone that Jay William and Catherine were very good students, and she encouraged Marjorie send them to school more frequently. She pointed to Jay William's arithmetic skills and his exceptional ability to instantly add sets of numbers together. She said she had never had a student with that skill.

Marjorie was very happy to hear how well her children were doing in school. They were her only two to attend school. She expressed her appreciation to Mr. Watson for insisting she enroll them.

The meal consisted of fried chicken, mashed potatoes, green beans, homemade biscuits, and gravy. The dessert was Catherine's choice—blackberry cobbler made from the berries she and Jay

William had picked for canning the previous summer. Mr. Watson said it was the best cobbler he had ever eaten. Wanda blushed when he said that, because she had made the cobbler.

Ethel and Otto got a great deal of attention from the group. The Watson family now knew the twins would be leaving as soon as the adoption process was completed. No one spoke about this, however, because the subject was out of place at the celebration for Catherine.

Miss Armstrong said she had to leave so she could get home before dark. Jay William and Catherine asked if they could walk part of the way with her. "Only to the first fork in the road," Marjorie said, "because you still have a few chores to do before nightfall."

The children had a pleasant walk with Miss Armstrong because they trusted her and nothing was said about the twins leaving. Catherine told Miss Armstrong how much Jay William knew about the states and their capitals and asked if she would hold a bee on that subject. "Catherine, that is such a good idea," Miss Armstrong said. "We could call it a geography bee. I will give that some thought."

Jay William was excited at Miss Armstrong's response. He wondered how he could learn all the names of the states and the capitals. He wasn't sure how many he had heard mentioned. *The next time we go to school, I'm going to ask Miss Armstrong how I can get the names of all forty-eight states and capitals,* he thought.

"I'll beat you home, Jay William!" Catherine shouted. "We'll leave at the same time from the big tree up there, okay?" They got to the tree and started running, reaching the lane to the house at about the same moment. Neither one declared victory, but the fresh air and exercise gave them increased energy. Catherine helped Jay William with the chores, and they went into the house to play with Ethel and Otto.

"How much longer will Ethel and Otto be living with us?" Jay William asked Marjorie. She promised to tell him when she got the answer. When the children were asleep in bed, Marjorie began to sew a sailor suit for Otto and a sailor dress for Ethel, using matching fabric. She wanted them to look their best when they left to live with new parents.

Marjorie felt so many emotions and didn't know exactly which way to turn. She thought she might try to talk to Miss Franklin again soon.

CHAPTER 13

M ARJORIE HAD SENT word to Jerome earlier in the week, asking him to take her to Randolph to meet with the adoptive parents' attorney to finalize the adoption. Although Marjorie had not met the parents, Miss Franklin had assured her they were a stable couple. They attended a church, but Marjorie did not object because she trusted Miss Franklin's promise that they were good people. They wanted a quick adoption. Marjorie understood that and was happy to find a good home for the babies.

After she had signed the adoption papers, Jerome took Marjorie home. There was little conversation. Jerome was grateful that the illegitimate twins were leaving the area. He told his momma to send word if she needed help again.

When Jay William came home from school he could not contain his excitement about the geography bee Miss Armstrong was planning. She had given him permission to copy a map of the United States so he could learn all the states and their capitals as well as rivers, lakes, and other geographic details. He had skipped recess to get this done. He wanted to win more than anything he could imagine.

Catherine had promised to help by drilling him on the material. Marjorie said nothing to them about her trip to town but told them to get their after-school chores finished while she made supper for them.

They played with Ethel and Otto for a while after completing the chores. The twins were crawling all over the house, and Catherine and Jay William were assigned to keep them out of trouble. They loved to clap their hands to the songs Catherine sang.

After supper, the twins went to bed, tired from their fun time with Jay William and Catherine. Jay William got out his map and copied the names of the New England states and their capitals on a box lid to study. He recited them to himself while Catherine and Wanda sewed dish towels. Wanda showed her how to make them out of feed sacks.

By dark, Jay William was tired and took his geography notes to bed with him. He fell fast asleep as soon as his head hit the pillow.

Five in the morning seemed to come earlier than usual. He was milking the two cows when he noticed the oil lamp shining in the kitchen window. As he brought the milk into the kitchen, he saw that his momma and Wanda had a large breakfast ready.

Marjorie had opened a new jar of blackberry preserves to spread on the hot biscuits. Momma made an announcement: "Otto and Ethel will be leaving us for their new home probably this week."

Jay William suddenly felt a tight knot in his gut. His appetite was gone and he felt sick all over. "Momma, you mean this week?"

Marjorie nodded her head. "I signed papers to give up my rights as their mother. They now have a new mother and a daddy too. They are good people, but I do not know their names. They are members of a church, and Otto and Ethel will be going to church with them. That is out of my control now."

"Well, I'm not going to school today, because I want to see them off," Jay William declared. "Will I ever be able to talk or play with them again?"

"No, Jay William, you will not," Marjorie replied.

He began to shake and cry. "Please may I be excused now?" he asked.

Jay William went to the barn and sobbed uncontrollably. "I'll never have a chance to be a big brother again. I'll never be able to prove to Jerome that I'm the good big brother he refused to be. I love Otto and Ethel, and I will never see them again after they leave our house. Why, oh why must life be so hard to understand?"

CHAPTER 14

BRIGHT AND EARLY two days after the meeting with the attorney, Jerome knocked on the front door while Jay William was milking the cows. He heard the noise and looked out the barn door. Sure enough, there was his big brother acting like he owned the place.

Jay William finished with the cows and took the milk into the kitchen. There sat Jerome eating a big plate of sausages and eggs with biscuits and gravy. "Hurry up, Jay William, if you expect me to save you some of this breakfast," he bellowed.

"What are you doing here, Jerome?" Jay William asked.

"Is that any way to greet your big brother, squirt?" Jerome replied. "Why, I just came to bring you some good news. Those illegitimate babies will soon be history around here. A boat is coming down the Mississippi River to take them away. Hurry up and you can go with Momma to take them down to the river. Catherine and Wanda are dressing them now in Momma's room."

Jay William raced into the room and saw the babies dressed up for their new parents.

"Momma, do they have to leave right now?" he asked. "I haven't eaten yet or even talked to them. I didn't know they were going today."

"Yes. Jerome brought word this morning. We'll take the twins down to the river, and then they'll go to their new home," Marjorie replied.

"Momma, Otto and Ethel did not have a choice in the matter, and that seems so unfair. I suppose I should be happy that you did not give me up for adoption, but this stinks," Jay William said. He was visibly upset, and Marjorie was also upset that the transfer of the twins had come so suddenly.

"Okay, Jay William, quit your smart-mouthing and eat your breakfast now," she said. "It may be a while before this is completed. Don't quarrel with Jerome. I need his help now because we have no other transportation. Do I have your word on this?"

"I'll do what you want. I don't want to quarrel with Jerome. How are we going to get down to the river? Is Jerome taking us in his wagon?" Jay William asked.

Marjorie did not reply and began to sing to calm herself down. She reverted back to the song "I Love to Tell the Story," and Catherine joined her.

Finally Marjorie, Wanda, Catherine, and Jay William were nestled in the wagon with Otto and Ethel. Jerome took the driver's seat and they headed toward the river. The boat was waiting for them, and Marjorie delivered the twins into the open arms of two ladies chosen by the new parents. They asked if Marjorie needed a little more time with the twins, and she said she would like Jay William and Catherine to join her with them for a few moments.

Jay William tried to be brave and not to cry. He took Otto aside while Catherine chose Ethel. They had thirty minutes before the boat left with the twins.

Jay William told Otto how much he loved him and wished him a happy life with his new parents. The time passed quickly and the good-byes were not nearly long enough for Jay William, but he managed not to cry.

Wanda and Jerome had already left with the wagon, so Marjorie, Jay William, and Catherine walked the mile back to the house. They decided to sing Marjorie's song, "I Love to Tell the Story."

As they neared the house, they heard yelling, screaming, and crying from inside. Marjorie's muscles tightened and she walked more quickly. Jay William was filled with fear and trembling.

As they entered the home, Wanda was screaming, "Leave us alone!" She was scratching and kicking her brother as he threw punches at Fred Watson. Then Mr. Watson walked through the door, grabbed both men by the backs of their necks, and demanded they stop fighting. He told his son to go home.

With much emotion Fred replied, "I will not leave without my wife. Wanda and I got married a few weeks ago, and I want her to live with me. I came over to help her gather her belongings. Jerome blocked her from her room, and that's what started this fight."

"Jerome, get out of the way and let Wanda get her things," Mr. Watson said.

Marjorie swayed a little bit and groped for a table to support herself. She finally stumbled into a chair at the shock of the news. *The Watsons have caused our family more pain than good*, she told herself.

Jay William and Catherine looked at each other and headed for the kitchen. There they hugged and allowed the tears to flow. "What's going to happen next to our family?" Jay William asked. "I'm scared to think about it."

He thought about Otto and Ethel and wondered what it would be like to attend church as they would be doing soon. *Perhaps if Momma gave them to parents who would teach them about God, she might not be so opposed to believing in him anymore*, Jay William thought. *Maybe she believes in God now. If my daddy were here, he would help her believe in God. Oh, my questions are many, but I don't know the answers.*

"I know," Catherine said, "but at least we have school to think about. Do you have any geography questions ready for me to quiz you on before the bee this week? Jay William, I really want you to win the geography bee."

"I copied the map with the states and the capitals, and it's in my room," Jay William said. "Why don't we check on Momma? Then we can go outside and work on that."

They went into their momma's room and found her asleep. It sure seemed strange not to have the twins around.

CHAPTER 15

J AY WILLIAM HAD many unanswered questions, but Marjorie did not feel she could even begin to address them. Marjorie had not felt well for some time now but refused to admit it. She struggled from one day to another. Jay William noticed that his momma's skin had yellowed and that her hands, face, and legs were larger than usual. He asked Catherine if she noticed these changes and their momma's slowed pace. They tried to help her as much as possible but hated to miss school.

Jay William walked with Johnny Moore to his house after school and told him he was worried about Marjorie. He asked Johnny if his mother, Lorene, would mind checking on his momma. Lorene took Jay William home in her wagon and visited with Marjorie while the two boys did the milking together.

When they brought the milk into the kitchen, they heard the ladies in deep conversation in Marjorie's room. Catherine was cooking a meal of fried potatoes, biscuits, and white beans for all of them. She opened home-canned peaches for dessert. It was a simple supper but tasted very good, according to the two boys.

Mrs. Moore helped Marjorie with a few odds and ends around the house, making sure to get home before dark so she could finish the evening chores at her place. Jay William and Catherine got their clothes ready for school and went to bed early as did Marjorie.

The next morning, Mrs. Moore came to check on Marjorie.

She was even weaker than she had been the evening before. "Marjorie, I want to take you to a Memphis hospital to have you examined by a doctor," Mrs. Moore said. "I think you have what my mother had years ago. It's a disease called dropsy. This hospital will often help even if you cannot pay for it."

She helped Marjorie into the wagon, and the two ladies left for Memphis. Marjorie found breathing very difficult during the trip. At the hospital she was seen by a doctor, but he said that he could not help her and that she should go home and get her affairs in order.

Marjorie died as soon as the children got home from school. Jay William's world came crashing down and he felt helpless. The burial was the next day. Jerome built a wooden casket for his mother, and Loretta and Wanda helped with the burial arrangements. Marjorie was laid to rest by a large tree overlooking the Mississippi River.

The next day the sheriff was called to the house to find a home for Jay William and Catherine. The adult children were unwilling to take them into their homes. Sheriff Johnson quickly discovered that the orphanages were overflowing and could not accept any more children.

He arranged to have Mrs. Moore take Jay William and Catherine for a few days while he tried to find their father. Mrs. Moore was a widow and could barely afford to keep her place up and running. Sheriff Johnson returned several days later with news for the children. "I'm sorry to tell you this," he said, "but your daddy is just not around here anymore. I've checked the surrounding counties and have found no information about him or his whereabouts."

"What are we going to do and where will we live?" Jay William asked with much emotion.

"Well, I'm going to find out more about your Aunt Sophie and her husband, Hilton Henderson," Sheriff Johnson said. "They have a nice farm and could help us out until something else shows up. Now children, please don't cry. I'll do my best for you. Your aunt is your mother's sister. Her two daughters are married and both live in Dyer County. Did your mother ever talk about your aunt?"

"I haven't heard much about her," Catherine said. "I just heard our momma had a sister who did not talk with her at all. I don't think she would like us either, sir."

"Now, Missy, you don't know that to be true. We'll drive up to their farm and talk with your aunt and uncle now. Please don't assume it's going to be a bad situation. You must think the best until proven otherwise. That's what I always say. Now you two have each other, and that's not going to change. I won't separate you, and you can count on that."

Jay William was frightened. Catherine squeezed his hand to reassure him. He tried to think hopeful thoughts, but that was getting tougher to do. *Momma is gone and I just don't know how this is going to work out. I'm happy Otto and Ethel have a home,* he thought. *It's too bad Catherine and I couldn't have gone there too. I wish Momma had believed in God because I could sure use his help now.*

When they arrived at the farmhouse, Sheriff Johnson told the children, "Perhaps you two want to sit here while I go to the house. I will come and get you later."

Jay William watched as the sheriff took off his cap and knocked on the door. He was greeted by a woman who used her hands to show her annoyance at his words. The solemn look on the sheriff's face deepened as she spoke. After a few seconds, the lady pointed to the squad car and became overly dramatic. She shook her head and finally shrugged in resignation. Then a man with a clenched fist appeared next to her.

Jay William was terrified now. *He reminds me of Jerome when he's angry. I don't think he's happy to hear about us,* Jay William thought. He continued to watch as Sheriff Johnson put his cap back on and returned hesitantly to the squad car.

The sheriff opened the car door and said, "Okay, kids, I'm going to take you up to the house now, and you'll be living here for a short while."

"But sir, I can tell they don't want us to live with them. I don't like this at all," Jay William said.

Catherine put a protective arm around her little brother. "It will be okay, Jay William," she said. "I'll be with you."

The two walked slowly with Sheriff Johnson up to the house. Once inside, Jay William watched the sheriff walk back to the car and hesitate before he left.

"I didn't expect this to happen, and I'm not sure it will work out," Aunt Sophie told the children, "but the sheriff says it's the law. We'll make the best of this, I'm sure."

If those words were supposed to make Jay William feel better, they did not work because he felt even more frightened. Aunt Sophie had a stern look on her face, and Uncle Hilton appeared angry.

"Okay, children, follow me up the stairs to your new home," Aunt Sophie said. "It's not much but it's probably better than what you had before you got here."

When they got to the top of the stairs, Aunt Sophie said, "There are two beds up here, and you are responsible for taking care of this room." With that, she charged down the stairs.

Jay William overheard her say, "Their clothes are clean but otherwise hideous, not suitable for our home. If we must care for them, they can work for their room and board. This could work out well for us if we plan it right."

He whispered to Catherine what he had heard Aunt Sophie say.

"It will be all right," Catherine told him. "Come on. Let's lie down for a while." She held Jay William on one of the beds until he fell asleep. Then she rolled over on her side and was asleep right away.

CHAPTER 16

THE TWO YOUNGSTERS slept all night from sheer fatigue. They had not eaten since noon the previous day and were very hungry. They were afraid to go downstairs, so they made their beds and sat at the top of the stairs, waiting until someone called for them. At 6:30 a.m. Aunt Sophie opened the door at the foot of the stairs so quickly they almost fell over.

"Well good morning to you! I see you are awake and waiting to go to work" she said gruffly.

"Yes, Aunt Sophie," Catherine replied in her sweetest voice. "Jay William and I are really hungry. May we please have something to eat?"

"Let's get something straight right now," Aunt Sophie said. "This is not a hotel; if you want to eat you must work for it."

She saw Jay William looking out the screen door toward a large red barn. "Jay William, follow your Uncle Hilton to the barn, and he will teach you how to work like a man," Aunt Sophie said. She then turned around as though she had forgotten she had spoken to him or as if he were never there. He hurried outside toward the barn.

Jay William found himself running to keep up as Uncle Hilton strode across the cropped grass. The barn was not enormous but was crammed with equipment and animals. Stalls lined each side, and Uncle Hilton led horses out of each one and through the barn opening.

Jay William kept out of his way as best he could, finding shelter behind a plow. When the last horse passed, he started to follow it out to the pasture. He took in the hilly farmland for the first time. It was breathtaking, rolling toward a long line of trees in the distance. Only a pond some fifty yards away broke the green of the grass.

"Get back in here, boy. There is work to be done," Hilton said. He tossed him a pitchfork, but Jay William scurried out of the way rather than try to catch it. "First, get all of this animal dung out of here and put down clean straw." Jay William struggled to complete the job to suit Uncle Hilton.

"Now milk the cows and feed all the other animals in this area," Uncle Hilton said. "Get a move on. Don't be so slow about it." *I believe he's meaner than Jerome*, Jay William thought.

"I've finished doing all the things you told me to do, sir," Jay William said, stuttering. He noticed Uncle Hilton seemed annoyed at his words.

"Okay, go in the house and grab something to eat," his uncle said.

Jay William hurried into the house and noticed his sister's eyes were red from crying. He said nothing but wondered if her morning had also gone badly. The meal consisted of two biscuits covered in milk gravy with a glass of milk. After they had eaten, Jay William asked politely if he could have more.

"No, no, and no," Aunt Sophie replied. "I will tell you when you can have more. Now wash the dishes and get back to work."

Jay William was happy to help his sister, but Uncle Hilton grabbed his arm. "Not you, boy," he said. "You're going outside with me. We have more work to get accomplished."

Jay William wanted to prove himself to his uncle, so he worked furiously. The harder he worked, the easier it would be for him and Catherine, he thought.

In the house, Catherine scrubbed pots and pans and had them shining in a short while. Then she swept and mopped the floors.

She helped make supper. Aunt Sophie swatted her a couple of times for peeling the potatoes too thick. *Oh, Momma, why did you have to die and leave us? I don't think we'll survive here,* she said to herself.

By evening, both children were exhausted. The evening meal was the roughest, especially for Catherine. She helped kill, pluck, gut, and cut up a chicken. She put salt and pepper on it and rolled it in flour. Her mouth watered as she fried it. Aunt Sophie told her to put the food on the table.

She found that the table was set for only two people. She gave Aunt Sophie a questioning look. "You and your brother will wait in the kitchen until we have finished our meal," her aunt said. "You are then welcome to eat what's left over. Now get in the kitchen and wash the pots."

Catherine could not believe her ears.

In fear, she and Jay William did as much as they could while their aunt and uncle were eating. In due time, they were called to take the leftovers into the kitchen and told they could eat all they wanted. They saw an empty space where the chicken had been, and the corn on the cob was gone. The remaining food consisted of some green beans, a few cabbage leaves, two spoonfuls of potatoes, three biscuits, and a scant amount of gravy in a bowl. "Unbelievable," declared Jay William.

Catherine quickly placed her hand over his mouth and said, "Hush. We must not complain because I think they'll beat us. Aunt Sophie is so mean; she spanked me three times just for asking questions about how she wanted me to do jobs for her. Please, I can't take this anymore. Let's eat this food and go upstairs to our room."

When the kitchen was spic and span, Catherine asked, "Please, Aunt Sophie, may Jay William and I go up to our room in the attic now?"

"Not yet," Aunt Sophie said. "First pump some water into the large pan hanging on a nail by the window on the back porch.

Get a rag out of the rag box there and scrub those dirty bodies. You better put everything back into place because I can't pick up after you. I expect you to go upstairs without talking. Tomorrow will be a very busy day."

The poor children were so tired they didn't talk much. Once again, they lay down on one bed, put their arms around each other, and slept until morning.

CHAPTER 17

THE CHILDREN WOKE up before daylight. They were cold and wet. Jay William had urinated on the bed.

"Oh, no," he said. "I think I peed on the bed. What's going to happen now?" He cried softly because he was so upset and did not want Catherine to get in trouble along with him.

"Wait. Let's think this through," Catherine said. "You poor fellow. This happened because you were in such a deep sleep and were stressed from yesterday."

"I haven't done this in a very long time, so I suppose you're right," Jay William said.

Catherine tiptoed down the stairs. She looked into her aunt and uncle's bedroom, and they were both snoring.

She went quietly back up the stairs and took the sheet off the bed. She carried it downstairs and onto the back porch. She pumped water into the pan and rinsed the sheet. She wrung it out and brought it back to the attic room to dry out during the daytime.

They came down for breakfast when they heard their aunt and uncle get up.

"Didn't I make myself clear? Can't you follow a simple instruction? You were supposed to hang up the pan after you washed it out!" Aunt Sophie shouted. "I'll teach you what happens when my rules are not obeyed. There will be no breakfast for you two kids."

Catherine and Jay William were happy that she did not know he had urinated on the bed. "We're sorry," Catherine said. "It won't happen again."

Catherine was able to retrieve a biscuit from Aunt Sophie's plate; she had taken only one bite from it. Catherine knew Jay William would be working outside, so she wrapped the biscuit in a rag on the porch instead of feeding it to the chickens. She managed to show it to Jay William on his way out to the barn. He stuffed it into his mouth and kept walking toward Uncle Hilton without getting caught.

Aunt Sophie gave Catherine pillowcases, aprons, and other simple items to iron. She used a dress to demonstrate the proper ironing technique and had Catherine iron another one while she watched. Catherine did a good job with only minor mistakes, so Aunt Sophie decided that ironing was now Catherine's job. On ironing days, Aunt Sophie would help clean the kitchen and do all the cooking.

Out in the barn Uncle Hilton had Jay William wash all the garden tools and protect them against rust by oiling them with a soft rag. Jay William was not familiar with the task and asked for further instructions. Because he feared his uncle, he stuttered.

Uncle Hilton became gruff, which made Jay William's stuttering even worse. "Get over here, boy, and ask me again what you want to know. No stuttering this time," his uncle said.

Jay William didn't get too far with his question before stuttering again. "That's it. I'll stop this nonsense," Uncle Hilton said. He pulled a razor strap from his overalls and hit Jay William with it. The boy was so frightened he ran from him.

"Boy, I'm going to give you to the count of ten to get back here," Uncle Hilton said.

Jay William dragged himself back to his uncle. "I'm sorry, sir," he stammered, "but when I get scared it happens." Uncle Hilton hit him once again, and Jay William fell to the floor.

"Okay, boy, I'll help you up, but I hope you understand that I can't have you stuttering like an idiot while you're working here. Someday you'll thank me for taking the time to correct you. Go out and feed the animals in the pasture. That's a job this old man is happy to give you. Now go!"

Jay William ran to the pasture and introduced himself to the animals. "Hey, Bully. My name is Jay William Hawkins and I'm happy to make your acquaintance," the boy said as he led the big bull out from a fenced-in area to the other cows. "Now I want to introduce you to the prettiest female animal on this farm. This is Flossie, the best milk cow around here. Over here is Molly, the next best one."

He pumped water and took it out to the horses, which were feeding in the tall grass. "Okay, Herman," he said, "I know your name but I don't think you know mine. I'm Jay William Hawkins, and I want you to know I know that you work hard. My momma just died and that's why I'm here. I want to be a good worker because I will grow up to be a good husband and daddy. My daddy is gone and I don't know where he is."

"Jay William, it's time for lunch!" Catherine called out. He hurried into the house. He had had a good time with the animals and looked forward to doing that job again.

Lunch consisted of white beans and cornbread. The children were reminded of the days before Momma died. "I heard Uncle Hilton tell Aunt Sophie we are going to plant a garden this year," Catherine said. "I sure hope that works out, because we will be together again."

Sure enough, after the dishes were washed, Uncle Hilton called Jay William to the house to help plant lettuce. He showed him how to use a hand plow to make the ground soft enough to plant the seeds. The children gave the seeds a light covering of dirt and watered them using a can with holes in the bottom. Waiting until Uncle Hilton had left for another job, they played a quiet game as they prepared the garden.

The game was Jay William's idea. He started by saying, "Let's spell *tobacco.*"

Catherine replied, "T-o-b-a-c-c-o." When it was Catherine's turn she said, "Let's name the capital of Massachusetts."

He replied, "Boston."

They continued the game until Aunt Sophie came out and said, "How do you expect to finish this if you keep talking? Let's have more work and less play."

The pair then dug holes in the ground and put in tomato plants that Aunt Sophie had started in her kitchen window with the previous year's seeds.

"These better grow because Aunt Sophie will think we did something wrong if they don't," Catherine said with a laugh as she watered the plants. Jay William filled in the holes with freshly plowed dirt.

They also planted carrots, cabbages, and potatoes. Aunt Sophie and Uncle Hilton came out to check their work. "For a couple of kids, it looks good," Uncle Hilton said, "but we aren't finished yet. We have more to plant, and we'll have to keep out the weeds and water the garden if we don't get enough rain."

Jay William and Catherine tried to hide their happiness. They did not want Aunt Sophie and Uncle Hilton to know how much they enjoyed working together for fear they would be denied another opportunity.

"This was a much better day for me than yesterday. How about you, Jay William?" Catherine asked.

"Mine was good for two reasons," he said. "One, I got to work with animals, and two, I got to work with you."

CHAPTER 18

THE FOLLOWING WEEK, Jay William met one of the farm workers, Johnny Maddox, who came to plow the fields with a team of mules. Uncle Hilton told Johnny to show Jay William how to hitch up the mules. Jay William was less stressed with Johnny showing him how to do it. He preferred Johnny's way to Uncle Hilton's overbearing manner, which made him so nervous.

Jay William did not stutter once while talking with Johnny. The boy also talked to the mules while hitching them to the plow; even they were relaxed, Johnny said.

"Why are you here, Jay William?" he asked.

"My mother died, my father can't be found, and my older brother and sisters aren't willing to let us live with them," Jay William said. "My momma and Aunt Sophie are sisters, but I didn't know Aunt Sophie or Uncle Hilton. Sheriff Johnson brought us here."

Johnny suddenly said, "Okay and thanks for your help." He had spotted Uncle Hilton approaching them.

"Okay, boy, go do your work in the pasture. Lead the cows there, carry some water out to them, and then come back here for your next assignment," Uncle Hilton said. "Let's not mess around, because there is much work to be done around here."

"I'm on my way, sir," Jay William replied.

He loved the smell of the clean pasture and was amazed at all the wildflowers in bloom.

If Momma were here, I would pick her a bouquet of flowers, but I don't think my aunt would appreciate one, Jay William thought. He pumped the water and recited the states and capitals he could remember.

He filled the water troughs and brought Flossie out first. "Flossie, I'm happy that I can do this job, and I hope you like me because I like you very much," Jay William said as he led her to the green pasture.

Next he led Molly out. "Molly, I used to go to school and I liked it a lot," Jay William said, "but since my momma died, I must stay here and work. I don't think that's fair. Life is not fair. That's what Miss Armstrong said when she found out we were losing Otto and Ethel to their new parents. They were adopted because Momma couldn't take care of them. They will be going to church. I wish Momma had let us go to church."

Suddenly Jay William heard Uncle Hilton calling his name.

"Yes, sir," he said. "I haven't brought the bull out yet. When I get him out I'll be right there."

"I need you to come now!" his uncle shouted.

Jay William ran as fast as he could to the barn where Uncle Hilton was waiting for him. "Boy, I need you to run this lunch bag and bottle of ice water out to Johnny Maddox in the lower field," his uncle said. "Now don't poke around. Go, and then get back so you can eat before the food is gone."

Jay William ran the food to Johnny and then washed up in the pan on the back porch and entered the kitchen.

"You are all wet and smelly. What have you been doing, Jay William?" his sister asked.

"I just ran about a mile and a half to take Johnny Maddox his lunch," a winded Jay William said.

"What is he like?" Catherine asked.

"He's real nice and he showed me how to hitch the mules to the plow."

"I think we're going to work together in the garden again if I heard correctly. I sure hope so because I can smell spring in the air and it will be good to get outside. I know Uncle Hilton brought back new plants from town."

"But I haven't completed my animal chores yet. It's hard to get everything done when he keeps adding new jobs."

"You two will get more accomplished if you don't talk so much," Aunt Sophie said. "Now finish up in here because you two are going to plant vegetables. We have green beans, butter beans, and cabbage to get in the dirt today. Jay William, you must take the bull out to the pasture as soon as you can."

He swallowed the rest of his food and ran out to the fenced-in area where the bull was being kept. "Okay, Bully. We're going out to join the girls in the big pasture. I sure hope you enjoy the extra space to run. There's water waiting for you out there," Jay William said as he led the bull, using a rope around its neck.

"Get a move on, boy, and put those new plants in the ground because it's supposed to rain this evening, and that will give them a head start," Uncle Hilton said.

Jay William grabbed his straw hat and joined Catherine, who was already in the garden area.

After plowing the ground, Jay William took a deep breath and said, "I love the way the dirt smells after it's plowed. It smells so clean and fresh."

"Yes, but I think we're being watched, so we better work steady," Catherine said. "We can talk low while we work. I wonder how Miss Armstrong is doing. I know she misses us in her classroom. We learned a lot from her in every way, didn't we?"

"I sure wish we had that McGuffey Reader. I loved the stories. Did you?" Jay William asked.

The two worked until it was dark. Uncle Hilton and Aunt Sophie appeared from time to time to check their progress. During their hushed conversation, the children pledged to put into practice what Miss Armstrong had taught them about developing good character including honesty, kindness, and learning from mistakes.

Uncle Hilton told them to go to the pump and remove most of the dirt from their bodies before stepping onto the porch. Aunt Sophie had pumped bathwater into her laundry tubs on the porch, and the afternoon sun had warmed it. The homemade lye soap made the children feel clean after a busy afternoon. They ate a meal of beans, potatoes, and cornbread before doing the dishes and going to sleep.

CHAPTER 19

JAY WILLIAM AND Catherine had been living with the Hendersons for nineteen months. "Some days are worse than others," Jay William said, "but no matter how hard we try, we still annoy our aunt and uncle. Ants labor continuously, and they too face obstacles that make their work difficult. They get stepped on and pushed back, and they must take the same steps again, and yet they work at a steady pace."

"I remember that story from the McGuffey Reader," Catherine said as they prepared to leave their attic bedroom. "I know I'm going to help Aunt Sophie clean the kitchen today, because she told me so yesterday. The bottoms of her pots are black, and I'm going to see if she cleans them the way Loretta and I did for Momma."

Catherine told Aunt Sophie how her mother and her sisters kept their pots and pans sparkling clean with a monthly treatment of river sand to remove the black substance from the bottoms. She convinced Aunt Sophie to let her try this method once. If it worked, Catherine said, she would be happy to do this chore on a regular basis.

The next day Uncle Hilton brought a wheelbarrow of river sand out to the backyard for Catherine's experiment. Catherine rubbed the bottom of a pot in the sand, putting all of her weight onto it. Then she wiped off the sand and furiously buffed the pot with a rag. The bottom shined. Within an hour the black substance had just about vanished from all the pots, and they looked nearly new. Aunt Sophie could not hide her delight and admitted this was a marvelous idea.

Catherine knew Aunt Sophie was happy with her and thought, *Perhaps I should strike while the iron is hot.*

"Aunt Sophie, I know you are happier with me and my work than when I began here. Do you think maybe Jay William and I could have a little more food? We would especially like some meat—perhaps once or twice a week?"

"Little Miss Catherine," Aunt Sophie said in an acid tone, "do you think you can manipulate me into giving you more than I do just because you made me happy? Well you are completely wrong, and I am disappointed in your attempt to get on my good side. The answer is no. You are getting all I want you to have. My husband and I still make the decisions here, so don't try that again."

In the barn, Jay William was in big trouble because the hog had gotten out of its pen and had eaten a row of lettuce.

"Okay, boy, you've done it this time." Uncle Hilton's face was beet red and he was shaking with anger. "You have tried my patience beyond measure. This requires a severe punishment. How often have I told you to check the pens for security and for signs of wear and tear? The hog rooted under the fence and got out that way. You should have seen that coming because he didn't do it all at one time! Grab some rope from over there, and go out in the grass by the hog pen."

Poor Jay William was sick with worry over what was ahead, but he knew he must obey his uncle. He quickly handed the rope to him. He said nothing because he feared he would stutter and anger Uncle Hilton even further.

"Follow me outside and do what I say. That will make it easier for both of us. Lie down there on your back, and give me your hands and then your feet." Uncle Hilton tied Jay William's hands and feet securely together. Then he picked him up and threw him into the hog pen. "Now you stay there for the rest of the day," he said.

Uncle Hilton filled in the hole under the pen with dirt and then sat down under a shade tree with a tall glass of water and watched Jay William. The boy struggled to defend himself from the hog. He yelled and squirmed, trying to get out of the hog's way. Suddenly he thought about his momma's words concerning the twins' adoptive parents: "The twins will go to church with them, and that's okay with me."

Jay William whispered, "God, if you are real, please protect me and don't let the hog eat me." The hog suddenly retreated to a corner of the pen away from Jay William and lay down to rest. As the sun was setting, Uncle Hilton removed Jay William from the pen and threw him into the grass. He said nothing until he untied the boy's hands and feet.

"I hope this has taught you a lesson. Check all pens for security every time you are near one, and always secure the animals."

"I will do just that," Jay William said with a stammer.

"Do you want more punishment?" Uncle Hilton asked. "I will have none of your stuttering around here. Don't worry, though, because you've had enough for today." Jay William decided that, at least for the moment, Uncle Hilton was right: he had suffered enough.

Jay William went to the pump and washed all the mud and hog dung off of him. Uncle Hilton gave him a rag and homemade lye soap. He told him to sit down and drink from the water jar he had brought. Jay William fell asleep under a tree. When Catherine awakened him, she did not know what had happened but could tell by looking at him that he had had a bad experience.

CHAPTER 20

JAY WILLIAM AND Catherine were in anguish over the hog pen incident.

"Jay William, I never will understand how they can continue to give out such severe punishments to us, especially to you," Catherine said. "You could have died from that last one. We do our best, and still we have to eat leftovers and cannot eat at the table with them."

"I would love to have some meat," Jay William said. "I still remember how good it tasted. I know your favorite was fried chicken, but I think we'd both be happy with any kind of meat. Actually I don't think I want to eat with them, because I'd probably get punished for the way I chewed my food or for something else." They laughed.

"I know one thing for sure," Catherine said. "I want to leave this place as soon as we can. I promise you, Jay William, we'll find a way to get out of here. It's like a prison. There seems to be no escape. Do you think Miss Armstrong ever thinks of us? How about Loretta and Wanda? Do you think they do? I know Jerome doesn't care about us."

"Jerome seems nice compared with Uncle Hilton," Jay William said. "We'll keep doing the best work possible, and perhaps the punishments will become less frequent. I think we should go to sleep. It's quiet downstairs, so it must be late. Good night, Catherine!"

"Good night," Catherine said, giving Jay William a big hug.

The next morning after breakfast, Aunt Sophie said, "It's going to be cold soon, and I know the two of you need bigger and warmer clothes. You've been here for two and a half years and have grown like weeds. Catherine, you can wear my shoes from last year. They have a lot of wear left, and I'd like a new pair for Christmas anyway. I also have enough flour sacks to make you two dresses and some outing to make a new nightgown for you.

"Jay William, it seems you'll need a new pair of overhauls. You'll have to work extra to pay for them. Uncle Hilton's shoes will probably fit you. If they don't, we can stuff them with rags. We're doing this for you, and we expect you to appreciate it."

"Okay, if you're done talking, Sophie, I need Jay William to get started on his chores and the farmwork," Uncle Hilton said.

"If it's okay with you, sir, I'll milk the two cows and take them out to pasture," Jay William said.

"Sure, if that's okay with Sophie."

"I'm finished, Hilton. Let the boy get started on his work."

Uncle Hilton told Jay William to wait for him in the barn because he wanted to have a word with him. That made Jay William nervous, but he did his work and waited.

When Uncle Hilton got to the barn, he told him Aunt Sophie might get a little testy with Christmas coming soon.

"If that happens, stay out of her way and warn your sister, too," Uncle Hilton said. "Even our two daughters have suffered at those times. They moved away to Dyer County to avoid Sophie's moods. She is a good woman but can be a handful at times. I just wanted you to know."

"Thanks, Uncle Hilton," Jay William said. "Is it okay if I take the cows out to pasture?" Uncle Hilton nodded. Jay William was grateful to escape because his uncle sounded strangely different this morning.

"Hey, Miss Flossie," Jay William said to his favorite cow, "I'm getting new overalls that will cover my skinny knees. Now how about that? I'll be wearing Uncle Hilton's shoes. I hope they aren't too big for me. I must tell you about my Christmas a few years ago. We had a Christmas tree and I got a handmade wagon. Catherine got a new doll. It was the best Christmas ever for us. Do cows know when Christmas arrives? I've got to get Mollie before Uncle Hilton thinks I'm wasting time. I'll be back soon."

When Jay William got to the barn, Uncle Hilton grabbed him by the scruff of the neck and said, "Boy, what was taking you so long out there? I've got to take Sophie into town, and you better have this work done when we get home. Do you understand?"

"Of course," Jay William stammered.

"There you go again. You're talking like a boy with half a brain. I haven't got time to whip you now, but you've got one coming!"

Jay William worked furiously while his aunt and uncle were in town. He wanted to do all his chores well so he could avoid a whipping. He cleaned out the stalls and put in new straw for the animals. He winterized the tools, fed the cows and horses, and returned them to their stalls. Then he went to the kitchen and told Catherine what Uncle Hilton had said to him about Aunt Sophie's moods at Christmastime.

"She was in such a good mood, and we cut out two dresses for me before she left," Catherine said. "She's going to teach me to make her special blackberry jam cake. She said she won a first-place ribbon with it at a fair. She had me put beans on for supper and told me to fry some potatoes and to make cornbread. It's done, but I dare not let you have any ahead of time. I know! Why don't you get us apples from the apple tree? Doesn't that sound delicious?"

Jay William did just that, and they finished eating the apples on the back porch just before Aunt Sophie and Uncle Hilton returned in the wagon. They had some items for Jay William to bring into the house. Catherine set the table for them and served the food.

After washing the dishes, the kids got permission to go to the attic. Catherine asked if she could sew her dresses. Aunt Sophie said she should wait for better lighting the next day. Uncle Hilton told Jay William to try on his new overalls and his shoes.

Jay William ran to the attic, and in a short while, he came down wearing the overalls and the shoes. Both the pants and the shoes were slightly large on him.

"Come here and let me see if they'll work," Aunt Sophie said. She put a large rag in the toes of both shoes and had Jay William roll up the legs of the overalls. "Perhaps Catherine can put a hem in the legs for you," she said. "The way you are growing, I was afraid to get anything smaller."

Aunt Sophie dismissed Catherine and Jay William, and they went up to the attic.

"Boy, I was afraid we would never get away from them," Catherine said.

"I'm happy I finally have bigger overalls," Jay William said. "I think I'm taller than you now."

"I know you're tall. Boys are supposed to be taller than girls," Catherine said.

"Do you think Otto and Ethel will have a nice Christmas with their new parents?" Jay William asked. "I wish I could see them just once again. They'll go to church on Christmas. I wonder if I'll ever get to do that. Miss Armstrong worked hard to put together a Christmas program at school, but Momma refused to let us be a part of it."

"I know, Jay William," Catherine said. "When we get a little older, perhaps we can go to church if you still want to do that. Momma probably would have permitted it if she hadn't become ill and died. I miss our house in Randolph. I miss my doll too. I'm thankful to Mr. Watson for taking Momma to town so she could learn how to make new things like our Christmas tree."

Jay William called Catherine over to the attic window. "Look at that big moon," he said. "It's a harvest moon. I remember hearing about that when we were going to school. Isn't it the most beautiful sight you've ever seen?"

"I'll beat you to bed," Catherine said, ignoring the moon.

She ran to her bed, but Jay William stood looking out the window and thinking about his life. After a few minutes, he got into his bed and fell asleep.

CHAPTER 21

A S THE WEATHER grew colder, Jay William had been getting in trouble without trying. Uncle Hilton was convinced he could beat the stuttering out of him. Aunt Sophie wanted new wallpaper in two downstairs rooms before her daughters and their families visited the farm. She did not want Jay William to do the job, because he was not old enough. "Besides," she said, "he does such a good job in the barn, and I want you in here with me, Hilton. We've always enjoyed wallpapering the house together."

Jay William was happy to go to the barn by himself to talk with his animal friends. He had named them all, and they liked him as much as he liked them. Their stalls were clean, and the animals were always fed and watered before noon.

Uncle Hilton often went to the barn to escape his wife's agitated moods. One day he arrived there and found everything clean and smelling fresh. He was irritated that he could not find a reason to yell at Jay William. He asked him if he liked girls, and Jay William said, "The only ones I ever knew were my sisters, and I loved them because they were nice to me most of the time. Why do you ask?"

"Because if you're smart, you'll stay away from girls until you're older. I shouldn't have married so soon," Uncle Hilton said. "Sophie never says anything nice to me anymore. Boy, do you ever whittle?"

"I don't have a knife or know how," Jay William replied.

"Tell you what, boy. I have an extra one, and I'll give it to you so we can whittle together. Would you like that?"

"I sure would, sir," Jay William replied. "Can you show me how to do it?"

Uncle Hilton took a piece of wood and began to make a whistle. He got one started for Jay William too. The boy was a natural and hollowed out an area for the wind to pass through just as his uncle had showed him.

"Okay, Jay William, here is the rule. Never whittle unless I give you permission and am with you. Understand, boy?" Uncle Hilton said.

"Yes, I always follow your rules, Uncle Hilton, and I'm glad you're being good to me today."

"Well, don't expect it every day because I won't always have time for whittling or other nonsense."

"Hilton, Hilton Henderson," they heard Aunt Sophie calling. "Where are you hiding? Did you know you have to finish painting my kitchen door? Get in here and leave the work in the barn to the boy."

Aunt Sophie said Catherine could sew one of her new dresses if she baked the blackberry jam cake. She did a good job on both, and Aunt Sophie was pleased with her. They also baked two hams, made potato salad, and baked bread with yeast. Catherine was happy that she had learned to do so much under Aunt Sophie's guidance.

The Christmas tree was up, and Jay William recalled his family's Christmas tree in Randolph and how Mr. Watson got them all involved in the festivities. He hoped he and Catherine could join the Henderson family in celebrating the holiday.

On Christmas morning he awoke to Catherine shaking him. "Jay William, you better get out of bed because I can hear them yelling at each other downstairs. We sure don't want to irritate them today," she said.

Jay William got up, went quietly to the barn, and milked both cows before he had breakfast. He took the milk into the kitchen as he usually did. He heard Aunt Sophie telling Uncle Hilton he had done a bad job on her kitchen door and was getting lazy since he had Jay William doing most of his work.

Uncle Hilton was so angry that he grabbed Jay William without warning and chained him to the front porch. Then he got his horsewhip and beat him with an uncontrollable rage. It was the worst beating Jay William had ever received. He cried out to God, "If you are really there, please help me."

Jay William could hardly breathe, and Uncle Hilton was still swinging the horsewhip.

He was not aware that his younger daughter, Sarah, had arrived with her two children. He did not hear her horse buggy. She walked up to the porch and shouted, "Daddy, kill the boy and get it over with because I can't stand to see him suffer anymore."

Uncle Hilton stopped immediately, released Jay William, and sent him to the attic.

Sarah told Catherine to take a pan of warm water to her brother and to help him clean his wounds. She gave her clean white rags and salve to put on the gashes. Aunt Sophie bit her tongue for once and permitted Catherine to help her brother.

Jay William lay on his bed in terrible pain; his wrists were bleeding from the deep cuts left by the chain. He did some serious thinking and praying. "God if you are real, please get Catherine and me out of this place while we are still alive," he whispered. "Show us how we can escape."

Sarah fixed a large plate of food for the children. She included a generous slice of ham and the famous blackberry jam cake. Aunt Sophie did not say a word.

"Catherine, if you find a way to get out of here, take it, and then try to get help for me, okay?" Jay William said.

"Jay William, if you can find a way out, please don't wait for me, because you have suffered more. I can't stand the way he beats you," Catherine said, hugging her brother. "Perhaps you can escape when you're in the pasture with your animals."

The winter months offered no relief from their situation, but they knew it had to come soon.

CHAPTER 22

A T NIGHT IN the attic Jay William and Catherine spent much time discussing how they could escape the Hendersons' farm. Catherine was now thirteen and was quite pretty with red hair, a milky white complexion, and large brown eyes.

Jay William still found much comfort and peace when he was in the barn with the animals. He especially enjoyed the smell of the fresh straw. Uncle Hilton seldom had to ask him to work, because he was dedicated to the everyday tasks and completed them without being told to do it.

Jay William also enjoyed whittling with Uncle Hilton. The boy whittled Flossie the cow's image, impressing Uncle Hilton. The piece was their special secret and it stayed in the barn.

When planting season arrived, Catherine noticed that Johnny Maddox, the sixteen-year-old farm worker, was watching her intently during trips to the pump. His good looks did not escape her, and she got goose bumps all over her body when he headed in her direction one day. She had never had this feeling before, but it was a nice one.

Johnny smiled warmly at her, and she noticed his dark brown eyes and his dimples. "Catherine, I live with my widowed sister up the road three miles north of here. I told her all about you and about how much I love you and want to marry you and take you away from the Hendersons' place. I told her how pretty you are and how nice you and your brother are to me. She liked the way

I described you, and she said that if we got married we could live in her extra bedroom."

Catherine blushed as she listened to Johnny.

"I know we're young, but we can make it work," he said. "I could give you a better life than you have now."

Catherine could do nothing but smile at him.

"Meet me here at the pump at this time tomorrow, and we'll go to Piggott, Arkansas, and get married," Johnny said. "Don't let your aunt and uncle know what you're doing. I love you so much, and I want you at my side for the rest of my life."

"I want to do this, Johnny, but if they find out about it before I leave, they'll make trouble for both of us," Catherine said. "If I'm not here, it will only be because my aunt gives me a job that I can't avoid or because she found out about our plans."

That evening in their room, Catherine said, "Jay William, there's something I have to tell you. Johnny has asked me to marry him, and although I don't know much about marriage, I like him very much. I'm supposed to meet him down by the pump tomorrow. What do you think about this?"

Jay William squeezed her hand and said, "Catherine, Johnny is a nice person, and if that's what you want to do, you must do it. It will be your way to escape. Perhaps after that, you two can arrange for me to leave here as well."

"I promise you, Jay William, that I will try to get you out of here as soon as I can," Catherine said. "I'll meet Johnny at the pump tomorrow, and I'll try to take my clothes with me. I may need some help getting them downstairs without Aunt Sophie noticing."

The next morning Catherine took her clothes downstairs and hid them near the garden under a tree. She waited for Johnny, and the two made their exit. When he learned what had happened, Uncle Hilton fired Johnny fired from his job on the farm.

With Catherine's elopement, life became more difficult for Jay William. Aunt Sophie made him do the chores Catherine had done. Jay William continued to milk the cows and take them down to the pasture. Aunt Sophie taught him to iron, and he did that weekly task under her watchful eye. She feared he might also try to leave, so she kept him busy in the house.

Jay William was saddened that his sister did not make contact with him as he thought she would. He missed working with her in the garden. Aunt Sophie became his partner in that job. He found her scolding easier to tolerate than Uncle Hilton's beatings. During angry outbursts, Aunt Sophie would pull his hair and his ears, but that was nothing compared with Uncle Hilton's savagery.

Jay William helped his aunt can the produce from the garden and liked doing it. Uncle Hilton still needed his help with butchering and in the smokehouse. However, his aunt and uncle would still not give him any meat to eat. Jay William was determined to escape and watched for opportunities.

His chance finally came at Christmastime. Aunt Sophie and Uncle Hilton were planning a visit to their daughters in Dyer County, and Jay William would be left on the farm to take care of the animals.

As he helped pack up the wagon, Jay William noticed his aunt had left three hams for him to load. "Aunt Sophie, since I'm going to be alone for Christmas, could you leave me a slice or two from one those hams?" he asked.

"Absolutely not," she said. "You are getting a little bold, don't you think? We will be taking the smokehouse key with us to remove any temptation."

It took all morning to pack up everything Sophie wanted to take with her. Uncle Hilton worked just as hard as Jay William. He looked completely exhausted, and Jay William felt bad that his uncle would have to drive all afternoon with Aunt Sophie in such a sour mood.

"Boy, I sure wish you could have some ham and other things for your Christmas dinner," Uncle Hilton said, "but you know your aunt. She is a hard-hearted woman. At least I know the animals are in good hands. You are the best worker I have ever had on this farm. If I had a son, I would want him to be like you, Jay William." Uncle Hilton patted him on the back. "Oh, I hear Sophie calling for you, boy. You had better run and see what she wants."

"Aunt Sophie, do you want me for something else?"

"Yes, Jay William. I want to make sure you have water ready for me when I get home in three days. I'll need a hot bath after all the travel. And make sure the ironing is done."

"Yes, I'll remember to do that."

"Go get Hilton and tell him we need to be on the road now."

Jay William was happy to see them leave for Dyer.

CHAPTER 23

JAY WILLIAM TOOK Chester, the horse, down the road to see if Catherine was still living with Johnny's sister. He was disappointed to find the house empty.

"I can't believe Catherine didn't bother to tell me she was moving away," he said to Chester. "I'm going to leave while my aunt and uncle are gone to visit their children. It will be my only chance to escape, and I was hoping to tell Catherine and Johnny."

Jay William returned to the farm and decided to visit with his animal friends to tell them his plans. First he went to see Flossie. "Hey, pretty lady, I must tell you I'm leaving in three days for greener pastures. Ha! I bet you would like that, wouldn't you, Flossie? I'm going to miss you very much. Christmas Day I'm going to fix myself a good meal and eat in the dining room. I wish I had some gentleman's clothes to wear, but my overalls will have to do. You know, Flossie, I feel free already and I feel so grown up. I must show you the figure I whittled from wood. It's supposed to look like you. I'll take it with me on the way to my new life." Flossie looked at him with her large eyes as though she understand every word he said.

Back at the house, Jay William packed an extra pair of overalls that Johnny had given him a year earlier. He checked the flour supply and decided Aunt Sophie would be giving him a Christmas gift after all. He would bake a pillowcase full of biscuits for his trip to freedom.

Jay William wanted to have a good supper. He opened two jars of green beans that he had helped can and put two tablespoons of bacon grease in the pot for seasoning. He baked a pan of biscuits and opened a jar of peach preserves. Then he sat down at the dining room table, using good dishes. Jay William felt a little guilty about sitting there but did it anyway.

"At least I can eat like a gentleman," he said with a big smile. "Someday I will be a gentleman and wear nice clothes and a pair of dress shoes."

Jay William went out to the barn again and talked with his animal friends. He found a choice piece of wood, got out his knife, and carved a replica of the barn. "This will be a good thing to have on my journey to the promised land," he said. "I don't know what that means exactly, but it sure sounds good."

On Christmas morning, Jay William did his regular chores and then gave himself the promised gift from Aunt Sophie. He took one of her old pillowcases and baked the biscuits, using plenty of bacon grease for added flavor. He filled the pillowcase completely with biscuits and secured it with string from the barn.

On the day Aunt Sophie and Uncle Hilton were due home, Jay William got up at two in the morning and fed the animals. He tearfully told them good-bye and a left a note for his aunt and uncle. telling them he had completed his assignments and would not be coming back.

CHAPTER 24

T HE JOURNEY BEGAN at four in the morning. Jay William did not have a concrete plan and wished he could ask someone for advice, but he knew he might not have another opportunity for a long time. Hoping to find Catherine, he decided to go by Johnny Maddox's house one more time. The place was still empty. He knew Catherine would want him to do this and would be happy that he had escaped. Yes, he was going to find a better life than the one he had been living for three years.

Based on his trip with Sheriff Johnson to the Hendersons' farm, Jay William knew he was about twenty miles from Randolph. He decided the road would not be a smart choice, so he traveled in the woods next to the road. But the woods were pretty bare, and he feared he could be seen in the daytime. *Perhaps I could go a little deeper in the woods and not travel in the daylight hours*, he thought.

Into the woods Jay William went with his pillowcase filled with biscuits, his extra overalls, and two flannel shirts on his back. He knew the Mississippi River was on the east side of the road. He would remember that and watch the sun's position to guide him.

The sun came up and he had probably traveled only a short distance. *I must keep moving because I don't want Uncle Hilton to find me*, Jay William told himself.

He had taken his pocketknife with him along with a sharp knife from the barn to help him cut brush. Jay William felt guilty about not asking permission but believed he had no choice. The sun was up and it was warm for a December day. He stayed deep enough in the woods but was constantly checking to make sure he was still on the same course as the road.

By 5 p.m., Jay William was tired and hungry and ate two biscuits. He found a ditch to hide in near the road but still in the woods and pulled brush over himself. When he awoke it was dark, and he went to the road and ran southeast toward the river. He ran until he was tired and then slowed down and walked until the sun came up.

As Jay William walked deeper in the woods, his mind overflowed with memories. He wondered why his older siblings never bothered to come to see them at Aunt Sophie and Uncle Hilton's place. *Perhaps they didn't know where we went*, he thought. *Anyway, they have their own lives to live.* He recalled his momma with mixed emotions. He thought she had never expressed much love for any of them.

Jay William was grateful to Mr. Watson for getting his momma to send him and Catherine to school. He wished he could have had more time there. *I wonder if Mr. Watson ever thinks of us or even the twins. Catherine said he was their daddy. That's what Wanda told her. Grown-ups sure keep a lot of secrets from the kids*, he thought.

I suppose if Momma had me adopted by someone like she did Ethel and Otto, I could be in school and not running without knowing where I will end up. Jay William thought about how Ethel and Otto always made him feel good about himself. They would laugh at his attempts to be funny. He was suddenly very lonely and missed Flossie and the other farm animals. *I can't go back. I'll be punished, and I don't want to live there.*

Jay William checked his position and got back on a path near the road. He spotted a gorge, threw his pillowcase in there, and found brush for a covering. Then he sat down on a log and dug into his pillowcase. He ate three biscuits.

I helped Uncle Hilton put all that meat up in the smokehouse, and I didn't get even a bite of that meat, he told himself. *I'm sure Catherine has had meat to eat since she left. I sure miss her. I'm going to figure out a way to find me a rabbit or squirrel to eat.* After pulling the brush over himself, Jay William went to sleep.

When he woke up it was dark and he felt thirsty. *I should have thought of water, but I didn't.* He spotted an abandoned sharecropper house, went to the back porch, and found a pump along with a canning jar with a lid. He pumped water, drank from the jar, and then refilled it. Jay William looked around the place, hoping to find something useful. He found a book and placed it in his pillowcase for future use. As he left the yard he discovered some hickory nuts. He stopped and filled his pockets with them.

Jay William ate a few of the nuts and continued on his journey. When daylight came, he was ready for a rest. He found a ditch and crawled into it, pulling brush on top of him. He woke up a few hours later feeling very cold. Jay William peeked through the brush and saw snow. At first he was frightened because he knew snow would slow him down, but then he thought, *If Uncle Hilton has men looking for me, they will also be slowed down.*

Jay William remembered hearing a history lesson for the older students about how the Indians would build a fire with sticks. They would rub the sticks together, causing friction. They would place the sticks on a pile of dry grass and gently blow on it till the sticks began to burn. *I know I can do that,* he told himself. He pulled out grass that had been his bed, took two sticks from the brush that sheltered him, and rubbed them together.

To Jay William's surprise, the sticks began to burn the grass. He blew gently on it and soon he had a little flame. He added sticks, and after a while he had a warm fire in the ditch.

Jay William decided to rest a while and opened the book he had found. It was a geography book and he could read most of the words. He put snow in the jar and melted it by placing the jar fairly close to the fire. He then had drinking water. Jay William took the three pairs of socks Uncle Hilton had given him and rubbed off the dirt in the snow. He wrapped his feet in the extra shirt. Jay William was happy that things were working out so far. His socks looked much cleaner, and he wrung them tightly and hung them on a branch to dry.

I must look for some flint rocks like the ones the Indians used to make arrowheads. I can use them to start a fire later, he thought.

Jay William saw a rabbit hiding near a tree. A piece of that rabbit sure would taste good, but he wasn't quite sure how to make that meal happen. He would have to think on it for a while.

A few more hickory nuts and a biscuit satisfied his food craving, and he stayed put for the time being. Jay William felt warm and comfortable but was afraid to sleep. When his socks were dry, he put them on his feet. He waited for darkness to arrive before he traveled down the road. He kept an eye out for wild animals or anything else that might hurt him. Jay William hit an icy spot and turned his ankle. Using his knife, he cut off the bottom of his shirt and made a bandage secured with sticks to support his ankle. With Uncle Hilton's high-top shoes providing further support, he began his journey again.

Jay William took off one pair of socks and placed them on his hands for warmth. He discovered some frozen elderberries and ate a handful of them. By daybreak, he was tired and his ankle throbbed. Jay William found a stick for support and hobbled over to the woods, looking for a deep hiding place. He picked up an empty burlap sack and carried it to the place where he chose to spend the night.

With his ankle hurt, Jay William's progress was slowed down considerably. He went as far as he could but decided he had to be smart and not aggravate the ankle injury. Again he built a fire using sticks and grass. He pulled leaves off of branches, shook them dry, and added them to the grass and sticks. The fire provided enough warmth for him to get a little sleep.

On the fifth day of the journey Jay William saw familiar

landmarks. He spotted a few buildings on the horizon and suspected he had found Randolph. He avoided the town because he was still afraid Uncle Hilton might find him. He took a dirt path that led to the area where his family and the Watsons had lived. *Perhaps Wanda is there and she can help me with my foot,* he thought.

Before reaching this area, he heard a voice behind him. It sounded a little familiar, but he was not sure, so he ran as fast as he could with his bum foot.

"Hey, stop running for a minute, will you?" the voice said. "I won't hurt you, but it looks like your foot is hurt."

Jay William slowed down and then stopped because of the pain.

A man approached him and asked, "Are you who I think you are? Are your Marjorie's boy, Jay William?"

He was taken aback by the mention of his momma's name. He wondered if he had been caught by one of Uncle Hilton's workers.

"Here, take my coat and get yourself warm before you get sick," the man said.

CHAPTER 25

"You look tired and cold, and I know you must be hungry," the man said to Jay William. "I'm Fred Watson and I just visited my daddy's grave. I couldn't come to the funeral last week. Wanda and I have a house in Dyersburg now. We have a little boy, Paul William, who's two months old. Wanda will be happy to know you are okay."

Jay William was stunned and saddened to hear that Mr. Watson had died. He felt he owed this man a lot. But he was happy to hear about the baby. "I guess that means I'm Uncle Jay William now," he said. "I want to go to my family's old house to see it, but I don't want to get caught by my uncle Hilton and dragged back to his place."

"Relax, boy. I just heard from a reliable source he's not looking for you."

"Are you sure? I've tried so hard to hide from him."

"Yes, I'm sure. Besides, the house you lived in was torn down. What are your plans now, Jay William? Did you know the law won't let you live by yourself?"

"Why was the house torn down?" Jay William asked. "It was our home and I loved it."

"Actually it belonged to the Johnson family, and Jerome tore it down for more cotton fields," Fred said. "Jay William, put on that coat. I have a sandwich I don't plan to eat. I'm sure you're hungry.

You can relax because I won't report you to the Hendersons or to the county sheriff."

Jay William was so tired and sore he did as he was told. He sat on a log and ate the sandwich with his water. As he ate, he allowed his thoughts to roam free:

So Uncle Hilton isn't looking for me. I wonder why not. How can he manage the farm without my help? I did learn a lot from him. No other man spent as much time as he did teaching me how to work. I also learned that I must respect authority or pay the consequences, that a nagging wife can make you crazy, that a clean place is a good thing, and so much more.

Fred interrupted his thoughts. "Please come with me," he said. "I have a place up in the hills where you can stay until springtime." Tired of running, Jay William went with him.

Fred took Jay William deep into the woods, and the hike took a few hours. Finally they entered an amazingly warm cave. Fred showed Jay William to a table with a platter of fried squirrel and potatoes and a glass of cold milk. Jay William was so hungry that he ate the entire platter. "Thank you for the food," he said. "That was the first meat I've had since Momma died."

Fred went to the kitchen and returned with a warm coat, new overalls, two new shirts, shoes, three pairs of socks, and a warm blanket.

"Why are you doing this for me?" Jay William asked.

"Your clothes are dirty and threadbare, and you need new clothes that fit," Fred said. "I'd like you to work for me and my partner here in the hills until spring. Is it a deal?"

"What kind of work would I be doing?" Jay William inquired.

"It's an important job, and I think you'd be very good at it," Fred replied. "It takes a quick mind and fast feet, and I know for sure that you have both. You'd also have to be able to find a good hiding place in the woods. I know you can do that."

Jay William was a little suspicious. "Before I agree to the job, tell me exactly what I must do," he said.

"Come and meet my partner up the next hill," Fred said. "He'll make the final decision on hiring you, so we'll tell him you're older than you are. Thinking you're older will keep him from asking too many questions, so go along with me when I give him your age. We have a small manufacturing company up here in the hills and feel our product is an important service to our friends and neighbors." Fred gave nervous laugh. "There is one thing problem: the federal government wants to shut us down. We think the government has begun to spy on us. They want to find out exactly where our company is located. They're not sure, but the feds are smart and vow to stop our production."

Jay William looked confused and Fred capitalized on this. "Jay William, have I told you that Wanda is the mother of a little boy? Oh sure, I remember mentioning that to you. She loves to show him off to our families and friends. I want to support my family in style. I never want my son to grow up as poor as we did. Wanda would like a better house and new furniture, and I want to give her those things. With my income, I can do that," Fred said.

"If you work for us, you'll have a warm house, hot meals, and new clothes, and sometimes I can give you cash. Now can I introduce you to my partner to see if he feels the way I do? Follow me and I'll show you the rest of the place."

Jay William followed but remained on guard. They walked through an opening in the wall, and Jay was surprised at the cave's vast size. The room they entered had three beds, a stove, a table with chairs, and shelves stocked with food. Jay William spied two large hams hanging on the wall.

"The next step is for you to meet my business partner, Hershel Smith," Fred said. He led Jay William outside and up a steep hillside. "Up here, deep in this cave, is where our product is manufactured," he said.

A tall man with a long beard emerged from the cave. Jay William could not figure out the man's age. He was pulling a wagon filled with jars of a light brown liquid. Fred picked up one of the jars, admiring its color and clarity.

"This is our product; we make the best in the state of Tennessee. Families need it for pain control, and it's an excellent cold remedy."

"Is that whiskey?" Jay William asked.

"Yes, and it's made from the best corn available anywhere," Fred said. "Your job will be to watch out for those federal men. Never lead them here; run in the opposite direction and do everything to throw them off track. Hershel, this is my brother-in-law, Jay William. I recommend him for our new lookout man. He is smart, quick on his feet, and can outrun just about anyone. He is sixteen years old and needs a place to stay and a job. I need you to approve my decision to give him the job."

Hershel offered his hand to Jay William and said, "The job is yours; just don't disappoint us."

Fred patted Jay William on the back and said, "Congratulations! I trust you with this job. You've always been a completely honest young man. I remember that you refused to swear and were teased about being a preacher boy. We won't take you to the still because that way if you're approached by the feds, you can honestly say you've never seen it. You understand if they find the still, I'll go to prison. I know you would never want that for your nephew's daddy."

"I'll work with you," Jay William told Fred, "and I expect the same courtesy from you. Is that understood?"

CHAPTER 26

IN HIS NEW job as a lookout, Jay William watched for suspicious-looking men who could be spying on the bootleggers. After one month, he was feeling much better physically and his ankle had healed.

Jay William read the book he had found at the sharecropper house shortly after leaving Uncle Hilton's place. It was geography textbook. He loved it and looked at it every night. He read about places he had not visited but wanted to see someday. Jay William thought he would be much better at a geography bee now than he had been at school. He certainly did not travel much now. Fred and Hershel discouraged him from leaving the cave except to look out for the feds.

It was now the end of February, and Jay William would be twelve years old in a few weeks. He was grateful for the place to stay and for clothes that fit, but he was restless and wanted more from life than hiding in a cave and venturing out only to see who might be spying on Fred and Hershel's operation.

Jay William told Fred he wanted to do more. "I feel I'm not accomplishing much around here," he said.

"What do you mean?" Fred asked. "You've never complained before. Aren't you relieved not to running anymore, not knowing who might be after you? This has to be better. I've given you substance for your labor. What's the problem, Jay William?"

"Before I started working for you, I worked like a man for

three years, and I feel I need to do more actual work," Jay William said. "Don't get me wrong. I don't want to sound ungrateful, but something doesn't seem right for me. I appreciate the hot meals, the nice warm bed, and the clothes, but something is missing in my life. You've been great to me, Fred, and I appreciate it so much, but I want more jobs."

"Okay, do you see those jars over there?" Fred asked. "I need you to deliver those tomorrow evening. I'll put them in a tote sack with rags around them to prevent them from breaking. You must be very careful not to break them. If they get broken, you'll pay for them. I'll give you specific directions about where and how they are to be distributed." He gave Jay William a hand-drawn map with the delivery spot marked.

"This is important, Jay William, so listen closely. You must have twenty dollars placed inside an envelope before you turn over the merchandise to these people. Count it yourself; do not take their word for it. They have never cheated me before, because they get good whiskey for their money. They have customers waiting to receive it, so the sale has to go smoothly. They're making a living just like I am.

"Now you go to bed early tonight. You must be well rested for the ten-mile trip. Study the map until you know it by heart. That's important because you could lose it during the trip. If you have any questions or doubts, now is the time to make them known."

"How will I know them? I might deliver the merchandise to a federal agent. If that happened, I would be in a heap of trouble."

Fred threw back his head and laughed. "Yes, you would be in trouble, but that won't happen," he said. "Let me finish giving you directions. You don't need to know their names, but you'll be giving the merchandise to two men. They'll be looking for the delivery. You start whistling 'Dixie' when you see two men. If they're the wrong men, that's okay because it's a popular song here in the South. If they are the right men, one of them will stand tall and sing the complete song. Be respectful and stand tall yourself. Please don't sing along with him. That will only irritate him. Just be polite and do as I say.

"When he completes the song, applaud and say, 'Sir, I'm from Dixieland.' Then say, 'Do you have the money?' When you have counted the money and know the amount is correct, put it in the envelope and hide it; then lead them to the merchandise. When the exchange is made, make sure there is no one around and head here right away with the money."

Jay William had a little difficulty going to sleep that evening. He knew he was in a predicament. Once again he found himself speaking to God, though he was not sure God heard him. "Please, God," he prayed, "if you are real, hear me and keep me safe because I don't want to go to prison, and I don't want Fred to go either."

The next thing he knew, Fred was shaking him, saying, "Get up now and get started." He handed Jay William a lard tin with a lid. "There are biscuits and sausage sandwiches in there for you. Eat them when the sun comes up, because you'll need the nourishment to do a good job. Good luck and watch out for the feds. If you suspect you've run into one, lead him the wrong way. Try to get home before dark. Do you have any questions before you get started?"

Jay William recited the directions Fred had given him, and Fred was satisfied that he would do the job right. As Jay William walked to his destination, he became nervous and afraid. Once again he prayed, "O God, if you exist, please hear me now. Help me get this job done without a problem. I want to be free and happy. I don't want a life of crime."

Jay William arrived at the contact spot and saw two men sitting on a log. He nervously whistled "Dixie."

The men laughed uncontrollably. Jay William started to leave when suddenly, the tall bearded man stood and sang "Dixie" with such beauty and emotion that Jay William wanted to cry. He had never heard a man sing like that. Jay William took off his cap and stood tall until the man had finished the song. Then he applauded and stammered, "I'm from Dixieland, gentlemen." He was terribly nervous. The short man asked, "Did Fred send you here to us?"

Jay William shook his head yes.

"So you need money to take back to him. Here it is." He handed Jay William four five-dollar bills. Jay William counted the bills, placed them in the envelope, and sealed it.

He then motioned for the men to follow him to a hidden tote sack containing the whiskey. The short man put his hand on Jay William's back and said, "Don't be nervous. We won't harm you. We were laughing only because you did such a poor job with the song. Don't ever try to make a living in the music field."

"We wish you the best in life," the tall man said. "Thank you for allowing us to have a little fun at your expense. You seemed to have no trouble counting the money, and you must be okay because Fred trusts you with his money. Make sure you give it to him when you get to his place."

Jay William was a little irritated at that last remark and said, "Of course I'll give Fred his money, because it's his. I'm just delivering it for him. Good day to both of you."

Now that it was all over, Jay William felt more relaxed. To his surprise, in the bottom of the tote sack, he found a lunch with a jug of cold water packed for him. He sat down on a tree stump and ate all of it.

He took his time returning and went down by the river. On a tree he saw a sign that said, "Attention: The United States government will pay a cash reward for the arrest and conviction of bootleggers working in this area. Contact the federal office in Memphis."

Oh my, that means Fred and Hershel could be in big trouble, Jay William thought. *Fred won't be happy about this news at all.*

About ten feet away was a sign in red, white, and blue letters. The large type at the top read: "Mississippi Barge Company." The smaller lettering underneath said, "Deckhands needed now." This excited Jay William and gave him renewed hope. *Perhaps this is God's answer to my prayer,* he thought.

Jay William would turn twelve in a few weeks. *I did a man's job at the Hendersons' farm,* he told himself. *Surely I can do a deck man's job on a barge. I'm big for my age, and Hershel thinks I'm sixteen years old now. Perhaps I could even pass for an eighteen-year-old. I would be traveling up and down the Mississippi River. Maybe I could be out on the deck and see all the beautiful homes I saw in the books at school.*

He was so excited that he ran all the way back to the cave where he had been living for the past few weeks. He took the money directly to Fred.

"You look pretty happy, Jay William," he said. "I think you like doing delivery jobs."

"It's a scary job, Fred," Jay William said. "I saw a sign that said the feds would imprison me if I were convicted."

Fred and Hershel laughed at him. "Of course, they're aware of bootlegging around here," Fred said. "That makes our job more exciting. We get a good feeling when we outwit those feds. We've been doing this job for more than a year, and we're still free men. Jay William, I've made more money in this past year than I've made in my entire life. No way will I give this up."

Jay William then told Fred about the Mississippi Barge Company sign advertising for deckhands. "I can pass for a man, don't you agree? I did a man's job for three for Aunt Sophie and Uncle Hilton at their farm. You even said I look like a man. Do you think they would hire me?" Jay William asked.

Fred's heart softened when he saw the excitement on Jay William's face. "I suppose you can give it a try," he said. "If you're afraid of being arrested, you clearly wouldn't be happy working with us. Keep the shoes and the clothes I gave you. You'll also need a warm blanket. It can get cold on the river at night. Do you know how to get to the beach near Randolph? I've seen the barge down there. Here, let me draw you a map."

"Thank you so much for understanding me," Jay William said with emotion.

Fred shrugged his shoulders. "You're welcome, Jay William. I owe you something. We were all a little rough on you when you were a small boy. I for one want to apologize for my actions. I won't worry about you informing the feds about us. After all, you never did see a still, right, Jay William?"

"Right, and I don't plan to do that now," he said. "I'm grateful for the good hot food—especially the meat—the nice warm bed, and all the things you did for me."

"Here, take this smoked ham and some beans," Fred said. "Who knows when you'll get a chance to eat again?" He packed up a few extra things for Jay William and sent him on his way.

CHAPTER 27

J AY WILLIAM TOOK the supplies Fred gave him including food, water, clothes, and the map that would guide him to the Randolph beach. Most important was the geography textbook he had found at the abandoned sharecropper house shortly after he left the farm.

Jay William followed the map until he arrived at the Randolph beach. He thought it looked amazingly familiar but wasn't sure at first exactly why. Then it occurred to him that this was where he told Otto and Ethel good-bye before they were handed over to a nurse who would deliver them to their adoptive parents.

It had been a little while since he last thought of them. His momma had said that she signed a paper promising no one would seek the twins. She did this for their well-being.

As he looked at the Mississippi River, Jay William was filled with awe at its size. The tall trees on the hillside seemed to beckon him, and he could not resist the urge to climb up the slope. He found a cemetery at the top. He checked out the tombstones and found names with birth and death dates. He was fascinated by this, though he was not sure of the reason. Some areas had only small metal posts with birth and death dates. He searched without success for a grave with his momma's notice and decided to find a shade tree where he could rest and eat a bite of food.

As he was leaving to go back down by the river, Jay William spied a grave marker with Marjorie Hawkins's name. He verified the date of death and began to cry. He wished he could see his momma now. He had so much to tell her and so many questions that needed answers. He also wished he could talk to Catherine. After a short time, he decided he must stop feeling sorry for himself and move on. He wanted to visit the site of the family's old house but feared he would be reported to the sheriff. He did not want to be returned to the Hendersons' farm.

Jay William went down to the beach and read from his geography book. He was surprised at how much information he found regarding the Mississippi River. As he gazed at the wide span of the mighty river, he suddenly felt very small.

The textbook said Robert de La Salle had explored the river in 1692, taking a group of men all the way down to the Gulf of Mexico. La Salle discovered four bluffs above the flood plain on the Mississippi River in present-day Tennessee, and he described the view as breathtaking. Randolph was bluff number two. The Chickasaw Indians occupied all four bluffs. Memphis was on bluff four. *I can't wait to find out more about my place of birth here on the river,* Jay William thought. *I bet Jerome doesn't know about this, because he never learned to read. Actually I'm not angry at him any longer.*

With the sun fading, Jay William needed to find a place to sleep. He carried his blanket to a spot under a tree near the beach and made his bed for the night. *I'm so glad I don't have to be concerned much about snakes at this time of the year,* he told himself.

Jay William thought about his day and about all the things he had discovered including his momma's grave. He thought about Otto and Ethel and tried to imagine what they would be like now after being taken from the family. *They have each other and a momma and a daddy to rely on and to learn new things from,* Jay William thought. *Momma said they would go to church, and she was okay with that. I wonder if Momma would have learned to believe in God if she had lived longer.*

He tried to remember what life was like when his daddy was with the family. His father believed in God and sometimes prayed. *I hope that there really is a God and that he loves me like my daddy said,* Jay William thought. He knew sleep would soon come, so he closed his eyes.

The next morning Jay William awoke to the sound of a foghorn from a big boat. He ran onto the beach for a better view. There to his delight was a boat with "Mississippi Barge Company" painted on its side. He waved at the men on deck and hollered, "Do you need deckhands? Are there any other jobs I can do?" They smiled and waved back at him.

Jay William noticed food floating on the river. He jumped into the water, gathered as much as could, and brought it to the beach. *This is a great meal,* he told himself. *I've got bologna, chicken, and vegetables. I won't starve to death!* He carefully divided the food into small portions, fearing he might not get many meals in the immediate future. He placed what he did not eat in a tin and hung it from a tree to keep it from being eaten by insects or animals.

He got out his prized book and read more about the Mississippi River. He discovered that the Chickasaw Indians had lived in the area for more than 125 years before the white man took their land.

Jay William closed his eyes and tried to imagine what it must have been like for the Indians. He felt bad that the white man had forced them out of this beautiful place. He stared at the wideness of the river and imagined the Indians fishing from their canoes. He could almost hear them.

I must not feel sorry for myself, he thought, *because I have it better than they did, and I have hope of better things. Perhaps I'll be hired by the barge company and learn a trade to support myself.* He closed the book and hid it safely before climbing the hill again.

He could see Randolph from the west side of the hill and the great Mississippi from the east. Jay William knew that Randolph was not available to him now and that the Mississippi River was his hope for a better life. He decided to visit his momma's grave and found himself talking to her. He told her about Catherine's marriage and said he was going to be a success in life. He sat on the hill for quite a while, thinking about all the things for which he could be thankful: Miss Armstrong, Johnny Moore, Fred Watson, and most of all Catherine. He hoped her life was good. He thought about Aunt Sophie and Uncle Hilton. Although they were cruel to him and Catherine, he learned much from them.

Jay William got up and ran down the hill and into the water. He enjoyed the spot where the Mississippi changed course and ran upward. He remembered the older children in his schoolroom being taught the reason for this phenomenon. It was caused by an earthquake in which two towns were shifted from Tennessee to Arkansas. Jay William was not sure about the details but decided he would find out someday. He wanted to know about so many things.

He decided to sharpen his arithmetic by writing long list of numbers and adding them up in his head. He wrote all the words he could remember giving to Catherine for the spelling bee practice. He tried writing sentences, knowing that they were not without mistakes but that he would do better someday.

Jay William thought about his daddy and the few memories he had of him. It seemed to him that his daddy was treated badly by the family, and this made the boy sad. Mr. Watson had changed his life by talking his momma into sending him and Catherine to school. But Jay William knew life could not continue as it was, and he prayed, "God, if you are there, please give me a chance to work on a boat soon. Thank you very much, sir."

Within a week Jay William realized the men were not throwing garbage from the boat but good food. They were friendly and shouted kind words to him. One of them asked why he wanted to work on a barge and what his qualifications were. Jay William replied truthfully and said he was a hard worker and needed a job.

One afternoon a boat stopped and he heard a loud voice say,

"I'm Captain Greene of Mississippi Barge 45. Come to the boat and talk with me if you want a job. My men will help you aboard."

Jay William swam as fast as he could to get there before the captain changed his mind about giving him a chance. When he got to the boat, the deckhands helped him aboard. He shook off as much water as he could. A man gave him a towel to dry off his clothes and escorted him up to the captain's quarters.

Everything about the boat looked fancy to Jay William. Brass railings led him to the captain's quarters. He suddenly glimpsed his reflection in a mirror in the hall. He looked shabby and unkempt with his long hair and tattered clothes. Would the captain even talk with him?

The captain was a large man with the biggest hands Jay William had ever seen. His well-manicured beard was dark brown with a few gray streaks. "I've gotten word that a young man has been on the beach for a week begging for a job on one of our barges," the captain said, offering his hand. "I'm told you are very insistent on this. You want to work for this company. Is that correct?"

"Yes, sir. It's a dream of mine and I need a job badly," Jay William stammered in reply.

"How old are you, son?" the captain asked.

Jay William wanted to say he was sixteen but decided against telling a lie. Before he realized what he was doing, Jay William told the captain the whole story. He told him he was an orphan. He told him about his hard work on the Hendersons' farm. He even told him about running away in hopes of a better life. Finally he told him he had seen a sign saying the company was hiring deckhands.

The captain smiled and told Jay William he could work on the barge for two weeks. If the crew liked his work, he would have a job. The captain said one of the men would take him in a boat to gather his belongings and would bring him back to the barge. The trip was quick. Jay William gathered his book, his extra shirt, and his overalls and put them in his tote sack, and they returned to the barge.

He was then taken to his space on the large boat. It was about six feet long and four feet wide and had a bed and a small locker for his belongings. One of the men told Jay William the captain wanted to see him at seven in the morning. Jay William put his few belongings in the locker and went with the man to eat supper. He was so excited about starting his job that he asked to be excused and returned to his cubbyhole. He thought about how wonderful it was to be on the boat. He could not wait for the job to start and had a hard time falling asleep.

The next morning Jay William met with the captain, who wanted the new crew member to know what he expected of him.

"Safety is the most important part of this job," Captain Greene said. "Don't worry about how much you accomplish. First and foremost, make sure you work in a safe manner. Safety is that important! You are the youngest man on this boat, and you must be thick-skinned because you'll be teased about your stuttering. Acknowledge it and hold your head high. The men will stop once they fail to get a reaction from you.

"You must keep your space tidy at all times. Inspections will take place at various times. Your job will sometimes require heavy lifting. Considering the farmwork you've done and your muscular physique, this shouldn't be a problem for you. I don't expect you to know everything about your job in two weeks, but I do expect you to do all that the deckhand boss asks of you.

"Jay William, don't do a job if you don't understand how to do it. Ask. There are no stupid questions. Stupid is not asking a question when you don't understand what is expected of you. Now relax. I'm going to call for Louis Miller. He's been with the company since he was fifteen, and he knows all about the job." The captain shook Jay William's hand again and asked, "Do you have any questions about what we went over?" The boy shook his head no.

Louis Miller's appearance surprised Jay William. He was small in stature, walked with a prominent limp, and wore thick eyeglasses. He looked at Jay William and said, "So you're the new lad I've been hearing so much about! We'll go downstairs and meet the others."

As they walked down to the galley, Louis said that the other men called him Old Louie and that this was okay with him. "I don't care what they call me as long as they do what I say and keep our number 45 the best in the fleet." He winked when he said that, and Jay William immediately felt comfortable with him.

"You'll start at the bottom of the stack and work your way up by doing a good job," Old Louie said. "Today you'll help the cook. Just do exactly what he says and you'll do fine."

Old Louie introduced Jay William to a very large man whom the crew called Fatso. He looked very tough, especially with a meat cleaver in his right hand.

"Put that knife down, Fatso, and meet your new assistant, Jay William Hawkins. Don't frighten him before you give him his duties for the day," Old Louie said.

The cook, whose real name was Adam Carter, put the knife on the table and offered a large hand to his new assistant. Jay William was intimidated by the tight grip and the strong handshake.

Fatso wasted no time in barking out commands. "I sure hope you're not afraid to work hard," he said. "Peel this bucket of potatoes and slice them for fried potatoes. Let me show you exactly how I want them cut." He demonstrated his preference, and Jay William had no difficulty doing just what he ordered.

By lunchtime, Fatso had seen enough to be impressed with Jay William's skills. "Boy, who taught you how to work in a kitchen like that, your momma?" he asked.

"No, sir. My mother died when I was only eight. My aunt taught me when I went to live with her," Jay William replied.

"She did you a favor. Did you know that?" Jay William simply shook his head up and down and kept working without looking up. The meal of ham and beans, fried beans, and cornbread was one of the crew's favorites. For dessert, there were fried apples.

Jay William cleaned the tables, washed the dishes, and let them air dry. He had worked a long day, but Jay William felt he had done his best and he was happy. He got a nickname when one fellow said, "Hey, that name Jay William takes too long to say. How about calling you just plain JW?"

That was fine with Jay William, and he became JW to all the men on the barge.

By the evening, Jay William was exhausted and was happy to go to his cubbyhole. He lay on his bunk and immediately fell asleep only to be awakened by a piercing alarm and cries of distress. The shouting was followed by lots of laughter.

He found out later that two jokesters had smeared motor oil on Old Louie's thick glasses and had sounded the distress alarm. According to the story, Old Louie put on the glasses and headed for the deck to deal with the emergency. He panicked, shouting, "I'm totally blind!," and grabbed a rail to avoid falling. The guys told him they had played a prank and offered to clean his glasses.

Poor Jay William saw no humor in this and was angry that Old Louie had been treated that way. He told him so in the morning. Old Louie said that life on the river could become monotonous after several weeks and that things like this were bound to happen every once in a while. "Sometime the joke may be on you, JW," he said. "You must not take it personally. Learn to laugh at yourself and you'll be fine.

The barge unloaded cotton and whiskey in St. Louis, Missouri. Several of the men got off the barge to have a few hours of fun in the city before they loaded the boat with nails and other products and headed for New Orleans, Louisiana.

Jay William took his geography textbook out on deck and read in the sunshine. He learned that Randolph had enjoyed its heyday in the 1830s. At that time, Randolph shipped out more cotton on the Mississippi River than Memphis did. Randolph had about a thousand residents, four hotels, three warehouses, saloons, and schools.

When Old Louie spotted Jay William, he asked him what he was reading, and the boy shared what he had just learned. Louie said his grandpappy had lived in Randolph and was told by his daddy that the town once had a fancy hotel called Washington Hall where the rich steamboat customers stayed. Louie's great-grandfather said a new steamboat arrived in Randolph almost daily. According to the weekly newspaper, *The Recorder*, in 1834, eighteen steamboats came through Randolph in one week.

CHAPTER 28

J AY WILLIAM LISTENED with fascination as Louie discussed Randolph's history. He had not known that the town played a big part in the Civil War. Louie said the Confederate army built two forts there—Fort Randolph and Fort Wright—using slave labor. The rebels tore down many of the town's abandoned buildings in the process. The Confederate army also operated boot camps there for Tennessee soldiers. Private (later General) Nathan Bedford Forrest began military training in Randolph, Louie said.

At this point the lesson had to stop because it was time to load the barge for the New Orleans trip. Louie asked Jay William if he wanted to watch the men do that. "Check with Fatso first," Louie said, "and if he can spare you come down to the lower deck."

Jay William was excited when Fatso told him to join Louie and appreciated his warning: "Stay out of their way because you are there only to watch."

Jay William hid his precious book in a pot in the kitchen and ran to join Louie as he supervised the men loading the merchandise. He watched as the crew placed large barrels of nails, food, and coal in the barge's storage area and secured them using ratchets, winches, and sledgehammers. The men then took a break for supper.

Jay William hurried to the kitchen to help Fatso put the finishing touches on the meal. To his surprise, Fatso had prepared beef roast, carrots, onions, and mashed potatoes with chocolate cake for dessert. After this delicious meal, Jay William cleared the tables and washed the dishes. Fatso asked him if he was the one who had put a book in a pot. Jay William admitted he was in a hurry to watch the merchandise being loaded and had put it there for safekeeping until he returned. "I'll let it slide this time, but don't let it happen again, JW," Fatso said. "The pot had been clean, and I had to wash it again before we could use it. That book must be pretty important to you. How come?"

Jay William said this geography book contained fascinating information about the Mississippi River and about his hometown of Randolph. He said he had learned even more from Old Louie, who had a grandpappy who had lived there and who knew a lot of the town's history.

"Well boy, I left that place when I was fourteen, and I've been working on a barge ever since," Fatso said. "I never had much of a life except on this river. I belong here and I love my job. I quit school when I finished sixth grade. Perhaps I can help you learn more about the Mississippi River and its history and commerce and how it made Randolph famous. If you want to work in this galley, I think I can arrange it with Captain Greene. I could use a good worker like you, and I could answer your questions about Randolph's history. Would you like that?"

"I'd like to help you and hear your stories about all this, but I also like Old Louie. Would this mean I couldn't work with him anymore?"

"JW, Old Louie feels protective toward you, and he'll always find time for you. I want a man to help me here, and I need someone dependable like you. Why don't you sleep on it and let me know later? I'll talk to Old Louie and see if we can't work out something for you." Jay William took his book and headed for his cubbyhole for the night.

Morning came much too soon. Old Louie shook him and said, "No one is permitted to sleep late here. Wash your face, get dressed, and head down to the galley. Fatso and I have been talking, and he really needs your help there. I'll be available whenever you need me. Get a move on. Your two weeks are up, and Captain Greene wants to speak with you this morning. It's an important day for you, so shape up and get going."

"Am I in trouble? Will I lose my job?" Jay William asked in a frightened voice.

Old Louie patted him on the back and said, "I don't think so. Just hurry down to the galley."

Jay William raced to the galley, grabbed an apron, and asked Fatso what he should do first. "Start cutting those potatoes up for frying, and then I'll show you how I want the eggs scrambled," the cook said. "The captain has an announcement to make at breakfast, and we must get the meal ready before he comes down."

Breakfast was on the table before Captain Greene entered the galley. To Jay William's surprise, he sat down with the crew instead of having breakfast in his quarters. For the first time, Jay William was told to sit at the table with the other men. He was so nervous that he ate very little.

Captain Greene stood up and said, "I would like to welcome our newest permanent employee, Jay William Hawkins. Will you please stand?"

Jay William rose to shouts and applause from the crew. The men chanted, "JW, JW! You are trouble over and over again."

They slapped him on the back, and the next thing he knew they had shoved him into a chair and had placed a towel around his shoulders, and an elderly crewman was cutting his hair. One of the men shouted, "Shave him and make him look like a man."

Jay William hardly knew how to deal with all the attention, but he felt important for the first time in his life. The captain sat and watched with a smile on his face.

"Your position will be in the galley with Fatso," he said. "Old Louie has also asked to have access to you. We'll work out the details later. Now everyone get busy, and let's get this load down to New Orleans." The place emptied quickly, and Jay William started doing the dishes.

"I'm going to give you more responsibility since the captain gave me permission," Fatso said. "We're having beef stew for dinner, and you need to cut up those vegetables I placed over there while I slice the meat. If you could see yourself now, you would see what we see—a handsome young man instead of a scared boy. You did well with all the attention you got. Congratulations! Now let's get busy and make this stew."

Jay William did exactly as Fatso instructed him to do, and the stew was done to suit the cook's taste. He showed Jay William the way he wanted the biscuits made and was surprised at how quickly the boy learned to work with such large quantities of food. "Young man, if I'm not careful, you'll have my job soon," Fatso said. "Just look at the smiles on the crew members' faces as they eat what you've prepared!"

"You're just trying to make me feel good, aren't you, Fatso?" Jay William said with a grin.

"Perhaps," Fatso said with a laugh. "I know you had your heart set on being a deckhand, but this is a safer place right now, and I really do need you. Do you want to hear an interesting fact or two about Randolph while we get the kitchen ready for a busy day tomorrow?"

"Okay, that sounds good," Jay William said.

"The spot on the beach where we stopped to bring you to the barge is where Davy Crockett watched a large meteor shower on November 13, 1833. Many people thought the world was coming to an end."

"Are you telling me Davy Crockett lived in Randolph?" Jay William asked.

"No, but it's said that one of his best friends lived there and that he often visited him. Davy Crockett helped put together a proposal for a canal for President Andrew Jackson's approval. The canal would have connected the Tennessee River to the

Hatchie River. This would have meant an increase in business for Randolph, which is only a few miles from the point where the Hatchie River merges with the Mississippi. The canal would have been a big deal because the Hatchie was navigable as far inland as Bolivar. But President Jackson was against such government projects, and the canal never materialized."

"Boy, if that had happened, Randolph could have been as big as Memphis! Right, Fatso?" Jay William said.

"It's hard to say now, but our history lesson is over because it's time for us to crawl into our bunks. Morning will be here before we know it. Good night to you," Fatso said.

CHAPTER 29

J AY WILLIAM HAD grown into a sturdy young man with wide shoulders and large biceps. He looked much older than his fourteen years and had more life experience than most boys his age. He continued to work mostly in the galley with Fatso and to learn more about the town of Randolph and its part in the Civil War. One day Old Louie entered the galley and asked Fatso if he could borrow Jay William for an important task. The deck needed a good cleaning before the barge arrived in New Orleans.

Old Louie told Jay William there were usually many boats in the port, so he wanted the barge to look its very best. "Son, you always take pride in whatever task you're given, and that's why I'm assigning this job to you," he said.

"Exactly what do you want me to do?" Jay William asked.

"You're going to give this deck a scrubbing like it's never had before," Old Louie said. "When you finish, this barge will outshine all the boats in New Orleans. Captain Greene will be the envy of all the other captains, and he'll be happy with me for choosing you to do the job.

"Okay, here's the first thing you must do. Take one of those wide push brooms and that dust pan and bring them out to the deck. I want you to push all of the debris off of the deck and onto the dust pan and place the debris in that large can over there. Make sure you don't leave even a hair on the deck. When you've finished that, I'll explain the next step."

Jay William worked as thoroughly and as efficiently as he knew how. He pretended Uncle Hilton was going to check the work with his horsewhip in hand. By three in the afternoon, he had completed phase one. Old Louie came to check on his progress and said, "JW, you never cease to amaze me. Go get something to eat and then we'll discuss the completion of this project."

Jay William returned to the galley where Fatso was busy making supper. "You arrive only when I'm almost finished preparing this meal!" Fatso wailed.

"Didn't Old Louie tell you he had me working out on the deck?" Jay William asked.

"Sure he did, but I have to give you a hard time so you won't forget me in here," Fatso said with a smile. "JW, I thought of something I meant to tell you about Randolph and the Civil War. There is still an underground magazine in Randolph where the Confederate forces stored gunpowder. You must ask someone to show you where it's located. I saw the magazine once when I was a lad, but I'll probably never get back there."

"Okay, I'll do that, Fatso. Hey, did Old Louie tell you he needs me out on the deck for phase two of the job I'm doing?"

"He sure did, and he plans to use you for a couple of days. Be careful that you don't get sunburned out there. You're not used to the sun anymore. I'm going to let you have the supper menu since you missed lunch."

Jay William enjoyed his meal very much and asked Fatso for seconds. Old Louie entered the galley and asked, "Aren't you done eating yet, boy? I forgot to check on you earlier, and I'm sorry you missed your noon meal. Are you too tired to start the second step? I think it would be better to wait until tomorrow morning. Is that okay with you?"

"I don't mind, but in the meantime could I go out on the deck and watch the river? I love to watch it when it's calm like it is today."

"I'll walk out with you and we can discuss tomorrow's project."

Opening a closet, Old Louie showed Jay William a large mop and a bucket with a wringer on top for excess water. He also pointed to a large bottle of detergent that would remove all the dirt and grime on the deck. He said the crew had painted the deck just before Jay William was hired.

"I've been here more than three years," Jay William. "I can hardly believe it. Sometimes it seems I've been here only a short time, and other times I think I've been here forever. I remember when I got off the barge in St. Louis and bought a pocket watch and announced the time to the guys got back on the boat. They were angry with me, and my watch disappeared. That was the only money I ever spent from my salary, and it was gone in less than twenty-four hours. No one ever said a word about what happened. I believe Old Man River has a pocket watch."

"JW, pay attention to what I'm telling you now. This job is very important to me," Old Louie said, interrupting his musings.

"I'm sorry. I think all the fresh air I got today stirred up things in my brain," Jay William said.

"You must change the water whenever it begins to look dirty; otherwise you won't get a clean deck," Old Louie told him. "The last step is to rinse the deck with clear water. Captain Greene himself will inspect the deck when you finish tomorrow. A good job is more important than a quick job. I'm going inside to check on a few things. Do you have any questions?"

"I don't think so," Jay William said.

The sun had nearly set when Old Louie returned to the deck. "What are you doing out here in the dark?" he asked. "You should have joined the deckhands in the break room."

"I'm still not comfortable around those guys unless you're with me. I don't mind being by myself," Jay William said.

"You must associate more with the other men," Old Louie said.

"Sir, I don't know how to talk with them. They're always laughing and telling jokes I don't understand."

"JW, learn a lesson from Old Man River: listen and go with the flow. Old Man River doesn't get upset because he's not in control. Sure he sometimes throws a few rough waves, but for the most part, he flows gently with the tide. I hope you learn to do that soon. You're still young and most of the men know that, but you should try a little harder, okay?"

"I'll try!" Jay William said. He wanted to get along with the other men, but his lack of confidence held him back.

The next morning, Jay William joined the deckhands for breakfast in the galley and then went to the closet to get the supplies. He cleaned the deck meticulously. He wanted it to look good when Captain Greene inspected it.

Later that afternoon, Jay William completed the task. He was very pleased with the way the deck looked, and he hoped Old Louie would be too. Jay William put the mop and the bucket back in the closet and stopped by Old Louie's office to ask if he would check the deck.

Old Louie walked out to the deck and was more than pleased with the way it looked. "JW, you did a fantastic job here!" he said. "The deck looks as good as new. Why don't you go spruce up? Put on fresh clothes, comb your hair, and come back here. I'll give you a few minutes. I want you to be here when the captain takes a look."

Jay William washed up, put on clean clothes, and made sure his hair was combed before he returned to the deck. Old Louie and Captain Greene arrived shortly after he did.

Jay William was a little nervous but felt he had done a good job. He saw Captain Greene smile when he inspected the deck. "Young man, the deck couldn't look any better than you have it looking," the captain said. "I'll be the envy of my peers when I get to New Orleans. Sometimes we give a bonus for superb work.

You deserve one for this job. Thank you for all your hard work. I'll add the bonus pay to your regular salary."

After winning the captain's praise, Jay William seemed to hold his head up a little higher. He spent more time on deck than in previous years and received respect from the other men.

When the fifth anniversary of his employment arrive, Jay William was acknowledged by all the crew members. They told of watching him grow from a frightened boy into a hardworking man. Their stories turned his thoughts to Randolph and his siblings. He decided he would talk to Fatso about getting off the boat and going home when the barge docked in Memphis on June 1.

A few days later, while the two were making breakfast for the crew, Jay William told Fatso about his plan.

"You're the best man I've ever trained in the galley, and I don't want to start over with a new man," Fatso said. "But I won't try to talk you out of leaving. When I was younger, I often thought about leaving, but I never did. That's why I never had a wife and children. I stayed on the boat and cooked for the crew. It's been a rewarding job, but I'll always wonder what my life would be like if I'd left. Would I have been a good husband and father? I'll never know because I'm too old and set in my ways even to consider such a thing now. I will say this: if I'd had a son, I would have wanted one exactly like you. You're so eager to learn, and you learn fast. I hope you continue to learn and to seek your dreams. Go look up your sister, Catherine, and perhaps together you can find your dad."

Later, Jay William asked Old Louie for his thoughts.

"JW, you've gotten past many struggles, and you have a good job here now," Old Louie said. "Before you resign, make sure you really want to do this. Jobs aren't easy to find, and plenty of men would love to have your job. Have you considered what you will do when you get off this boat? Do me a favor before you resign. Get a pencil and paper and write down the advantages and disadvantages of working on this boat. Take your time and concentrate on what you're doing. After you've done that, bring me the list and we'll look at it together. Don't go to Captain Greene until I talk with you again."

The following day Jay William returned to see Old Louie with the list. He had spent much time writing out the pluses and minuses. Old Louie was sure Jay William had decided to look up his family, so he gave him some advice.

"JW, there are swindlers who prey on young men with money in their pockets, and they will rob you," Old Louie said. "Here's how to avoid that. First, you should have the captain give you your salary in large bills. Hundred-dollar bills would be best because they are less bulky. Stuff that money in your socks before you get off the boat. Practice walking with a little bulk in your shoes now so it won't be obvious that you have something in them. Here, take this folded paper and slip it inside your shoe. That should do the trick. When you leave, go straight to the general store a block north of the boatyard and buy good clothes. Then go directly across the street to the First Bank of Tennessee. Open a savings account and put most of the money in it. Do you have any questions?"

Jay William had taken notes as Old Louie spoke. He read them back to Old Louie, who saw that Jay William had understood his instructions.

"Please don't talk to the captain until I've given you the okay," Old Louie said. "Fatso and I are to be the only people who know what you're planning."

Jay William left his office and went back to work.

CHAPTER 30

THE FOLLOWING WEEK, Captain Greene called Jay William into his quarters and asked if the rumors of his impending resignation were true. Jay William was taken aback by the question because he thought Old Louie would prepare him to meet with the captain before the subject arose.

"It is okay, JW," Captain Greene said. "I've talked to Louie and Fatso. They both said that you were an excellent employee and that they would definitely hire you again. That's all I need to mark your file 'Will Rehire.'

"I agree with them. I'm proud to have hired you, and I'll be sorry to see you leave. However, I agree that it's time for you to return to Randolph to try to locate your family. You are leaving for all the right reasons, and you can come back to work anytime we have an opening. Do you want me to hold your salary in the safe until your departure?"

"Yes, sir, and I'd like big bills because I plan to put the money in the bank as soon as I'm properly dressed to visit it. Old Louie said I should do that, and I value his opinion."

"That's a smart choice," the captain said. "Come up to my office just before we dock in Memphis."

Jay William felt good inside when he left the captain's quarters. He had gotten everything in order for his departure from the barge. He knew he was a lot smarter and more skilled than he was when he first came aboard.

The next two weeks seemed to fly as Jay William labored beside Old Louie and Fatso. He sensed some of the men were looking at him differently, but he could not put his finger on what had changed. When Jay William awakened on June 2, 1930, he realized this was the day the barge would dock in Memphis. He looked at his list of tasks and knew he best check it twice. He had breakfast to serve, and then he would go down to the loading dock and help unload products before leaving right after lunch.

When Jay William went down to the galley, he heard laughter and wondered what was going on. As he entered the room, the crew sang "For He's a Jolly Good Fellow," and then two of the biggest men hoisted him up and stood him on a table by the door. The crew called out, "JW, give us a parting speech."

He hardly knew what to say. The men called out more loudly. Finally Jay William stammered, "I want to thank all of you wise guys for putting up with the young boy who came aboard this barge. Thanks to all of you, I'm a little more prepared to face the world than when I got here. Now can I go and help Fatso get the food on the table one last time?"

"No, you can sit and be served by Fatso himself," the cook said.

Jay William was joined at the table by Old Louie and Captain Greene. It was a morning he would always remember. The captain said Jay William would be off the boat as soon as it docked. Jay William started to protest, but the captain said it was best this way. He told Jay William to see him after he had gathered his belongings.

The men shook his hand and wished him good luck. Then Jay William met with Captain Greene. The captain gave him $1,000 in cash for his five years of service and told him to put $950 in a savings account. He advised Jay William to keep the money there until he needed it for something important.

Jay William never looked back after he left the barge. He hurried to the department store on the corner near the bank and purchased a handsome suit, a dress shirt, and a good pair of shoes. He went to the bank and opened an account with $950. Then he returned to the store and bought overalls, two work shirts, socks, and work shoes. He also got a suitcase and put his extra clothes in it once he left the store.

A group of young men snickered as he did that. "Did you get off that boat this morning?" one of them asked.

"I don't know what you're talking about," Jay William said. "I'm headed for Randolph and must hurry to catch my ride there."

Another man patted him down, looking for money. Finding nothing, the group shoved him around and then left. Jay William was happy that his money was in his sock.

He was a little shaken by the experience and was happy that his mentors had cautioned him about the city's dangers. He returned to the bank to find out where he could get transportation to Randolph and spotted the banker who had helped him earlier.

"Mr. Jones, I'm Jay William Hawkins and I just opened an account with you this morning."

"Yes, of course, Mr. Hawkins," Mr. Jones said. "I remember you and marvel at what a smart young man you are to have saved your money. How can I help you now?"

"Sir, I need to find transportation to Randolph, and I wondered if you had a suggestion. I've been away for eight years and I don't know where to find a ride from here to there."

"It just so happens that a customer from Randolph is finishing up some banking business, and I don't think he would mind your company on the trip home. He's about your age. If you wait here a minute, I'll see if he's willing to give you a ride."

Mr. Jones returned shortly with a young man whom he introduced as Mr. Moore. Jay William shook hands with Mr. Moore, who said that he would be delighted to take him to Randolph and that his wagon was just down the street.

The pair left and got into the wagon without saying too much more. As they headed out of Memphis, they kept glancing at each other. Finally Mr. Moore spoke up. "Would your full name be Jay William Hawkins?" he asked.

"Yes. How did you know that?" Jay William asked.

"I'm Johnny Moore and we walked to school together. Our mothers became friends, but your mother died shortly after that. You had a slightly older sister, Catherine. I was a little sweet on her, but I never told anyone. Is she coming back to Randolph too?"

"No. She got married and I haven't seen her since. I'm trying to find her. Do you know if any of my other siblings is in the Randolph area?" Jay William asked.

"I've lost track of my old neighbors because I'm so busy helping my stepdad, Herman Smith, on his farm. He owned the farm we lived on, and when his wife died, my mother married him. He's good to me and calls me his son. I'm his only son because he and his first wife had no children. Hey, where should I take you? We're almost in Randolph?"

"How about the old Watson home? Is it still there?"

"Yes. The younger son, Ted, lives there alone since his father died. He is trying hard to keep it up. He has a pair of good-looking horses and often works with them. Here we are. That's Ted coming out to the road now. Should I stop here?"

Ted Watson was surprised to see Johnny stop. "Who is your passenger, Johnny?" Ted asked.

"This is one of our own, Jay William Hawkins, and he wanted to stop here," Johnny said.

"Well sure enough," Ted said. "Get out, Jay William, and shake my hand. You look like a gentleman all dressed up like that. My girlfriend would like to see me in that suit you're wearing. If that's your suitcase, you might as well grab it because you're spending the night here so we can catch up on what's happened since you left."

Jay William got out of the wagon and asked Johnny what he owed him for the ride. "Not a thing," Johnny said. "I was coming here anyway and I enjoyed your company. But I do have to get going to the farm. See you around, Jay William." Johnny hurried off.

That evening Jay William and Ted talked about everything that had happened since Marjorie died. "My dad passed away about four years ago, and I've had a hard time managing the place since his death," Ted said. "Fred doesn't come around much. He and Wanda and their three kids live in Covington now. Perhaps we can arrange to visit them this week. I have two great horses with hand spans of sixteen each. We could ride them into Covington and visit with Fred and Wanda for a few days. They can help you find the rest of your family. How does that sound, Jay William? You must, however, prove to me that you can ride well, because these horses are my pride and joy. I can't let just anyone ride them. The horses were a gift from my dad, and they're an investment for me. Tomorrow morning, we'll ride them in this area."

The next morning, the pair saddled up the two horses and headed into the countryside. Jay William had forgotten how much fun a day out in the forest could be. They stopped by a spring and filled up on water for themselves and the horses. They sat down on a log and talked about their childhood years and family issues. Ted asked if Jay William ever wondered how Ethel and Otto were doing.

"I think of them on occasion," Jay William replied, "but I know I couldn't have a relationship with them if I found them. Besides, Momma signed a paper saying no one in our family would attempt to find them."

"It sure was sad that it worked out like that," Ted said. "Hey, how did you like life on the Mississippi? Do you have any exciting stories you want to share, Jay William?"

"Not now," he said. "We should get going because the horses have rested long enough and I'm anxious to learn about my siblings."

"I think you should know that I have a girlfriend, Carolyn Carter," Ted said. "I plan to marry her as soon as I can figure out how I can get her to agree. She takes cares of her younger brothers and sisters. She's the prettiest girl in Tipton County."

"I'm happy for you," Jay William said, "but I don't want a girlfriend until I get things straightened out in my head regarding my family. Hey, let's ride up to Covington in the morning and see Fred and Wanda. I think I've proven I'm an okay rider."

"We can do the chores early and head to Covington," Ted said. "Now I'll race you to the store. You can buy food and show me what a good cook you've become working on that barge. I'm tired of cooking for myself, because I'm not that good. Let's get started."

Jay William kept up with Ted's fast pace, which surprised them both.

CHAPTER 31

TED AND JAY William got up at four-thirty the following morning and quickly completed their chores. They put extra clothes in a bag and headed into town to purchase potted meat, pork and beans, and a package of crackers for the trip. Ted had a sweet tooth and added a few fried pies to the stash. Then the two men headed for Covington, which was about twenty miles from the store. Jay William felt he was about to discover his family and was excited about what lay ahead.

Fred and Wanda were living in a shotgun house. It had a large front porch, a living room, one bedroom, a kitchen, and a back porch. Fred had escaped when the feds found the still he and Hershel were operating. He was now trying to make an honest living for Wanda and the kids. He was working for Jerome McCardy, the older brother of Wanda and of Jay William. The family was relieved that Fred had not gone to prison.

Wanda was thankful that Jay William was alive and could hardly believe how grown up he looked. She happily introduced her three children to their uncle. The oldest was little Freddy. He was followed by Herbert and Hannah. Jay William played with the children briefly as did Ted, who was also an uncle to the trio.

Jay William considered asking Wanda about Ethel and Otto but never mentioned them because he knew it would be pointless. He asked Wanda if she ever heard from Catherine, and Wanda said Catherine lived in Dyer County in a small town called Bogota. Jay

William asked for directions, and Wanda said he could take a bus to Dyersburg and get further directions there. Wanda told him Loretta and Charles lived in Tipton County just five miles from her place and had a boy and a little girl. Jay William got directions to their house and asked Wanda if he could return to her place and visit later in the day.

"Of course. I don't mind," she said. "Why don't you see if Loretta and Charles want to come for supper here tonight? Perhaps Ted can ride out to Jerome's place and ask him and Sue to come. It would be great to have most of Momma's children in one place."

That night the siblings and their families ate a meal together and talked about earlier times. Jay William said he wanted to head for Dyersburg the next day to see Catherine and Johnny. "Spending time with all of you makes me want to see her too," he said. "Would you all be okay with that?"

Ted understood how important it was for Jay William to see his sister and agreed to take both horses home to Randolph so Jay William could leave from Wanda's house the next day.

Finding Catherine and Johnny's place didn't take much work. The town had a store, a church, a school, and a population of three hundred. Most of the residents were sharecroppers, as were Catherine and Johnny. Jay William arrived at their house at suppertime. Catherine set a plate on the table for him and served up fried squirrel, potatoes, and green beans from the garden. Jay William was overwhelmed with emotion at seeing his sister and Johnny and their four-year-old son, Ernest, and did not eat much.

Because it was planting season, Johnny was in bed by eight o'clock. He took Ernest with him, giving Catherine and Johnny an opportunity to catch up on what had happened in their lives since Catherine left to marry Johnny.

"I've got to be honest with you," Jay William said. "I would really like to find our daddy. I feel we were cheated and so was he. I vaguely remember Jerome hitting him repeatedly on the head before he finally agreed to leave that morning. Do you remember how Daddy came back to our house that Christmas with gifts?"

Jay William became upset as he spoke about these events. Catherine took his hand and said, "I know it's painful for you to remember all that we suffered, but Johnny told me that if our daddy wanted to see us he could have done it. There are two possibilities: he didn't want to see us or he was no longer alive. Jay William, you must stop torturing yourself with these thoughts. Yes, it was terrible, but we lived through the tough times and we need to quit reliving them now.

"Speaking of bad times, I'm sorry I escaped Aunt Sophie and Uncle Hilton's farm and left you to fend for yourself. I promised to try to get you out of there, but Johnny was ordered off their land, and we had to move away without telling you. Was it worse after I left?"

"I did okay, but I had to leave," Jay William said. "I took my chance on the Christmas just before my twelfth birthday when Aunt Sophie and Uncle Hilton went to visit their daughters. I made out just fine. I got a job with the Mississippi Company Barge and worked on a boat for five years. I grew up fast and learned a lot from the older guys there."

"I heard from Wanda that Fred found you in the woods nearly frozen and took you to his whiskey still and kept you there until the weather got warmer. He never knew for sure what happened to you after you left his place, but he hoped you were able to get a job. Oh, Jay William, I'm so happy you're safe. You look great and I'm so proud of you. Little Ernest is going to love you a lot because he looks like you. Jay William, you must stay with us for a while since we have so much to catch up on, but right now I have to go to bed. I need to get up with Johnny at four in the morning and cook his breakfast."

Jay William slept on a pallet in the living room because there was no extra bed. He lay awake for long time thinking about the events of the last few days. *If only Ethel and Otto had been there, everything would have been complete*, Jay William told himself. *I must quit thinking about them. I can only hope they're happy with their adoptive family.*

It seemed he had just fallen asleep when Ernest jumped on him and said, "Uncle Jay, I want you to play with me."

Jay William saw the sun shining in the window. It felt good to be with Catherine and her son. As Catherine had predicted, Ernest liked Jay William, and Jay William enjoyed spending time with his nephew.

Catherine and Jay William spent ten days discussing all that had taken place in their lives while they were separated. Jay William discovered that Catherine had fallen into a deep depression after losing a baby in the first year of her marriage. She was overjoyed to become the mother of Ernest, whom Jay William soon came to love dearly. The boy eased the pain in his heart over having lost Ethel and Otto. They played every day while Catherine watched them with pride. Johnny worked hard in the fields and was very tired in the evenings. It was difficult for Jay William to leave Bogota for Randolph, but he felt he must decide on his next step in life.

CHAPTER 32

WHEN HE RETURNED to Randolph, Jay William still had plenty of cash and offered to pay Ted Watson a dollar a week in board and to help with the chores. Ted was happy to have the company and took him up on his offer. Jay William helped Ted in the vegetable garden, milked the cow, and fed the horses. He was excited to be with farm animals again and to work in the garden. The two men enjoyed riding the horses and being together.

Ted often walked to the Carter house, which was about two miles down the road. One evening he came home bubbling over with excitement because Carolyn Carter had agreed to marry him. She was the oldest daughter of Edward Carter, who had been widowed for several years. Carolyn had been mother to the youngest daughter, who was only five years old when her mother died.

"Just think, Jay William, the prettiest girl in Tipton County has agreed to marry me," Ted said. "I'm the luckiest guy in the state of Tennessee."

He was carrying on so that Jay William hardly knew what to say. He thought about his momma; she was beautiful but had a short, miserable life.

Finally, Jay William said, "I'm not sure I can talk with you about this, because I haven't experienced what you say you're feeling. All I can say is that I hope you're making a good decision. You're my friend and I wouldn't want to say anything to burst your bubble. When I choose a wife I don't care if she is pretty or not. I want her to be kind, honest, and loyal. I want her to be willing to work hard to make our home a good place for our children."

"Jay William, I know your home life was filled with a lot of anger and bickering," Ted said. "I understand your thinking on this. But I want you to meet Carolyn. I believe you'll change your mind about my feelings toward her. She takes such good care of her baby sister, and she wants her to live with us after we're married. I'm going to their house tomorrow when our chores are completed. Why don't you go with me and meet the Carter family? They would enjoy seeing you. Why don't you sleep on it? We'll talk about it in the morning during our ride on the beach."

After morning chores, the two men saddled up the horses and went to the grocery store for food. Then they rode to the beach. When the sun got hot, they stopped in a shaded area just below the place where Marjorie was buried. Jay William got quiet and Ted asked what he was thinking about.

"I came upon my momma's grave by chance when I was waiting here, hoping to get hired by the Mississippi Barge Company. Finding it was such a surprise," Jay William said.

"How did you feel when that happened?" Ted asked.

Jay William wasn't ready to share his thoughts about his momma, so he quickly changed the subject. "Why don't you tell me what to expect if I go with you this evening to the Carter place?" he asked.

"You can expect to be welcomed by the family," Ted told him. "There are five girls and four boys in the family. Earl Carter is a small-framed man with a kind heart and a big smile. Carolyn is the oldest girl and is pretty much in charge of the house, but all the girls work together so well. Mr. Carter is very proud of his beautiful girls, and their maternal grandmother has taught them how to be gracious, kind Southern women. They all cook, wash and iron the clothes, and tend the garden. In the front hallway you will notice a photograph of Mr. Carter's late wife at the age of seventeen. She was very pretty lady. We should probably head for the house so we can get ready to go."

Jay William jumped up first from the grass. They rode to the Watson place and finished the chores early. Then they each took a quick bath.

"Jay William, wear the fancy clothes you had on when you arrived from Memphis. You looked like a city gentleman, and I think the girls would really like that," Ted said.

"Why? I've never noticed you dressed like that when you walk to their house in the evenings," Jay William said.

"The girls are hoping to go to Randolph for a brush arbor meeting," Ted said. "I'm wearing my best tonight."

The two men walked to the Carter house in their best clothes. Jay William was nervous, fearing he would embarrass himself and Ted too. He decided to follow Ted's lead during this social call since Ted seemed so much more confident.

Jay William was amazed at Mr. Carter's friendliness. He shook Jay William's hand briskly and made him feel at home. The girls were all smiles, and he was surprised at how much attention he received from the family. The house was bigger than most and was shiny and clean. Jay William was shy and found conversation difficult. Mr. Carter sensed his discomfort and invited him out to his barn to see his new wagon, which had arrived that day. Jay William had never seen a brand-new wagon and was impressed.

Mr. Carter asked Jay William to tell him about his work on the barge. Jay William was surprised that he could talk with him so easily.

"Jay William, Ted has talked about you ever since you've been back in the area," Mr. Carter said. "He tells me you're a good friend to him and help him out at his place. That's commendable, but I'm more impressed with you for sticking with a job on the barge for five years. I admire you for doing that. Very few men in this area stick with a job for long. My girls seem impressed with your good looks." That remark made Jay William blush. and he could think of nothing to say in response.

"My girls would like to go to the brush arbor revival meeting being held in Randolph. It's supposed to be a weeklong event, and all they've talked about this week is the event's opening tonight. It appears that all their young friends are attending, and they want to join them. Please, will you drive them there tonight?"

Jay William looked at him in total disbelief.

"I trust you completely, young man," Mr. Carter said. "There isn't another man in the county whom I trust to drive my daughters there, and that includes my own sons. You have a reputation for being level-headed and honest."

"Sir, thank you for your kind words," Jay William said, "but I'm shy and don't how to act around girls. I was embarrassed and didn't know what to say when your daughters spoke to me inside. That made me feel foolish, and I don't like that feeling."

"You are anything but foolish, young man," Mr. Carter said. "I'm very protective of my pretty daughters, and I find your humble attitude refreshing. Most of the young men I know are cocky and too sure of themselves."

"To tell you the truth, sir, I don't know what a brush arbor meeting is. Can you tell me?" Jay William asked.

"From what I know, it's like a church service held in a countryside setting," Mr. Carter said. "Limbs are cut off trees to build a shelter or an arbor to protect people from the elements. People sit on flat boards placed across tree stumps. The roof is brush piled on top of the shelter's frame, keeping out the wind and the rain. I don't want to discourage them from attending. The girls like the singing and most of the preaching. Their mother was a good Christian lady, and I'm trying my best to raise them as I think she would want. Granny Knight has been a lifesaver for me. I have four boys and five girls, and she has been a big help with them, especially for my girls. They all know how to keep a clean house, to sew, and to garden."

"I have a confession to make," Jay William said. "I've never been to church and wasn't taught about God, but I've been trying to find evidence that he is real. I've even prayed when I was troubled at times in my life."

Mr. Carter was silent for a moment, and then the pair walked back to the house.

At five o'clock the new wagon left the Carter home filled with five happy young women accompanied by two young men. Jay William was in the driver's seat. Wilma Carter sat next to him in the front seat to direct him to the revival meeting. Jay William found driving the wagon easy because he had driven Uncle Hilton's wagon several times on the farm. The problem for him was his fear of stuttering; he said almost nothing to Wilma, only nodding his head occasionally.

The girls had packed a picnic basket with all sorts of good food. They had brought cold fried chicken, homemade bread, potato salad, baked beans, pickles, and two blackberry cobblers. Jay William enjoyed the picnic with the girls. They talked softly and he gradually relaxed.

Wilma was twenty years old, and she seemed to be the one who kept everything running smoothly. She went out of her way to make Jay William feel at ease. She took it upon herself to make up his plate and offered it to him with a warm smile. At dessert time, she served him a double portion of the blackberry cobbler. Jay William was surprised at all the attention she gave him. He felt comfortable and happy with Wilma at his side and was not bothered that she spoke about God as though he was her best friend. She often used the phrase "Thank you, Jesus."

"How is Jesus different from God?" Jay William asked her.

"Jesus is the Son of God, who came to earth as a baby and who taught the truth from God to many people. He died on the cross and was brought back to life by his father, God," Wilma said.

Jay William had never heard this explanation before, and

somehow he accepted it. He felt she must know what she was talking about because he believed she had spoken sincerely.

Wilma asked Jay William about his work on the river and was fascinated by his stories about his time on the barge. He told her about the expensive pleasure steamboat he had seen docked in New Orleans. "Ladies were dressed in beautiful ball gowns, and the gentlemen wore very expensive attire," Jay William said. "They danced to music, and there was much laughter coming from the boat."

She asked if he had ever been on a fancy boat.

"No," he replied. "We were on the deck of our barge at least thirty feet away from the boat. That's as close as I've ever come to a fancy boat."

The brush arbor was only a short distance from the picnic area, and the seven of them arrived at the meeting just as the sun was setting. Jay William was surprised as they entered the area. He counted fifteen wagons, and he had never seen so many young people in one place before. They were talking and laughing and seemed to be having a lot of fun. The girls were dressed in pretty clothes, and the men wore their best. All of this made Jay William feel happy. The group quickly found seats, and he was glad that Wilma sat beside him.

The service soon began. The woman at the piano smiled and began to play a song that almost everyone seemed to know. Later they sang a hymn about how God kept his eyes on a sparrow. The line "I know he watches over me" nearly brought Jay William to tears.

Jay William recalled the times he had escaped death. He thought about his afternoon in the hog pen with his hands and feet tied together; he knew the hog could have killed him. He remembered how he prayed to God for help. *It was God who protected me from harm that day*, he thought.

Other songs followed, and the young people began to clap their hands as they sang. They all seemed happy. The preacher read from the Bible about how God had sent an angel to close the lions' mouths to protect Daniel. Jay William wondered if God had sent an angel to close the hog's mouth that afternoon. So much was beyond his comprehension, and yet he believed all of it was true. He felt tears in his eyes and hoped no one could see them.

When the preacher had finished, he invited those who wanted to know more about God or who wanted prayer to come up front. Jay William was interested and watched several people step forward. He stood and wiped away the tears as they trickled from his eyes. Jay William was not sure what had occurred, but he knew in his heart that God was indeed real, and he desired to know more.

The Carter sisters had good, almost godly natures, and yet they were fun to be with that evening. They joked and laughed on the way back to their house, but Jay William's mind was on the things he had seen and heard for the first time in his life.

God is as real as the wind, he thought. *I can't see the wind, but I can see the results of the wind, like the tree limbs blowing. That must be how it is with God; I can't see God, but I understand what God does for those who trust him as Wilma does. Perhaps I should have walked up front with the others.*

As they neared the Carter home, Wilma put her small hand in his and asked, "Jay William, are you okay?"

He nodded yes.

"Jay William, I'll pray for you tonight before I sleep," she said softly. "I'll pray for God to give you peace and comfort. Would like to go to the meeting again? I think I'd like to go tomorrow evening. Would you?"

"Maybe so," Jay William replied.

They ate the rest of the picnic food and talked on the front porch. Because it was late and they were exhausted after a long day, Jay William and Ted accepted an invitation to sleep on the porch. As he lay listening to Ted mumble in his sleep, Jay William could not get Wilma off of his mind. *She is sweet, smart, kind, and pretty,* he thought. *She'll be a good wife for some lucky man. She knows all about God and told me that Jesus died and was buried and was brought back to life.* He trusted her and wanted to see her again and thought perhaps he would go to the meeting the next evening.

That means Ted and I have to do the chores quickly tomorrow, he thought. *And we won't have time to ride the horses, but that's okay with me.*

Jay William woke up the following morning to singing coming from the barn. According to the sun, it was only about six o'clock. He walked to the barn and found Wilma milking a cow. He noticed she had already gathered a basket of eggs.

"Good morning, Wilma. I'm surprised to see you up so early," he said.

Wilma jumped when he spoke, because she thought she was alone in the barn. "Good morning, Jay William," she said with a reddened face. "How did you sleep last night? I suppose the hard porch made it difficult for you to rest comfortably."

Jay William thought she looked pretty. "Actually it wasn't bad. I slept well," he told her. "May I help you with the chores?"

"Yes, if you wish," Wilma said with a smile. "All the others are still sleeping including my daddy and my brothers." She pointed to a large bucket of scraps and said she would appreciate it if Jay William slopped the pigs.

By the time the others woke up, the pair had breakfast on the table. They had cooked smoked ham, a platter of fatback, fried potatoes, eggs, milk gravy, and three pans of biscuits. That was plenty for the large number of people around the table. Jay William was thankful that Fatso had taught him to cook for a big group.

As everyone gathered, Mr. Carter asked Wilma to pray a blessing over the food. Jay William felt a little awkward because he was not sure what the family expected. Wilma came to his rescue. She quietly told him to take her hand and the hand of the person next to him and to bow his head. She then thanked God for the family and friends at the table and for the food that he had provided. Everyone said amen and began to pass the food.

During the meal, everyone seemed to be in a happy mood and there was much laughter. Jay William thought, *This is what I always wanted, a happy family. It's so different from how I grew up.*

Mr. Carter said, "Okay, who votes for Jay William to go back to the meeting tonight?"

All those who had gone the evening before raised their hands. Even two of the Carter brothers raised their hands. "What do you say, Mr. Jay William, are you up to another evening with the Carter bunch?" Mr. Carter asked.

"Sir, I would be honored," Jay William said. "You have a nice family and I enjoy being with all of you."

Wilma squeezed Jay William's hand. When he looked at her, she blushed and smiled.

"Okay, all of you have work to do around here," Mr. Carter said. "All the chores must be completed before the wagon leaves the barn this evening."

The Carters cut down weeds from around the vegetables in the garden. Ted and Jay William helped to repair a few fences. Then they asked to be excused so they could go to Ted's place and do their chores. The two men hurried to the Watson farm. The animals appeared happy to be fed, especially the cow that Jay William milked. He thought about Wilma and the service he had attended with her at his side. He smiled to himself just as Ted entered the barn.

"Looks like Jay William has something to smile about this morning," Ted said. "So what did you think about my Carolyn? Is she not as beautiful as I told you?"

"I think all of the girls are pretty," Jay William said.

"But Carolyn is the prettiest one," Ted said. "You seem to be favoring Wilma. Is that true?"

"I think she's special," Jay William said.

"Let's shower before we leave. I've filled the big barrel with water, and the sun will have it just right by two o'clock. I have to wash my clothes now and get them ready for this evening. Do you need any done too?" Ted asked.

"I think I am okay," Jay William said. "I still have some in my suitcase that I haven't worn yet. Do you mind if I take a quick nap? I'm tired and I want to be revived before we leave."

Ted woke him up an hour later, saying, "Okay, I've had my shower and there's water left in the barrel for you. I want to be at their place at around three o'clock. Can we do that?"

They got to the Carter home at three and found a meal of baked ham, sweet potatoes, and vegetables waiting for them.

"Since you men seemed to enjoy the blackberry cobbler last evening, I made another one," Wilma said. "Would you like to try it first?" She turned and smiled directly at Jay William.

He felt his cheeks turn pink. "I suppose," he said.

The others noticed they were both blushing as Wilma served him and then the others. The girls did the dishes while the men went out to the barn with Mr. Carter.

Mr. Carter shared a story about how Ted and Carolyn's engagement occurred. "They were walking from church on Sunday evening," he said, sharing her account. "They usually took the long way home, so they walked across homesteads instead of taking the roads. Normally when they got to a fence, Ted would lift Carolyn over it. They got to a fence and he said, 'Give me a kiss and I'll lift you over it.' Carolyn replied, 'Now, Ted, you know we can't kiss until we're engaged to be married.' Ted repeated, 'Give me a kiss.' Suddenly she said, "Ted, are you saying you want me to marry you?' Ted replied, 'Yes, that's what I'm trying to ask you. Carolyn, will you marry me?' 'Of course,' she said. They got to the house and woke me up. Ted asked for her hand in marriage. I think it's a good match. I'm pleased with my daughter's choice for a husband."

When the men returned to the house, the girls were dressed

up for the meeting at the brush arbor. Jay William noticed that Wilma looked especially nice dressed in his favorite shade of blue with white dots. Wilma noticed Jay William staring at her and she blushed. She was tiny, not quite five feet tall and a mere eighty-five pounds. He smiled warmly at her. She gave him a quick smile and turned away.

Everyone was excited about the evening ahead. Mr. Carter instructed Jay William and Wilma to sit up front in the wagon. Their group was the first to arrive. Jay William thought the place looked strange without all the young people there.

The preacher was standing close by. He was tall and rather young looking. "Hello. I recognize you from last evening," he said. "My name is Joseph Sparks, and I'm so happy you are here again. Did you enjoy last evening's service? I suppose the fact you are here means you did, right?"

"We enjoyed it very much," Wilma said. She then introduced the group to the Reverend Sparks.

The Reverend Sparks shook hands with Jay William and asked Jay William if he would help him for a few moments. Jay William agreed and followed the preacher inside the brush harbor. The Reverend Sparks gave Jay William songbooks to place at every other seat for the service.

Jay William saw a song with the title "The Old Account Settled." As he read the words, he realized he should settle his account with God. Tears came to his eyes as they did the night before. He wanted the joy and contentment Wilma had.

He felt a tap on his shoulder and heard the Reverend Sparks say, "Is something troubling you, brother? Would you like to talk about it?" He pointed to the front of the arbor and motioned for Jay William to follow. "Let's move to the front so we can have a little privacy."

"I've been wondering about the existence of God since I was a child," Jay William told the preacher. "My mother told us there was no God and wouldn't permit us to mention him. Momma died when I was only eight years old, and my daddy was gone long before that. After meeting the Carter family, I do believe there is a God, and the preaching last night explained much about how God has protected me. I want religion so I can feel the way Wilma Carter does."

With the Reverend Sparks guiding him, this was Jay William's prayer:

"Dear God, I need you. I'm humbly calling out to you. I'm tired of doing things my way. I want to start doing things your way. I invite you into my heart and my life to be my Lord and Savior. Fill my emptiness with your Holy Spirit. Make me whole. Help me to trust you and to love you. Help me to live my life for you. Help me to understand your goodness, mercy, and love. Give me peace in my heart."

When Jay William had finished his prayer he was amazed at how much lighter he felt. Someone seemed to have cut away a heavy rope that had been wrapped around his heart.

When he looked back, Jay William noted that several people were sitting in the brush arbor. The preacher gave him a New Testament and told him to read the book of John first. He said the best way for him to learn more about God was to attend a Bible-believing church.

"Introduce yourself to the pastor and tell him you would like to be baptized," the Reverend Sparks instructed Jay William.

"What do you mean by baptized?" Jay William asked.

"Now that you have given your heart and your life to God, you need to take the next step in your walk with God," the preacher said. "The Bible tells us that when we are baptized we are doing what Jesus told his followers to do. You enter the waters of baptism to show the world you have made a decision to die to your old sinful ways; when you rise up out of the water you show the world you are with Christ as a new creation."

Jay William had a new look on his face when he joined Wilma, her sisters, and Ted. He had a calm, peaceful appearance.

He smiled warmly at Wilma, saying, "I know God is real, and he now lives inside my heart."

Wilma squeezed his hand and said, "I'm happy for you." They held hands during the preaching and listened intently to all that the Reverend Sparks had to say. Wilma wanted to protect Jay William and also had romantic feelings for him. After that evening Jay William was at the Carter home almost daily reading the Bible with her.

Jay William was baptized the following Sunday at the Grace Tabernacle Church where the Carters were members. It was a wonderful experience for him.

When Ted and Carolyn married, they moved into the Watson house. Laura, the youngest Carter sister, came to live with them. Mr. Carter invited Jay William to join his household. Jay William worked with the Carter men as they prepared the ground for planting. He held the New Testament in one hand and the plow in the other. He seemed unable to get enough of God's Word.

One day Mr. Carter said to him, "Jay William, you are like a son to me, and I need to know something, son. Do you plan to marry Wilma?"

Jay William was caught completely off guard. He stopped what he was doing and looked directly at Mr. Carter.

"You know she's in love with you and is ready for marriage," Mr. Carter said. The fact that you're living with us makes this complicated for her. If you don't plan to marry her, you need to let her know. She's waiting for you to ask her to marry you. You are good friends and I see that you enjoy being with her. Those things are important in a marriage relationship."

"Mr. Carter, I hardly know what to say," Jay William finally replied. "I do love Wilma and cannot imagine my life without her. She has taught me so much. She is such a good person—loyal, kind, and all the other things I desire in a wife. But I'm afraid I know nothing about being a husband, and I don't want to hurt her. She deserves the best." By this time, he was trembling and crying.

Mr. Carter put his arm around Jay William and said, "Son, relax. I'm not trying to pressure you. I just need to know what your intentions are. More important, Wilma needs to know what your plans are regarding marriage. She is hoping for you two to marry, and she wants a family soon. Don't rush into it if you're unsure, but don't string her along if you don't have marriage in mind. This has been awkward for all of us."

CHAPTER 33

THAT EVENING JAY William dressed in a new shirt and slacks he had been saving for an important occasion and asked Wilma if she would take a walk with him. She must have sensed something was special about this walk and said, "Yes, I will, but I want to freshen up a little."

In less than an hour, Wilma joined Jay William on the front porch dressed in the blue outfit with white dots, the one Jay William had admired during the brush arbor event. Her long, thick hair was loose and shiny with a pretty blue ribbon tied securely in it. *She looks so sweet*, Jay William thought.

The two walked hand in hand toward the meadow. In his free hand Jay William carried a small picnic basket that Wilma's younger sister, Mary, had packed at his request. Their conversation was casual and he quoted Bible verses he had recently memorized.

When they got to their destination, Jay William put down a quilt he had tucked under his arm and opened the picnic basket. They shared light sandwiches and iced tea. Jay William prayed silently for the right words to say to Wilma. He took her hands in his and said, "Wilma, I love you very much and I would like to be your husband, but I'm afraid I don't know how to be a good one."

"If you want me to be your wife, you must ask me," Wilma said gently. "If I accept your proposal, your next step is to ask my daddy for permission to marry me. He likes you very much, and I'm sure he will say yes. He knows you are a hard worker and will take good care of me. We will then get married. Most of my family and friends have traveled to Piggott, Arkansas, for the ceremony. There you can get a marriage certificate for two dollars, and there is no waiting time as here in Tipton County.

"Jay William, just so you know, I want a large family with at least four children. I will always put God first in my life, and you will be my second love. I promise to do my best to make you a good wife and to be a good mother to our children."

"With God's help and yours, I will be a good husband and do what is right for you and our children," Jay William said. "Will you marry me, Wilma?"

"Yes, I will be honored to be your wife," she said.

Jay William gave her a gentle kiss on the lips. Then he took her by the hand and said, "Let's hurry and see your dad right away."

When they returned to the house, the entire family was assembled in the living room. "Mr. Carter," Jay William said, "I am asking for permission to make Wilma my wife very soon."

Everyone applauded when Mr. Carter gave his blessing for the wedding.

On August 30, less than a month later, Wilma became Mrs. Jay William Hawkins. They lived at the Carter home for a few weeks as they waited for a house to rent. They soon decided to move into a sharecropper house rather than wait. They purchased new furniture for the house. It was great to be together in their new home. Two months after their marriage, an excited Wilma told Jay William he was going to be a father. Their baby was due in May, which gave her an opportunity to help him pick cotton. Wilma sold a few of her quilts in the Covington area. She gained a reputation for doing excellent work. Her pregnancy was going well, and she began to sew baby clothes.

They were picking cotton late in October about a mile from their home when Wilma spotted something in the east.

"Look, honey. I see smoke and it appears to be our home,"

she said. "Oh no, I hope I'm wrong because our new furniture will be lost."

"I best go and check it out," Jay William said. "You stay here and wait while I go to the house. No need to upset you or the baby if everything is okay." He ran toward their home.

Wilma could not wait long before following him. She met Jay William as he was returning to her.

He took her into his arms and said, "I'm sorry, Wilma. You were right. Our house caught fire and there isn't much left. Let's go to your dad's house for the evening and return with your dad in the morning to see if there's anything worth saving."

Wilma went with Jay William to her dad's house and was comforted by her siblings. Carolyn and Ted came to pray with the couple and to encourage them. The next morning, Mr. Carter got out the wagon and asked Jay William to drive it to the site of the house. Jay William and Wilma were heartbroken to see the house in ashes. There was no insurance on their belongings, but Jay William reminded Wilma that he still had money in the bank in Memphis.

"That money is for the house you want to build, not for furniture. I was hoping we could start building it before our baby is born," Wilma said, breaking into tears.

"Wilma, we may have lost our belongings, but we still have each other; most of all, we still have God. He has everything under control," Jay William said. "Please, let's go back to your dad's place. I want you to get some rest. You have our child to think about." Turning to Mr. Carter, he asked, "Sir, can we stay at your house until we find another? I also would like you to come with me when I go to Memphis to get money from the bank so we can buy clothes."

"Jay William, you can take the wagon if you wish," Mr. Carter said. "I don't have to go unless you want me to do so."

"Jay William, could I please go with you?" Wilma said. "I haven't been to Memphis since I was a child, and I'll help you choose my clothes. First I want to borrow something from Mary to wear there."

The pair left for Memphis to get money for much-needed items.

CHAPTER 34

O N THE WAY to Memphis, Wilma sat close to Jay William with her hand in his. She sang hymns and tried to be cheerful. She discussed with him what she thought they should purchase first. "I need fabric to make two new dresses, and I want to find fabric for quilting," Wilma said. "I want you to purchase another suit with a dress shirt and tie plus dress shoes and socks. I need a good pair of shoes for church too."

"How much will all those things cost us?" Jay William asked.

"I think fifty dollars should cover it all if we shop wisely," Wilma said. "I'm asking God to help us find the things we need on sale. I would like your permission to speak to the store manager for an additional discount."

"I trust you, Wilma. You are a special gift to me from God, and I know he'll help us. Here we are now. I'll help you down and then park the wagon and tie the horses. Go into the store and start looking for the things we have to buy, but wait for me before you make your final choices."

Jay William went into the bank and withdrew a hundred dollars from his account, assuring the bank manager he would restore the money shortly. He then joined Wilma at the general store. She was smiling sweetly at him as he entered. She had chosen a blue fabric with white dots to make another dress like Jay William's favorite. Her next choice was a green-and-white-striped fabric that was only ten cents a yard.

Wilma asked if she could help Jay William choose a suit, noting she had seen a charcoal-gray one at half price. They chose a blue shirt and a gray-and-blue-striped tie. Wilma looked for fabric to make baby gowns. When they had all their choices together, Wilma asked if the store manager was available. The manager was also the owner of the store.

"Hello, my name is Harvey Smith and how may I help you?" he asked.

Wilma introduced herself and her husband to him and said, "Sir, we're from Randolph and work hard in the cotton fields, plus I make quilts. Our house burned down while we were in the field yesterday. All our belongings were lost including our new furniture. I'd be happy to make a quilt to display in your store if you'll permit me to take orders from your customers. You would be doing them a great service. For that privilege, all I ask from you is an additional discount on my fabric and thread. Can we work that out with you?"

Mr. Smith was impressed with Wilma's straightforwardness and said, "Yes, ma'am, I think it would be a great service because our city ladies don't like to sew or to quilt. I'll give you a 10 percent discount on your supplies plus half of the purchase price of the quilts when sold. We've had a bin of fabric here for more than a year. If you can use the fabric, I'll throw it in for nothing."

Wilma could not contain her joy and gave God thanks in the store.

On the way home, Jay William said, "Lady, your God sure watches out for you."

Wilma sang "His Eye Is on the Sparrow," and the couple returned to the Carter home with a mission.

The Carter family had a meal of beans, ham, fried potatoes, and cornbread ready for them when they arrived. Wilma was tired but planned two quilts with the quilting blocks. Jay William said he would help her in any way he could.

The next morning he asked her to stay home, saying he would

pick her portion of the cotton. He left before the sun was up. When Jay William checked on Wilma at noon, he was amazed to see she had a dress partially sewn.

"Wilma, please rest this afternoon. I think you try too hard to help make money. I'm the husband and I'll take care of my family," Jay William said.

She surprised him by sobbing. Jay William didn't know how to respond, because this was not how Wilma normally reacted. He quickly returned to the cotton field and filled his sack in record time. Then he got on his knees and cried out to God for the wisdom to know how to help his wife. Jay William decided to ask Mr. Carter's advice.

At six in the evening Jay William added up what he had picked for the day and discovered he had 452 pounds of cotton. He was pleased with that and tracked down Mr. Carter.

"Good evening, sir. May I have a word with you? I need some advice," Jay William said. Mr. Carter asked how he could help.

"I asked Wilma to stay at the house today and rest instead of going to the field with me. She worked on sewing and designing a quilt. I felt it was too much for her to do and asked her to rest this afternoon and not to sew. She started crying and that scared me. I went to the field because I didn't know how to help her. Now I fear she's upset with me."

"Go into the house, freshen up, and tell her just what you told me," Mr. Carter said. "Wilma will understand. She's like her mother—understanding and kind."

Jay William followed his advice. He went to their room and found Wilma resting on the bed with her hymnal beside her. She stirred and opened her eyes. They were puffy and she looked sad. Jay William sat on the bed beside her and said, "Wilma, I was so confused today when you began to cry. I didn't know how to react, so I ran away. I should have stayed with you until you felt better. I did what I thought a husband should do for his wife. I picked cotton with more energy and determination than ever before. I totaled 452 pounds today, but that isn't important since you look so sad. Wilma, I am so sorry I made you feel so sad that you cried. Will you forgive me?"

"Of course, Jay William. I love you. I'm happy to be your wife, and I want to help you support us. I love to make quilts, and I think God gave me the talent to do just that! I know you want to build a house for us, and this will help us get there faster. Perhaps you can help me with this project."

"I will seriously think about that," Jay William said. "How about taking a walk? Are you up for that?"

Wilma got out of bed and dressed, and she and Jay William went out into the sunshine. "Jay William, may we go down to the meadow where you asked me to marry you? I want to feel that happy feeling we experienced that evening," Wilma said.

They grabbed sandwiches and a jar of cold iced tea to share once they got there. Jay William was cautious about every step Wilma took. He held her hand and had a blanket roll with the iced tea and the sandwiches inside it over his shoulder. They hardly spoke until they got to the spot where he had asked her to marry him.

"How can I help you with your quilting project, Wilma?" Jay William asked when they were settled there.

"First, I want you to help me put markings on the cloth I want to embroider," Wilma said. "I've drawn up designs and need you to put straight pins through the paper they are on. I'll draw the lines on the cloth from there. That will be a slow process for me by myself. I think it will go better if we both work on it. What do you think?"

"I would have to have you show me how to do that," Jay William said. "My hands are big and could be clumsy. Why don't we try it out when we go back to the house? I want to get in the field early in the morning."

"Let's go now before it gets dark," Wilma said.

The couple left for the house after they had eaten the

sandwiches and had shared the tea. Wilma was so happy that she practically skipped back to the house.

They worked together until they were sure the project would go as Wilma planned. Jay William caught on quickly and had an entire quilt top ready for her to embroider before he went to bed. Wilma began to embroider by a coal oil lamp while he slept.

The next morning, Wilma said, "I'll go to the cotton field with you because you were so much help to me last evening."

"I would rather you stay here and work on your quilting," Jay William said.

"No, I insist on going with you," she said.

Against his better judgment, Jay William took her with him to the field. He decided they should quit early for lunch, and once they were back at the house he told her, "If you want me to help with the quilts, you must stay here this afternoon and rest."

Wilma frowned, but Jay William said, "Wilma, you said you wanted me to be the head of the house, and that is my decision. We'll work together tonight, okay?"

Wilma smiled at her husband and agreed to do as he asked.

Jay William picked 250 pounds of cotton that afternoon and was tired when he finished for the day. Wilma had hot bathwater on the back porch for him and told him this night it was his turn to rest. He went to bed at seven-thirty. Two of Wilma's sisters helped her embroider while he was sleeping. Their plan was to help her finish the work by the weekend so she could get the quilt to the store in Memphis.

On Saturday, Wilma and Jay William took the two sisters along with them to Memphis. The city was busy with shoppers, and the girls were happy to accompany Wilma and Jay William as they took the finished quilt into the store.

Mr. Smith came out to see the quilt and asked Wilma to place it on a bed in the store. He was amazed with the colors she had chosen and with the fine workmanship. Wilma had used a repeat pattern of a lady with a parasol in pastel shades of blue, green, and pink. Mr. Smith put a price of thirty-five dollars on it and told her to make another one because he already had someone in mind to purchase this one.

The three ladies were excited about the news and purchased more thread and material for all of them. Jay William went to the bank to deposit the money from his earnings in the cotton field. The ladies talked about their sewing projects all the way to Randolph.

On January 1, 1933, the family gathered at the Carter place to celebrate a new year. Ham, cornbread, potatoes, cabbage, and black-eyed peas cooked with fatback sat on the dinner table. Family members talked about the good and not-so-good things that had occurred in the past year and asked God to bless them with health and financial security in the coming year. Jay William had been hired at the cotton plant in Covington, and Wilma was selling her quilts regularly at the general store in Memphis. A new home was becoming a strong possibility.

At the end of January, Wilma lost her baby, a little girl. It was a sad time for Wilma and Jay William.

CHAPTER 35

THE WINTER WAS long but things were looking up for Jay William and Wilma. They had found a home near Covington where Jay William was working at the cotton mill. Wilma was happy making quilts and was also creating fashionable clothes for herself. She loved to design her own clothes and still had several yards of fabric from the store in Memphis. The store often gave her fabric that was not selling well.

The couple's greatest desire was to have another baby. Wilma began to make a few baby gowns and a baby quilt in hopes of having a child soon.

In March, Wilma discovered she was indeed expecting, and she could hardly wait to share the news with Jay William. He was excited to learn he would be a daddy, but he wanted Wilma to hold off another month before telling the family. That was hard for her but she obeyed his wishes. They prayed and read the Bible together more often, asking God for a healthy baby and mother.

Jay William worked the night shift, and during the day they planned their new house. They projected they would be able to complete the house by the fall and move in before the baby was born.

By May, Wilma was beginning to show, and they told Mr. Carter the good news. Soon the entire family knew and everyone was excited for the couple. The baby was due in mid-November. Wilma's sisters came over in the evenings after Jay William left to work at the cotton mill. They wanted to help her with her quilting so she would get more sleep and be healthy. Each sister had advice for her, and after writing down their suggestions, they prayed about each one.

The couple decided they had enough money to begin their new house. Jay William drew up the plans and the work began in June. The brothers-in-law and church friends helped him whenever they could.

The ladies enjoyed visiting the construction site and bringing food for the workers. Wilma benefited from having their company while the work was being done. The ladies noticed Wilma's legs were swollen and encouraged her to elevate them as much as she could.

The couple had a garden that Wilma tended in the early morning hours starting at daylight. She insisted on sharing the job with Jay William because he was spending so many hours building their new home.

The home was a super-size shotgun house. It had a big front porch, a living room, an extra-large bedroom, a larger-than-usual kitchen, and a back porch. There was an outhouse in the backyard.

The home was ready at the end of October. Jay William was proud of the cabinets he had built in the kitchen. He had also built a pantry for canned goods, a feature all of Wilma's sisters loved. Wilma and her sisters had made curtains for all of the windows, and the house was indeed pretty.

The church gave the couple a surprise housewarming party at which they received new linens and a new set of dishes. Wilma was happy with the blue-and-white floral pattern. She also received several gifts for the baby. The couple found it difficult to express their appreciation for all their church friends had given them.

By the middle of November, Jay William had dug up several trees from the woods and had planted them in the yard. Wilma was content to watch him from the swing on the front porch.

She was ready for the baby to be born and obeyed her husband's request that she rest frequently.

John William was born on December 5. He was an easy first baby. He mostly ate and slept for the first six weeks. The couple enjoyed their son and spent a lot of time with him. He talked early and walked by the time he was a year old.

Jay William continued his full-time job at the cotton mill. He had a chance to move to the day shift but decided to stay on the evening shift because it worked well for the three of them.

Jay William was not shy about sharing his faith at work when an opportunity arose. One fellow was upset about that and punched him on the cheek, decking him.

When Jay William got up from the floor, he told the man, "Now you can hit me on the other cheek."

"Are you a smart aleck or what?" the man said.

He walked back to his work area but returned soon after to ask why Jay William had offered him his other cheek.

"The Bible says, 'Whosoever smites you on the cheek, turn to him the other,'" Jay William explained.

The two later became friends and the man became a Christian.

Wilma and Jay William wanted to add to their family but were not successful. The couple decided to pray more fervently for a new baby. On November 1, 1937, Veronica Lee was born. She was a quiet baby and, like her brother, mostly ate and slept in her early weeks. John was proud to be a big brother and enjoyed helping with her care. He talked and sang to her when Wilma was busy. He also liked to help his mother by picking up his toys and putting them away.

In the spring of 1938, Jay William began to fast and pray for God to guide him in telling others about God's mercy and grace. Many people in rural areas had not heard about God's gift of salvation. As he prayed, Jay William felt God's calling to become a preacher and to share the gospel. He decided to wait and to pray more before telling Wilma what he believed God wanted him to do.

Jay William struggled over how to do this, but finally he came home from work one evening, woke up Wilma, and shared the news with her. He waited for her response, but before she could speak he suddenly asked, "How can I preach God's Word effectively when I stutter at times? How can that be honoring to God? Who will want to listen?"

Wilma took his hand gently in hers and said, "Jay William, if God is calling you to preach his Word, you must be willing to obey. God knows what he's doing. Leave the details to him. Jonah had fears and ran away from God, and you know what happened to Jonah. Moses couldn't speak eloquently, but God used him mightily to deliver his people out of Egypt. I'm your helpmate, and I'll always be available to you. I'll begin to pray sincerely about this. I knew when I met you that God had great things in store for you in his service."

Jay William was up early the next morning and asked God how to accept this calling. He talked to his pastor, who said he would be available if Jay William needed his help.

"I need to know how I can come up with a sermon to preach," Jay William said.

"Pray and ask God what he wants you to preach. Then let the Holy Spirit guide you," Pastor Mayberry said.

Jay William listened more closely for God's voice when he prayed. The first sermon he wrote was about prayer. He wrote that Christians are to pray without ceasing and to pray about everything. He titled the sermon "The Importance of Prayer."

He took the sermon to Pastor Mayberry, who told him it was good and asked if he would like to preach it on Sunday. Jay William said he would have to get his feet wet sometime, and he would preach.

Jay William rehearsed the sermon several times before Sunday morning. As usual, the Hawkins family got to church early. Pastor

Mayberry told the congregation, "Today I have a surprise for all of you. Jay William Hawkins feels called to the ministry and will preach his first sermon this morning. I ask each of you to pray that the Holy Spirit will lead him and will guide his words."

When the time came for Jay William to preach, several men walked up to the platform and prayed for him and then quietly returned to their seats. To everyone's amazement, he spoke without stuttering. His first sermon brought two people to the altar seeking salvation.

Over the next few years, Jay William was asked to preach at several churches in the area. The stuttering that had plagued him most of his life vanished whenever he preached, and it became less frequent in his daily conversations. Perhaps this was divine intervention because no other explanation seemed possible. He would preach at every opportunity, including on a street corner in town.

Jay William was ordained a minister in the Assemblies of God denomination and became a pastor at the rural Detroit Assembly of God Church. He continued working at the cotton mill as he pastored the church.

The couple's fourth child, Heather Marie, was born in July of 1940. She was a healthy baby, and Jay William and Wilma were happy to have another child to love.

The family vehicle was a pickup truck. Jay William built a shelter over the bed, connecting it to the cab, and installed two bench-type seats on each side of it. He added a wood stove with a vent system that carried the smoke outside the vehicle. The stove kept passengers warm in a smoke-free atmosphere. He often used the truck to take people to and from church.

One Saturday evening in December of 1940, Jay William was returning to Covington from a prayer meeting. Four women church members were in the back of the truck along with seven-year-old John. Jay William, Wilma, and six-year-old Veronica were in the cab. Five-month-old Heather was nestled in her mother's arms.

Jay William rolled down his window to yell at a truck driver who had ignored a stop sign and was quickly approaching the Hawkins vehicle. The warning came too late, and the truck hit his pickup.

No one appeared seriously injured, but Wilma was beside herself. Her baby had disappeared from her arms. Everyone got out of the two vehicles to search for Heather, but the baby could not be found. Wilma was hysterical and began to panic. She would no longer listen to reason.

Jay William spotted Heather lying face down in the road when the other vehicle was moved. He ran to pick her up and realized she was not breathing. Wilma refused to believe this was Heather because the baby's skin had darkened. She rejected Heather when Jay William attempted to place the child in her arms.

Everyone prayed for a miracle. In a short while Heather began to breathe and her skin became a healthy pink. Once again, God showed Jay William he could trust him with all of the family's needs.

CHAPTER 36

JAY WILLIAM'S FRIEND and brother-in-law, Ted Watson, was now also an ordained Assembly of God minister. The Watson family moved next door to the Hawkins family, which made Wilma and Carolyn very happy. The young cousins became almost inseparable. The families worked and played together daily. During this time Wilma discovered a way to have fun with the children and to bring in extra money for the family. She taught the older children how to make willow tree furniture.

She had them choose sturdy but pliable willow trees from those growing down by the river and taught them to bend the wet branches into shapes. The children made smaller versions of furniture. They most frequently sold tables and chairs. Jay William was proud of his wife's industrious nature and purchased a new Singer sewing machine to make her sewing jobs easier and to give them a more professional, finished look.

In July of 1943 Wilma went into labor. She and Jay William had two girls and one boy and wanted another boy to balance out the family. Carolyn had five children and was a big help to her sister.

The midwife arrived at the Hawkins home when Wilma's labor pains were five minutes apart. But Wilma did not progress, and the midwife discovered the baby was breech; the feet were in the birth canal, and the baby was not moving down. Poor Wilma grabbed the iron headboard and screamed in pain.

Jay William could not handle seeing her in so much pain. He drove to the nearest hospital and brought back a doctor to help his wife deliver their baby. The doctor examined Wilma and attempted to change the baby's position without success. He said he was sorry but he could not help Wilma deliver the baby. Jay William was so upset that he called for an ambulance to take them to Memphis.

There a doctor found that the baby boy had died, and he removed him. Wilma was gravely ill with blood toxicity. She was given antibiotics, but her body would not heal. The doctor was frank with Jay William and said it would take a miracle for Wilma to live. "We both serve a God who does miraculous healing," he said. Jay William and all of their family and friends prayed that Wilma would live.

Sarah and Jerome arrived at the hospital and asked if they could adopt Heather since their three-year old-daughter had recently died.

"Heather will lack nothing and will have a good life with us," Wilma said. She insisted that Jay William promise her he would keep the family together. Crying, she said, "Jay William, will you go home and bring our children here? I need to see them."

Within an hour, he had returned with the children, and she had a chance to hold them in her arms and to love on them for a short while. Wilma died peacefully soon after that with Jay William and her sisters at her side. It was a very sad time for everyone.

CHAPTER 37

J AY WILLIAM'S WORLD was turned upside down. "How am I going to live without Wilma at my side?" he cried. "She was the glue that held our family together. How am I going to care for our children and our home? How can I keep my job and still care for my children? How about our church? How can I be a pastor without Wilma at my side?"

Jay William then cried out to God, "I need you more than I've ever needed you before!" He sobbed uncontrollably.

Ted and Carolyn helped by praying for him. They prayed God would give him comfort, peace, wisdom, and strength, especially at this time.

With help from family members, Jay William purchased a burial plot and made funeral arrangements. Wilma's sisters helped take care of the children, comforting them and meeting their urgent needs. Jerome and Sarah asked Jay William if they could take Heather for a while. Jerome tried to convince Jay William that two children would be much easier for him than three.

Jay William lost his patience and shouted, "How dare you ask me this when Wilma made it very clear that her children would not be split up? Don't ever bring up this subject again. I will never separate my children!"

Jay William was distraught. This was the lowest point in his life. Mr. Carter came to see him and said, "Son, I know the pain you're feeling. When my beautiful Leone died she left me with nine children. It was tough for me to survive and to be a good daddy to them. I ended up inviting their grandmother, her mother, to come live with us. Things became much better for my children. Children need a mother in the home. Women know things about children that don't come naturally for us men. We're so busy trying to make a living and to discipline the children. This was the best thing I ever did for my children, especially the girls. Your children need a woman in their home. Jay William, I know Wilma would agree with me."

"Mr. Carter, I can't imagine ever marrying again," Jay William said. "Wilma was the love of my life and my best friend. I could never love another woman."

"It may be too early to talk about this," Mr. Carter said, "but if you find a good woman who loves your children, marry her. You'll have my blessing and I believe Wilma's blessing. I don't believe Wilma would want you to be lonely. You had plenty of that before you met her."

"Mr. Carter, there could never be another woman like Wilma," Jay William replied.

After embalming, Wilma's body was brought to the Hawkins home and placed in the living room as was the custom at the time. People could view the body and pay their respects from 4 to 8 p.m. Mourners brought food of all kinds so the grieving family would not have to prepare meals.

Jay William and his family endured a difficult two days, but they took comfort from the many stories people told about Wilma's kindness and love.

John was happy to have his cousins' help with the chores. Visiting with his cousins took his mind off of his mother's death. Wilma's sisters took Veronica and Heather to the store and bought them dresses for the funeral service. Veronica helped with her little sister, who was told that her mother was sleeping.

Since Wilma had been ill, the little girl was happy to see her mother looking so pretty in the pink box. She would greet friends at the door, saying, "Hi! I guess you came to see my beautiful mother sleeping."

She would take them by the hand, walk them to the casket, and keep chattering until Veronica gently asked her to hush. Veronica felt good about being a mother figure to her sister. This gave her a sense of purpose, which she needed now.

On the third day, Wilma's body was taken to the Assembly of God church in Mumford, Tennessee. The children sat huddled together beside Jay William during the funeral. The pallbearers carried the body about twenty feet from the church to its final earthly resting place.

John stood tall and refused to cry in front of his cousins, but he was hurting on the inside. He used the back of his hand to brush away the tears before anyone saw them. Veronica cried at intervals and was comforted by an aunt during the graveside service. Heather felt safe and secure in her daddy's arms as she observed how her siblings reacted.

As was the custom, the spouse was expected to throw the first shovelful of dirt onto the casket as it was lowered into the hole. Jay William stood Heather beside him to free his hands for this ritual.

Heather realized the dark hole now held her mother in the "pretty pink sleeping box," and she ran toward the grave screaming, "I want my momma!"

She had to be restrained for her safety. Jay William felt almost helpless and did not know how to handle the situation. He had received bad advice from family and friends on how to tell his three-year-old daughter about her mother's death. He was told that Heather was too young to understand the concept of death and that he should tell her that her mother was sleeping. In time the child would forget all about this tragedy, Jay William was told. In fact, Heather would not soon forget seeing her sleeping mother placed in a dark hole, and she spent most of the night crying for her momma. She was afraid to close her eyes for fear that she too would be placed in a dark hole and would be covered with dirt.

Heather cried a great deal and had temper tantrums. She would held her breath while crying and would pass out, leaving a puddle of urine on the floor. Three weeks after the funeral, Jay William took his three children to his sister, Catherine, about seventy-five miles away. He decided it would be faster and more fun for the kids to take the train. He tried to make the trip enjoyable by having their pictures taken in the train station's photo booth and by purchasing soft drinks for them.

Catherine was happy to help Jay William with the kids but was not feeling well when they arrived. The children were happy to see her and Uncle Johnny. They always enjoyed visiting their aunt and uncle. Jay William had to return to Covington to work at the cotton mill. He knew he could sleep on the train on the way back.

The next morning, Catherine woke up to discover she had hemorrhaged during the night. She knew she needed bed rest after the bleeding, and she sent Johnny next door to ask her neighbor Nancy Petty if she could help with the children.

Nancy was considered an old maid at twenty-one. A kind-hearted lady, she cared for her dad and her two brothers. She washed, ironed, cooked, cleaned, and helped out where needed in the rural community. Nancy was active in the Community Church of Dyersburg, which met in the school building on Sunday mornings. In addition to teaching a children's class, she sang solos during the morning worship service.

Nancy had helped raise several nieces and nephews and was a favorite of many local children. Since she loved kids, she jumped at the chance to help the Hawkins children, who had recently lost their mother.

Jay William worked five eight-hour shifts a week at the cotton mill, and at the end of that five-day stretch, he returned to Catherine's house to retrieve the children.

As Jay William watched Nancy care for his children, his heart softened. "Miss Nancy, you're so kind and gentle with my children, and they seem to like you. I really appreciate you being here for them," he said.

"Sir, you have very well-behaved children, and that's a compliment to you and to your late wife," Nancy replied.

"How about Heather?" Jay William asked. "She's become a handful since Wilma's death. She cries frequently, especially at bedtime. Do you have difficulty with her?"

"Actually, I insist she obey me," Nancy replied. "She needs guidelines, and punishments for bad behavior. At first, Heather resisted me big time, but she's come a long way in a short while. When she has her temper tantrums and urinates on the floor, I insist she mop it up. Then I pick her up and rock her. She talks about her mother, and I listen to her talk about her feelings. This seems to calm her and she often falls asleep. All three children need much love now. Losing a mother is painful, and children need love and understanding."

Jay William was amazed at her words and suddenly remembered Mr. Carter's advice about finding a good wife. *Nancy would be an asset to the Hawkins family*, he thought. He pondered this idea for a little while and then blurted out, "Well, Nancy, since you appear to love my children and they love you, how about packing up and going to Covington to take care of them?"

"Sir, I can't do that! You're a pastor; it wouldn't be right," Nancy replied.

"Oh, I intend to make it legal," Jay William said. "I'll marry you today. We can get on the train in Dyersburg, go to Piggott, Arkansas, and be back here in two hours as a married couple. Pack your belongings, and we'll leave for Covington in the morning with the children."

Nancy agreed to marry him and they left for Piggott and were back at Catherine's home in less than two hours. They brought their wedding license and showed it to Catherine before telling the children they were married.

Catherine made no attempt to disguise her anger. "Jay William, what were you thinking?" she said. "Nancy, I'm surprised you went along with his idea! Why, Wilma has been dead only twenty one-days."

"Jay William needs me and I need a husband. Most of all, those three children need me," Nancy replied. The five members of the Hawkins family left for Covington.

Since Jay William never had a good relationship with his mother, he could not understand John's attitude toward calling Nancy mom. John thought that calling her Miss Nancy was more proper. Furthermore, he thought that embracing her as his mom would be disrespectful to his late mother. Veronica agreed with him. Heather, however, ran into Nancy's arms and said, "Miss Nancy, you're no longer Miss Nancy. You're my new mother." John looked at her with disapproval as she clung to Nancy.

CHAPTER 38

THE HAWKINS KIDS were anxious to see Aunt Carolyn and could hardly wait until they arrived at the Watson home. John was so happy to see his four male cousins that he could hardly contain himself. He needed male companionship. When they arrived that hot morning on August 13, 1943, Aunt Carolyn welcomed her nephew and nieces with open arms and an open heart. As they exchanged hugs and kisses, Carolyn was puzzled by the presence of the lady with her brother-in-law and awaited an explanation.

When Jay William introduced Nancy as his new wife, Carolyn was more than surprised; she was furious. She grabbed Jay William's arm and led him into her kitchen.

"Sit down and listen to me," she said. "There are still tracks in the yard from the ambulance that took Wilma to the hospital in Memphis. How dare you bring another woman so quickly into her home, a home she loved and kept so beautiful?"

Jay William attempted to explain the reason for his marriage to Nancy, but Carolyn interrupted him.

"She loved you and her children as much as any woman ever loved her husband and children. Wilma was gentle, kind, and loving. What do you really know about this woman? She'd better treat those children well, or her troubles with the Carter family have just begun. We'll be watching her, and she better not harm those children. I am so disappointed in you."

Jay William stood up and said, "Surely this family knows of

my love for my children. I promised to keep them together, and I won't break the promise I made to my dying wife. Nancy was caring for them at my sister's home because Catherine became too ill to do that. The children like her and she treats them well. I felt I had no choice. For their sake I felt I must marry Nancy and bring her here in a godly and legal marriage. I felt that was the only solution. She is a good Christian woman and will help raise my children and care for the home. She can sing solos and teach Bible stories. She's been doing that in her local church. She will be a blessing to any church and to our family.

"You might also be interested to know that Heather has gotten better. She has fewer temper tantrums and sleeps better at night." Jay William exited the kitchen and walked across the yard to his home. He was tired and emotionally drained, but he had been moved temporarily to the day shift at the cotton mill and thought he might get a few hours of sleep that night.

Arriving at home, Jay William got a nice surprise. His children sat in the right places at the table. His place was waiting, and the food looked delicious. He did not feel hungry, but he ate in an attempt to bring normalcy to his home.

The following morning he left the house for the cotton mill. He felt confident God had everything under control and would take care of his family in his absence. The children spent as much time at Aunt Carolyn's house as possible after completing their chores. Most of the family took a dim view of "that woman," and the kids preferred the Watson home to their home.

Nancy was struggling in her new situation. She had not spent much time away from her rural community and was in unfamiliar territory. Nancy made the kids ask for permission to visit the Watson house and limited the time they could spend with their cousins. This angered the children.

Carolyn was most upset that Nancy made Heather mop the floor after she had urinated on it during a temper tantrum. She said Heather was too young for the task. The hostility between the two women grew.

Jay William found himself depending more upon Nancy for advice and comfort. They decided that for their marriage to survive, they needed to make a fresh start away from Wilma's family. They prayed daily together for wisdom and guidance.

Jay William wanted to relocate his family, so he called the headquarters of the Assemblies of God in Springfield, Missouri, to see if a pastor was needed somewhere in that state. He learned that a small rural church in the Ozark Mountains was looking for a pastor. Jay William wrote a letter to the Assembly of God church in Stoney Point, Missouri, attaching a résumé. He was invited to meet the congregants, who would decide if he was the man they wanted to shepherd them.

Leaving the children with the Watson family, Jay William and Nancy drove from Covington to Stoney Point in September of 1943. They arrived at about one-thirty on a Saturday afternoon and met with the deacons and the pulpit search committee. The couple felt that this was a good opportunity and that Stoney Point would be a good place to start over as a family with Nancy as the woman of the house.

A family belonging to the little church owned Garrison's Resort, which was located on a lake with a beautiful mountain view. The Garrisons offered to give Jay William and Nancy a cabin for the weekend. It was the first time either of them had stayed in such a beautiful setting. The lake was crystal clear, and they enjoyed watching others fish and boat there.

The chirping of the birds in the morning was quite different from the crowing of the family's rooster. The croaking of the frogs and the howling of the bobcats at night were also new sounds for the couple. They shared relaxed and shared a laugh. This was their first time together without the children since being married, and they felt free to talk openly.

The church was a humble building in a community of simple

mountain folks who were kind and worked hard to make a living. Many were lead miners. On the second Sunday in September of 1943 the church bell rang and beautiful music called believers to worship for the first time in nine months. The weather was warm and sunny, and the folks were anxious to hear the preacher from Tennessee.

Nancy soon discovered that her new husband had a zest for God. He was completely relaxed as he preached God's Word to those spiritually hungry people and spoke without a trace of a stutter.

Jay William delivered a powerful sermon about giving to God the things that belong to God and to Caesar the things that belong to Caesar. This proved to be a timely message, especially with World War II forcing people to make sacrifices to support American troops in Europe.

The church was full again on Sunday evening as Jay William preached his second sermon, this one on the powerful love of God for mankind. God gave his only Son as a sacrifice for sin, Jay William said, since this was the only way he could give human beings eternal life with him.

The congregants asked Jay William to be their new pastor, but he asked them to pray for a week before they made this choice. He promised to pray for God's will for the church and for the pastor. Within ten days he received a letter saying he had received 100 percent of the votes in the election for a new pastor.

Jay William said he would accept the opportunity but needed three to four weeks to settle his affairs in Covington. He had to resign as pastor of his present church and to give two weeks' notice at the cotton mill. The hardest part was breaking the news to his relatives, especially to Wilma's family. They received the news much better than he had expected. Carolyn and Ted knew a family that was interested in renting the house Jay William had built for Wilma.

CHAPTER 39

IT WAS IN the third week of October 1943. The weather was sunny and warm, ideal for moving day. Jay William had his truck packed to capacity and a trailer attached. Ted was at the wheel of another fully packed pickup. Everyone was ready for the trip from Tennessee to Stoney Point, Missouri. The girls were crying when they got into their daddy's truck. They were sad to be leaving their Aunt Carolyn and their cousins.

John was excited because he liked driving with Uncle Ted. He had mixed emotions about the move. His dad had made the mountains sound exciting, and he was anxious to find out if the place was as good as his dad said. He hated to leave the comfort of home and especially his cousins next door. He also hated to be so far away from his mother's grave.

Aunt Carolyn had made a sack lunch and had told John he was in charge of it. He could not wait until these trucks headed north to Missouri. He had been assigned to watch for hand signals from his dad and to relay them to Uncle Ted. John took the job seriously.

John thought of all the changes that had happened in a short time. He felt he was betraying his mother by calling Nancy mom, but his dad had insisted on it. He wanted her to be the nice Miss Nancy, not someone who bossed him around. She seemed to want everything done her way.

John hoped to have fun in the truck with Uncle Ted driving

and to stop thinking so much about things he did not like and could not change. He liked the way Uncle Ted sang old gospel songs. The loud and joyful sound made him feel good all over. Sometimes he would sing along, which made Uncle Ted laugh.

Shortly they crossed the Mississippi River on a ferryboat, Uncle Ted said, "Hey, John, your aunt Carolyn made you caretaker of that box of food. Give me a biscuit sandwich. It will be our little secret for a short while." John liked that and they ate three apiece before they stopped.

John thought about how grown up he had felt when he sold the family hog and chickens to a neighboring family. His dad had trusted him with the sale and said he handled it well. His father had taught him about money at an early age. John wished he had more time with his dad. He always tried to please him and to do what he said, but nowadays his dad seemed to be too busy. His mother had stressed the importance of obeying his parents. He could no longer talk to her about things that bothered him. He had no one to listen to him, it seemed.

"Hey boy, are you sleeping on the job?" Uncle Ted asked, interrupting this thoughts.

"What do you mean, Uncle Ted? John replied.

"I've asked you three times to look for something sweet in that box from my wife."

They laughed when John took out two pieces of chocolate cake. It felt good to laugh with Uncle Ted.

"I sure got a kick out of how your dad insisted he couldn't leave the milk cow behind and had you tie a rope around her neck and lead her into that trailer. Your sisters really like riding on her back. Your dad seems to have a language that the animals understand. So you'll still have to milk that cow two times a day. You can't get rid of that job so easily," Uncle Ted said with a laugh.

The truck ahead was signaling a stop at a country store on the right. They all got a bathroom break. Jay William went into the store and came out with two pounds of bologna and two loaves of light bread plus snack cakes. He also had a surprise—cold soft drinks in bottles. Everyone crossed the road and sat on a quilt Nancy unfolded. The store-bought food was a treat for the children. Uncle Ted said all they needed was a can of pork and beans to make the meal complete. Jay William gave John a quarter and told him to buy a big can of them at the store. Nancy found a can opener, small bowls, and spoons and the party continued. Neither John nor Uncle Ted mentioned anything about the box Aunt Carolyn had packed, because they were uncertain how much food was left.

The girls asked John to play tag with them, and they began to run. He pretended he could not catch them. Finally Jay William signaled it was time to get moving. The girls were happy not to have been tagged and this time got into the pickup with smiles. John was happy he had put smiles on their faces. His mother had taught him to be kind to his sisters, and he knew that was what he had just done.

Finally, their convoy pulled up a steep hill and into the lane where a rental house was waiting. The owner, Deacon Mosier, had given it to Jay William and Nancy for three months until they could find something they wanted. The simple rock house had two bedrooms, a kitchen, and a living room. The toilet was further from the house than the one in Covington, but it would have to work for now. Thankfully, there was a large back porch, and that was where the milk cow, Jersey, would dwell for the time being.

Uncle Ted whispered to John, "You don't have far to walk to milk her here, do you?"

John smiled and shook his head.

Uncle Ted helped bring in the furniture. Then he went to bed because he planned to leave early the next morning. He had checked the food his sweet wife had packed, and there was plenty left. John was sad when he left. He secretly wished he could drive back with him.

In the morning, Nancy made breakfast for everyone, but Ted

had left while it was still dark, and she was not aware he had gone. She felt bad that he had left without eating. The kids told her the meal of ham, milk gravy, biscuits, and cold milk was delicious. Now it was time to get to work. Jay William and John went outside to figure out where the cow would be happy. Nancy and the girls got the kitchen set up. Veronica put most of the dishes in the cabinet, while Heather put the silverware in pretty green mason jars on the table.

Within two weeks the place began to look like a home. The church congregation was kind to the children, and they seemed a little happier with the move.

One evening Heather sat by her dad and hugged his neck. He asked if she wanted to play their game. He pulled her up onto his lap, and she squealed with delight. The two of them laughed.

"Heather Marie, the prettiest little girl I ever did see— Hawkins!" Jay William said.

"Oh, thank you, Daddy," she replied.

Then Jay William said, "Heather Marie, the ugliest little girl that I ever did see—Hawkins!"

"No, Daddy!" she said and pretended to hit him. They repeated these lines several times, and the laughter got rather loud.

Nancy was tired of the nonsense game and said, "Okay, Heather, get down and let your daddy rest. This move was hard on all of us!"

Heather would not move, and Nancy again told her it was time to get off of her daddy. Heather began to cry on his lap. When the little girl remained obstinate, Nancy said rather harshly, "Okay, Heather, you know what happens if you don't obey."

Heather crawled down slowly from Jay William's lap, crying more loudly.

"Hush it up!" Nancy said and started toward her, but Jay William signaled her to stop.

Veronica took Heather away to play with her. It seemed she often mothered Heather. She wanted to keep her out of trouble.

Veronica was a sweet, tender-hearted little girl who always looked out for her sister.

John could hardly wait to finish milking the cow, because his dad had said he could try out the slingshot he had made with his cousin Kevin the day before they moved. The handle was made from a forked branch from John's favorite tree in the backyard. They had cut an old inner tube to make the elastic sling. John had already filled his pockets with stones. John soon adopted the ritual of milking the cow and playing with his slingshot.

Veronica and John were enrolled in the one-room school the first week after they arrived. Both were a little nervous on their first day, but they were less so when they recognized children from the church.

Miss Mary Long, the school's teacher, greeted them at the doorway. She smiled, but Jay William thought she looked tense. She was a tiny lady with long brown hair pulled up in a bun on top of her head. Her glasses were thick, indicating poor eyesight. He introduced himself and then his children.

"I've heard about you and have been expecting you here," she told him. "Welcome!" The children were led to seats assigned according to their grades. Once they seemed settled, Jay William left for home.

One afternoon shortly after, John came running into the house, telling the family he had found a creek nearby and had crossed it on a big fallen tree. He wanted everyone to walk across the creek with him. Nancy encouraged Jay William to take a break and to go with them, but he was busy preparing a sermon and said he could not do it. "Perhaps later, John," he said.

John asked if he could show the girls how he crossed the creek.

"No. Wait until I come with them," Jay William said.

The next morning after the cow was milked, Jay William asked John if he wanted to show him how he crossed the creek. John was excited and walked across the log with his arms out straight. His dad told him he had done this very well. Jay William recalled how he would run across a log when he was younger. John decided he wanted to be like his dad and do that. He began to practice running across the log after his chores were completed.

A week later, John was bored with running across the log by himself and decided it was time for the girls to join him. Jay William had not given them permission, but John decided not to tell the girls that. He brought them to the creek and showed them how he quickly he could run across the log. He told them they could do it and it would be fun. He told them they should not worry about falling into the creek, because it was not that deep. But Veronica and Heather were terrified and refused. John laughed and called them little babies.

Veronica could not handle the teasing, so she accepted John's challenge and discovered if she did not look down at the water but to the other side of the creek, the crossing was easy. Heather, however, would not attempt it. John finally gave her permission to crawl across the log. The girls did not tell Jay William about the adventure with their brother.

The fresh air seemed to make them all seem happy, and they enjoyed exploring the woods and finding little treasurers like broken pottery, pretty rocks, and wildflowers. Jay William was more relaxed than Nancy had ever seen him. She became less tense herself, and the children found them both more approachable. Jay William spent more time with the children, and Nancy enjoyed keeping busy in the house. She found ways to make the house more organized.

One afternoon Jay William and the kids were walking in an area they had not visited before and found land for sale. They walked up a hill and looked at the property. Jay William thought it would be affordable since it had a lot of trees on it. He decided he would find out who owned the land and would talk with that person. He waited until the kids were in school and took a ride to the general store to inquire about the property. The owner happened to be in the store and said he would be happy to go with him to see what he might be interested in buying. They looked at the land, and Jay William said he wanted enough to build a small house and a small barn and to plant a family garden.

Jay William sketched a house and a barn with a large garden plot plus a yard for the kids. The owner gave him an affordable price and said he would get his brother-in-law to clear the area Jay William needed.

"I'll discuss this with my wife and see you later today," Jay William told him. The two shook hands and set a time to meet again.

Jay William was so excited because this land was even less expensive than he had imagined, especially with free clearing of the trees. He drove home and told Nancy the news, and they took Heather with them to see the land.

Nancy liked the spot and said it would be nice to have a bigger house without a cow on the porch. They laughed when Heather said, "But where will Jersey stay? There's no barn or even a house here."

"We'll build both of them if we buy the land," her daddy said.

They drove to the owner's place, and Jay William asked about having some of the large trees cut into lumber to build the frames of the house and of the barn.

The man laughed and said, "Yes, my brother-in-law does that, but you'll have to pay him for the lumber. He does the other work for free for me if I let him keep the trees. I was going to pass the savings on to you since you're the new preacher here."

They drove to the brother-in-law's place, and Jay William got a price he could afford to pay. Nancy and Jay William agreed that God was blessing them. They could not wait to share the news with John and Veronica.

When the trees were removed, the family gathered daily after school and cleared the land of debris. Jay William and Nancy worked at the site when the children were in school. Heather did her part by picking up small rocks as her daddy demonstrated and placing them in a pile away from where the house would be built.

All the members of the family worked hard because they were happy to be building their own house. It seemed the family was uniting and Nancy was becoming a part of the family. They completed the siding, the roof, and the rest of the outside of the house and planned to finish the inside during the winter. Jay William was a hard worker and expected much more from his kids than the neighboring children were accustomed to seeing. It seemed the Hawkins kids didn't have time to play.

Their Sundays were always a time to relax, however, and the children were able to play with other kids in the afternoon. "Sundays are the best day of the week," they began to tell each other. Parenting was tough for Jay William and Nancy. Jay William had had a poor childhood with little love and much physical abuse; Nancy had never been a parent before she married and became the mother of three children. She never questioned any punishment Jay William imposed.

The Hawkinses moved into their new house at the start of March 1944. They were happy to have an extra bedroom and the outdoor toilet closer to the house. They had a small barn for the milk cow, Jersey.

One evening after supper, John called for his daddy to help him with a school project.

"Not right now, John. I'm talking with Nancy in the kitchen," Jay William told son. "She's helped me all day on the house, and she wants me to help her plan the vegetable garden now."

"Can you just come look at my work and tell me if I'm doing it right?" John asked. When there was no answer from the kitchen, John got frustrated. *Dad doesn't take time to answer me anymore,* he thought. John asked for help less and less often.

Veronica seemed happy to continue to mother her little sister and to play with her. John became less interested in doing family things. He did what he was told but otherwise kept quiet. He found his joy in the friends he made at school.

The church was growing, and Nancy joined her husband in visiting new families and inviting others to attend. Nancy taught Sunday school and sang solos during the services. People frequently asked to hear her sing "You Must Live Holy." She was quite animated and put much emotion into her singing.

Nancy encouraged the ladies at the church to quilt and to have lunch together on Thursdays. They were to bring a sack lunch weekly and a new lady visitor once a month. This was a fun time for the ladies and a great mentoring opportunity.

John often functioned as babysitter while Jay William and Nancy were out doing church work. The young man was going through a stressful time, and he often teased his sisters when their parents were not home.

John had the company of other males only when he was at school. The boys who befriended him were older and mischievous. They often got into trouble. They would deliberately give the wrong answers to the teacher's questions, causing everyone to laugh. They would put grasshoppers in the younger kids' lunch boxes. Occasionally an older girl would find a grasshopper in her hair and would scream, producing laughter. Someone once placed a dead mouse on the teacher's chair when she was writing one the blackboard. Another time Miss Long was hit with a spitball that no one admitted to throwing.

This was Miss Long's first teaching job, so when these boys made it tough for her, she got discouraged. They loved causing her to become frustrated. She was spending so much time trying to discipline them that she had no time to teach. The younger children got little instruction.

Miss Long sent notes home with the boys who caused trouble to inform their parents of the situation. She asked for the parents' help to stop this behavior, but no parent responded to her pleas.

One day Miss Long became so upset that she told the boys

if they didn't shape up, she would quit and there would be no school for anyone. That possibility intrigued the older boys, and they pushed her further into desperation, causing her to cry. She dropped her eyeglasses while wiping the tears from them, and one of the boys stepped on the glasses, breaking one of the lenses. Miss Long put on the broken glasses, and the boys clapped and laughed at her. This was more insult than she could handle. Miss Long cried harder and dismissed school for the day. The boys took their time getting home and invited John to join them in their fun activities.

John told Veronica she knew the way home and not to tell their dad about the school day. Poor Veronica walked home slowly because she knew she would have a problem explaining why John was not with her.

When she got home, Veronica discovered her parents were out visiting. They got home about an hour earlier than the time John and Veronica usually returned. Veronica was asleep but they didn't notice.

In the meantime Miss Long was calling on the parents of the boys who made trouble for her. She walked up the road to the Hawkins house and was warmly received by Jay William and Nancy. She told them the reason for her visit and wondered why they had not responded to her note. Miss Long explained that the school would close if she quit but said she would not allow the boys to destroy the school.

Jay William was mortified to learn that his son was involved. Miss Long discovered that John had not brought the note home and that his father had no idea his son had been rude and was one of those making her life miserable. Jay William promised her she would see a new attitude from John on the next school day. He assured her that all of the boys who attended the Stoney Point church where he was the pastor would receive teaching about respecting those in authority.

Miss Long thanked him and continued her mission to speak

to each parent of the boys who were involved. She felt assured she had this set of parents on her side.

When Miss Long left, Jay William was very upset. He walked into the woods, fell on his knees, and cried. He realized the children missed Wilma's gentle nature. It was a quality he did not possess. He was desperate for relief from the pain he felt. "O God, I pray in the name of Jesus, show me how to do what I must do," he said.

Before he finished his prayer Nancy came to check on him. She led him back into the house, washed his face with a cloth, and offered him a glass of cold milk to calm his frazzled nerves.

When John arrived home at his usual time, he did not suspect a thing.

"How was school today, son?" Jay William asked.

"Good," John replied.

"Anything you want to tell me about your day, John?"

"No. Just a regular school day, nothing special about it, sir. Why do you ask?"

Jay William looked at his son's straight face and suddenly lost patience. He was upset that John had lied to him so easily.

He called the children to the kitchen and said, "I'm embarrassed and shocked at John's attitude. I'm embarrassed by his actions at school, especially by his choice of friends. We came to this mountain area to share God's Word. My only son decided to run with hoodlums, undermining all we hope to accomplish in these people's lives." He was so angry that his face was red and he was shaking all over.

Jay William next took a page from Uncle Hilton. He told Nancy and the girls to go outdoors and to stay there until he called them. He then removed his belt from his trousers and grabbed John by the shoulders. He shouted at John as he swung the belt at his bottom.

"This one is for lying to me about school." Whack!

The next swing was harder. "This is for not giving me the note Miss Long wrote." Whack!

"This is for your nasty attitude." Whack!

"And this big one is for being mean to your teacher!" Whack!

Jay William kept swinging the belt because he was so angry. John refused to cry and never apologized for his actions until his father finally demanded that he do so.

Unfortunately, this was the beginning of a new style of discipline for the children. No one spoke to Jay William about how severe his punishments were. Even Nancy dared not interfere. John, Veronica, and Heather each felt their father's strap at some point. They learned to follow his rules and to avoid bringing any kind of embarrassment or shame to their father lest they suffer the consequences.

On June 27, 1944, Nancy gave birth to a baby girl weighing an ounce short of ten pounds. Martha Ellen was a beautiful child with dark, curly hair like her daddy's. Nancy happily lost weight long after the delivery, because she had been overweight most of her life.

The Hawkinses enjoyed the house they had built on the hill, but John's problems at school persisted. Jay William wondered if the family should move to school district that provided better discipline. He wanted the children to have a good education. He sold their place and moved the family to a rented house in St. Francis. The school in town provided a solid education.

Because there was no full gospel church in St. Francis or in the adjoining town, Dislodge, Jay William felt God was telling him to preach the truth any way he could. He purchased a tent and held a revival for six straight weeks.

During those services he asked other ministers to preach. Many people came to know Christ and asked the Reverend Hawkins to start a permanent church in Dislodge where they could worship regularly. However, he could find no building to rent for a church. The weather turned cold, and Jay William added heat to the tent so he could continue to hold services there.

During this time, Nancy became ill. She finally agreed to go to the hospital, but she had almost waited too long to seek care. The doctors found her gallbladder ruptured, and the entire bile duct was gangrenous, including a large area of her liver. The doctors doubted she would live through surgery. Jay William called every minister he knew and asked for prayer for a miraculous healing for his wife.

Once again he called upon his sister Catherine to help care for his children. Nancy eventually recovered, but her liver remained enlarged for the rest of her life. Nancy was happy to come home to Martha Ellen, who was now eighteen months old. Little Martha had contracted measles, with a grossly elevated fever producing seizures. This led to grand mal seizures that continued throughout her life. She grew into a beautiful lady, married a wonderful man, and had four beautiful children, but her seizures were a hardship for the family because they were frequent and violent.

Jay William was tested over and over, but the challenges seemed to make his faith in God stronger. He realized God was in control, and he often preached on that theme.

Since turning four years old, Heather had wanted to join Veronica and John at school. She was told she had to wait until she turned five. She was now five years old and looked forward to starting school, but the local kindergarten was eliminated due to war expenses. Heather was devastated as she saw her siblings go to school while she had to remain at home.

"Daddy," she asked, "please can't you tell the school that I can read and write and that I'm a big girl? I don't want to stay at home again. How am I going to learn more if I can't go to school?"

Jay William believed Heather was ready and promised to talk to the principal about her. The principal agreed to talk to the first-grade teacher. The teacher said, "She may indeed be ready to learn, but she may not be ready to be separated from her family members all day for school. She may cry and interrupt the six-year-old children. I won't have that in my room. But if she can sit and learn without crying, I'll be happy to have her."

Jay William was delighted to give Heather the news that she would begin school the next day.

"Oh, Daddy, I knew you could it," she said. "I'm so happy. I'll get smart like John and Veronica soon."

"There's one thing you must not do or they'll send you home," Jay William said.

"What is that?" Heather asked. Before her father could tell her, she lifted her chin and said confidently, "I know I won't do it because I'm a good girl, right?"

"Sure you are, but you can't cry for your daddy or for Veronica. Okay?"

"Daddy, I'm not a baby, so don't worry, I won't cry," she promised.

No one thought this would be an issue. That night Heather went to bed and was so excited she could hardly wait for morning. She was up and dressed before the older children. Jay William drove them to school and led her into the classroom. He got her settled and left with her smiling and waving at him.

As soon as her father left the room, Heather realized she knew no one there. She became frightened and began to cry. She was indeed not ready socially to attend school.

Jay William had just returned to the house when the phone rang. To his surprise, it was the school principal telling him to come get Heather because she was crying for him. Jay William turned around and left to pick up his daughter.

Jay William and Heather walked out of the school hand in hand.

Heather was the first to speak when they got into the car. "Daddy, I wanted you. I missed you," she said. "I didn't know anyone and I wanted you. Are you angry at me?"

"No," he said with a sigh. "I missed you too, but now I've got to go milk the cow."

"But Daddy, I can help you. I'll be your new best helper."

"Heather, you can't milk a cow yet because sometimes the cow kicks and she could hurt you. So you be a good girl and color me a picture while I'm gone."

Heather knew she needed to help her daddy because Nancy was still weak and he was doing the work of two. She sat at the table coloring, and suddenly she knew what she could do for the family. When Jay William returned with the milk buckets, Heather was quiet until he had finished pouring the milk into glass jugs. Then she said, "Daddy, I know what I can do. While you milk, I can wash the breakfast dishes for you because there are a lot here."

"Honey, I appreciate your wanting to help, but you're too short to reach the sink. No, you just be good, and that's a big help to me," Jay William replied.

Heather was persistent. "Daddy, if I stand on a chair, I'm tall enough. Watch!" She scooted the chair over to the sink.

The two of them figured it out together. Jay William placed three chairs in front of the sink. The dirty dishes were on Heather's left side, the soapy water was in the first sink, the rinse water in the second sink, and the drying rack to her far right. "Start to your left and keep moving to the right until the job is finished," Jay William instructed his daughter.

This arrangement of morning labors was the foundation for a father-daughter relationship that lasted until Jay William's death.

The following year the family moved to Cantrell, Missouri, where the rent was less expensive. The home was memorable. Next to it was a huge chat dump. This pile of lead mining waste was as tall as a three-story building at times. The neighborhood children used it as one would a snowy hillside. They climbed to the top and slid down the pile of chat, laughing all the way.

The year was 1946 and the three older children were all in

school. Yes, Heather finally made it, and school was a joy for her. Another joyful event for the family was the birth of a baby boy, Peter David. He arrived one day before his mother's birthday on August 22. Jay William was delighted to have another son, and John was quite proud of his baby brother. The family now consisted of three girls and two boys.

Jay William did not pastor a church but was a guest preacher at churches in the area and often held revivals. Money was scarce, and the family had to charge groceries at times. The store was right across from the school, and Nancy would sometimes give John a list of things to pick up after class. Once the food was placed in the bag, he would say, "Please put it on J. W. Hawkins's bill."

Veronica saw this happen once and was intrigued by the simplicity of the transaction. She thought it was magic. She shared her discovery with Heather, who refused to believe anything could be that easy. Veronica declared with a crossed-heart-and-hope-to-die pledge that the family never had to pay for food.

One day, when lunch hour arrived, Veronica looked up her sister, and the two of them went across the street and bought snack food to share with their classmates. Veronica told the store clerk, "Put it on J. W. Hawkins's bill," and they walked out with the goodies. The handouts made them so popular that they hit the store again at second recess.

Jay William was away at a two-day ministerial meeting, so John had to tell the news to Nancy. "The store owner asked me today if my parents knew the girls were charging snacks on the grocery bill. I told him I would let you know and assured him it wouldn't happen again," John said.

The girls apologized to Nancy, but she told them their dad would get the news and he would be angry. They clung to each other when they were sent to bed for the night. They found it tough to go to school the next day because they knew when they returned they could be punished. They were afraid of what their daddy would do when he came home.

To their amazement, Jay William delivered only a mild rebuke. "Never do that again," he told the girls. "You didn't know you were wrong. You should have, but you didn't. Let it be a lesson learned."

Then he shared good news with the family.

"A church down in the south end of the state needs a pastor, and I've been invited to preach there in two weeks," Jay William said. "If I get this position, we would be about two hours away from Tennessee. That's super exciting."

When the date arrived, Nancy accompanied Jay William to the church. They enjoyed meeting the people. Following the evening sermon, they drove back to Cantrell and prayed as a family that God's will be done regarding Jay William's appointment. One week later he received a call saying the congregation had voted to make him the pastor.

CHAPTER 40

WHEN THE SCHOOL year came to a close, the Hawkins family once again packed up its belongings and moved to a new town. This time it was Silverton, Missouri. The children's excitement reached an all-time high. Their new home was in the church parsonage a half-block from the church. It was built on a large lot and had a big garage with a full-size loft. There was also a small shed for storage. The house had three large bedrooms, a spacious living room, and a big dining room next to a large kitchen, and for the first time, they had indoor plumbing. The front porch wrapped around the entire front of the house. The front yard was huge, with several tall shade trees. The back porch was big and eventually was made into another bedroom. Concrete sidewalks connected the buildings.

This was the nicest home Jay William and his family had ever been inside, and now they were going to live there! Jay William was happy that his family was pleased. To add to his joy, he got permission from the owner to plant a garden on the weedy property next to their yard. The owner was happy not to have to care for the property any longer. Jay William's years of gardening for Uncle Hilton and Aunt Sophie had taught him about caring for the soil in order to produce an abundant harvest. One church member had a farm about ten miles away and gave him space in a barn for Jersey, the family cow. The place had beautiful pastures where she could graze.

Before Jay William became the pastor of the Silverton Assembly, the church had split over a rigid and stern teaching about women's apparel. The teaching by a visiting evangelist was especially discouraging to a group of new believers and caused hurt feelings. Those embracing this belief would not associate with those who did not abide by the rules they tried to establish. This had caused problems within families, and some people did not speak to their kin. The previous pastor refused to permit the more militant church members to teach from the pulpit. He said God had called him to preach the gospel and to tell of God's love in the community. He said he would not become a "clothesline preacher."

Some of the newer members quit going to church, which led to the pastor's decision to resign. The group that had promoted the new rules for godly women had left and had rented a building across town to start a new church, the Reformed Assembly.

When Jay William became the pastor he wanted to know more about the issue and prayed for godly wisdom to help him reunite the church. He then talked to members of the Reformed Assembly, who told him the details of the split. He even attended a service in their store-front church in hopes of learning more about these people's beliefs. He wanted to understand what they were teaching.

Jay William did not have an issue with the theology he heard during the service. On further investigation, however, he found these people were teaching that a woman sinned if she did not dress in a holy or godly manner as they outlined it. For example, they said she would be responsible if her style of dressing caused a man to lust. They insisted that a dress must be at least four inches below the knee and that the sleeve must touch the wrist. They prohibited nylon stockings and high-heeled shoes. Wearing any jewelry, including a wedding band, was sinful in their eyes.

Many of the ladies in the Silverton Assembly worked at the dress factory in town, and for a small fee they could buy dresses from a selection of those that did not pass inspection. They received an employee discount on the better clothes. The dresses were fashionable but modest, and the women found the prices within their means. They also wore an occasional piece of costume jewelry.

After spending time in prayer, Jay William thought, *I know God honors his word and looks inside a woman's heart, where the real woman resides. My wife dresses in a simple manner pretty much in line with the new teaching at Reformed Assembly. Fashion means little to Nancy.*

Then he thought about Wilma, who was modest in her dress but loved fashion and had a sense of style that he admired. Both women loved God and were good wives who respected him and had gentle spirits. *Being a helpmate to a husband and nurturing children in God's Word are what really matters. Clothing is not as important*, he thought.

Jay William invited to Reformed Assembly attendees to join him in a midweek service at which he would address the subject of godly women and their apparel. Reformed Assembly members said that they didn't want to return to the Silverton Assembly where he pastored but that he could preach in their pulpit on the subject. Jay William said he would give them an answer soon. He talked to his deacon board regarding the offer and said he was praying that God would mend the broken communication in families and in the community.

Jay William agreed to the Reformed Assembly's offer. A group of younger ladies from the Silverton Assembly also chose to attend the service. They wanted to hear the Reverend Hawkins preach on the subject.

Taking his message from the book of Proverbs, he titled his sermon "The Godly Woman."

" Solomon was a very wise man," Jay William began. "He writes in Proverbs that strength and dignity are a woman's clothing and that the fear of God is to be praised. He mentions nothing about this woman's dress or sleeve length. He says she wears fine clothing but opens her heart and hands to the poor. She respects her husband and her conduct is pure."

Jay William continued to show that God's Word says a woman's internal beauty is more important than her external looks; a woman with a gentle spirit and a forgiving heart is a woman of true beauty.

"This is how you grow in love for God and others," he preached. "Be gentle, kind, and forgiving. Older ladies are to teach younger ladies in love and by example. The Holy Spirit will convict the immodest. Let's not be so quick to condemn others. That's not our job and it can discourage others.

"Tonight, let the Holy Spirit speak to you heart. If you have been quick to judge or have been unforgiving, admit it, and let God heal your heart. Ask for forgiveness from the one you offended. Let God once again allow the church to be a light of truth in our community."

Ladies on both sides of the issue repented of bad attitudes, and healing started in their hearts that night. The church family began coming together, and the split eventually dissipated. Those who chose to wear long dresses continued to do so but did not judge sisters who liked a little more adornment worn with modesty. The younger ladies liked to dress fashionably, while the older ladies were not quite as stylish. The ladies were happy to be working together again. Judgment and discouragement were no longer issues in their church. The Reformed Assembly congregation returned to the Silverton Assembly.

Church attendance grew so quickly that the Silverton Assembly had to build an addition; Sunday school attendance went from 150 to 450, and larger classrooms were a must. The Reverend Hawkins dared church members to dream big. They built a large multipurpose hall and included a three-room apartment for visiting ministers such as missionaries and evangelists. They doubled church space to accommodate the increase in attendance and activities.

The construction work was done by volunteers, with the Reverend Hawkins on the top of the list. He watched over the faithful, visiting daily in the community, and new families began to attend the Silverton Assembly.

Nancy delighted in ironing Jay William's white shirts and did a professional job. She considered this her contribution to her husband's ministry. He wore a fresh white shirt each day with dress pants and a nice necktie. He was a well-dressed man. Jay William hummed happily when he was not talking. He was excited to see God working in the hearts of so many in the community. In addition to his ministerial duties, he raised cattle on the land he had rented in the country. He also spent more time with his children and their friends. Many of them joined in church activities due to their fondness for the Reverend Hawkins.

The church began a children's ministry with fun-loving but firm leaders. Parents were attracted by the program, and each week children learned God's Word with lessons on their level. The program was the catalyst for church growth.

The youth group called Christ Ambassadors was one of the largest in the area. The group's devoted young leaders taught teenagers how to live a Christian life and to enjoy doing it. A youth rally was held in a different church in the area each month. The church with the most points received a banner. The points were calculated by the number of young people present and by the miles they drove to attend the rally. The Silverton Assembly usually had about forty teenagers attending each month.

In August of 1948, Theodore joined the Hawkins family, weighing almost thirteen pounds at birth. He was a handsome fellow and was an especially welcome addition. This made it even—three girls and three boys!

The Reverend Hawkins was now preaching radio sermons and had many daily listeners. People responded to his sermons and visited from as far away as Illinois. Many later joined the church to worship with the congregation.

The gospel quartet the Brownings was well known in the area and was a favorite at the church. The Brownings had a big following, and their services were well attended. With the new multipurpose hall, the church could enjoy a meal on those special occasions. The Silverton Assembly had some great cooks, and their specialties were well known. Even the diet-conscious could not resist Sister Crystal's peach pies and her pineapple upside down cake. Grandma Lawson always made bread and rolls.

The Hawkins children blossomed in Silverton. Jay William never permitted them to skip a school day unless they were too ill to attend. A couple of them, Peter and Heather, received perfect attendance awards for five straight years. This always made him happy. He wanted his children to have the education he never received.

The family loved the community. As the years passed, more demands were made on Jay William and he spent less time with his children.

He reserved Sunday afternoons for them and for his famous Sunday afternoon drives. The children loved stuffing themselves into the Packard and heading out on the country roads with their daddy. Jay William gave Nancy the afternoon to herself while the kids went with him. He made special memories for the children during their many trips to the Mississippi River a few miles from home. He loved to share stories about the river with them.

The Reverend Hawkins celebrated Mother's Day with enthusiasm. He always had special gifts for the mothers. He gave prizes to the youngest mother, the oldest mother, and the one with most children. Almost every child wore a flower on Mother's Day. A red or a pink one honored a mother who was living, and a white one honored a mother who had passed away. Veronica and Heather wanted to wear one of each, but Nancy decided that would raise too many questions.

Jay William's Mother's Day sermons were some of his best. He had not had a gentle and kind mother who loved God, and this may have motivated him to encourage mothers to do their best. He also taught husbands to encourage their children to honor and to obey their mothers.

Jay William loved to celebrate Christmas, and the family enjoyed helping him prepare gifts for all the children attending services on Christmas Sunday. The girls loved placing an orange, an apple, and Christmas candy in a cellophane bag and tying it up with a pretty red bow.

One Christmas when the children were handing out gift bags, a parent asked the Reverend Hawkins if what her child had said about his daughter was true.

"I don't know," he said. "What did your child say?"

"She said your daughter didn't receive any gifts from Santa because you don't believe in Santa at your house," the lady replied. "I told her that the nice Reverend Hawkins would not do that."

"Actually," Jay William said, "she is correct. I teach my children not to believe in Santa because it's not the truth! Teaching my children to believe in Santa wouldn't be fair to them. I want them to know that at Christmas we celebrate Jesus coming to earth as a baby to make a way for us to go to heaven by his death on the cross. He is the only sacrifice possible to redeem us from sin. I teach them in place of Santa to give gifts of service to the poor and the needy as God gave us a gift of Jesus. They love doing acts of kindness."

"Sir, isn't that a bit much for children to handle?" the woman asked. "What harm would there be in allowing them to believe in Santa so their Christmas could be like Christmas for all the other children?"

"If I taught them to believe in Santa Claus and the Easter Bunny, I would be teaching them to believe in untruths," Jay William said. "I would rather tell them the truth now than not have them trust me in larger matters." The lady walked away without saying another word.

The Reverend Hawkins was often a guest speaker at community events including Silverton High School's graduation ceremonies. The day after one such ceremony he received a call from the school superintendent's secretary. She said the superintendent, James Long, wanted the pastor to join him for lunch at a local restaurant to express his gratitude for speaking to the graduating class. She said he enjoyed Jay William's timely message.

On Tuesday at noon the pair had lunch. "Your address was outstanding, and appropriate for this graduating class," Mr. Long told Jay William. "You must have known about the challenges these students face to give such a fitting address. 'Each step is preparation for the next step' was what they needed to hear. Can you tell me your source of information for this address?"

"Actually, God is my source," Jay William said. "The Holy Spirit inspired me to speak on this topic after much prayer. I'm God's messenger, and I live to give his message to this community."

Mr. Long looked a little perplexed at his response. Then he said, "Pastor Hawkins, I hope I don't offend you with what I'm about to say, but I'm most anxious to know where you received your theological degree. Where did you attend seminary?"

Jay William said he was ordained before seminaries were popular in the Assemblies of God denomination. "I do, however, highly recommend the seminary to all ministerial candidates," he said. "I'm helping a young man get into one in Springfield, Missouri. Our denomination's headquarters is located there."

"Where did you get your education, Reverend Hawkins? I'm most interested to hear your story," Mr. Long said.

Jay William said he had completed the seventh grade and had received only two years of formal education due to family hardships.

"That explains a lot to me," Mr. Long said. "I've noticed that in your addresses you often use the wrong verbs. However, you seem to have no difficulty with articulation and with theological terms."

"I'm sorry," Jay William said, "but I don't understand. Can you explain what you mean?"

"For example, in your address on Sunday, you said 'I were wondering' when 'I was wondering' would have been correct. In about the third grade, you would have learned that a singular subject takes a singular verb, while a plural subject takes a plural verb. With your permission, I'd like to give you this third-grade English book. I knew you would have an explanation for this, and I'm sorry about your family hardships. The book is yours to keep, and I hope you accept my sincerity in giving it to you. I've noticed that most of your children have had perfect school attendance. I know it takes a special effort to get them to school daily. I also know most of them are exceptionally good students. I know they would be happy to help their father with a new learning project. I'd be happy to meet with your again to check your progress. Based on the success you've in your church and in our community, I doubt you'll have any difficulty. You're an interesting man, and I wish you much success."

Jay William thanked Mr. Long for his time and interest and promised to meet with him in the future. The pastor studied daily and had Heather test him. He wanted to improve and felt blessed that he had attracted the attention of Mr. Long, a man he believed wanted to help him.

CHAPTER 41

JEROME MADE HIS appearance at thirteen and a half pounds. He was the largest of Nancy's babies. When he was born, Dr. Wilson told Nancy, "Jerome is the biggest baby I have ever delivered in my twenty years as a physician."

Nancy was proud of her big baby and was thankful she had kept so many of the other children's baby clothes. On the day he was born, Jerome fit into clothes for a six-month-old. He had long, curly black hair, and his deep dimples made him a hit with all the church family.

Things appeared to be going well for the Hawkins family. Jay William studied his English grammar book regularly. His last lunch with Mr. Long gave him encouragement. He was happy Mr. Long had noticed the improvement in his grammar.

Farming remained in Jay William's blood, and he had rented five acres to raise corn. John, now a high school junior, helped him work there. One day, after twelve hours of labor in the field, the pair called it quits for the day. John noticed his class ring was missing from his finger.

The pair walked from one end of the field to the other, looking for the ring without success. Jay William fell on his knees and prayed for God's intervention. There, shining in the moonlight right where he was kneeling, was the class ring. Once again, God honored this man's faith.

Those who looked at outward appearances, including the size

of his church, may have said Jay William was doing very well. He was handsome, with thick, dark wavy hair. He had a kind word for all he met. He believed everyone had a good side; he was forgiving to those who had gone astray. He had friends on both sides of the track. He had a great love for those who did not believe in God. He spent much time visiting and praying with those hurting people and was known to visit people of many faiths.

Jay William liked to drive a good-looking car. He put many miles on a car and often traded in one for another. His favorite car was a Packard. His deacon board saw how hard he was working for the church and hired an assistant pastor to help lighten his load. Bob Miller was a new seminary graduate. The son of a friend, he was recommended by Jay William. The young man moved into a comfortable ministerial apartment provided by the church.

Jay William thought his new assistant pastor talked too much of his own importance and not enough about the church's successful programs. Bob was overheard saying the Reverend Hawkins was uneducated and too old-fashioned. He often entertained younger church members in the apartment, and that annoyed Jay William. After he spoke to the deacon board about his concerns, the members decided to terminate Bob when his six-month trial period was over.

During this time Jay William developed headaches that could be relieved only by time in a cool, dark room. One Sunday afternoon, Heather was jumping rope near the room where he was resting. Each time she landed on the sidewalk, his head pounded more. Without warning, he got up and gave her a spanking with his belt.

He felt so bad afterward that he made a two-hour trip to talk with Catherine about the incident. She was always willing to listen to her younger brother. Jay William often thought she was more like a mother than a sister. As soon as he got out of the car, she sensed he was not feeling well.

Jay William poured out his heart. "Sis, I don't know what to do anymore," he said. "My head hurts so badly most of the time. I'm not good to my children or to anyone else when my head pounds with pain. I seem to lose all reason but can't help myself. What do you think is happening to me?" He began to cry.

"Now stop crying and let's talk about this,'" Catherine said. "Don't you remember that our dad had such bad headaches that he would lie in the barn where it was dark? Jerome used to have the girls make the problem worse with loud noises. Jerome chased daddy off during one headache episode. Perhaps you've inherited the problem from him."

"I think I remember that, but it was so long ago," Jay William said.

"Jay William, it's time you seek medical help. I heard a rumor that our daddy ended up in an old folks home with those headaches. Will you promise me you'll have Nancy go with you to a specialist for headaches?"

Jay William returned to Silverton and talked to Dr. Wilson. He sent Jay William into Cape Girardeau for help. The specialist hospitalized him so he could monitor the headaches and Jay William's response to medications. The headaches became more frequent, and the medications did little good. The specialist tried insulin injections but they did not work. Jay William's disposition was affected, and when he returned home the children walked on egg shells, fearing he would explode.

This caused Jay William to feel unsure and frightened. His physician encouraged him to take a break from his church duties so he could concentrate on getting well. His performance in the pulpit was not the same, and the pain seemed too much for him. Once he collapsed while giving a sermon. The deacons had a meeting to discuss how best to help their pastor. They decided he needed a break from preaching and made an appointment to visit him with a proposal. They asked Nancy to make sure the children were not at home during their visit.

The deacons had already contacted the Rev. Armin Smothers,

whom Jay William had recommended for assistant pastor. The action had been on hold due to Jay William's illness. Now the deacons wanted the Reverend Smothers to fill in as pastor for six months while Jay William recovered from his illness.

Nancy had told her husband the deacons were coming to visit him. He supposed they would be praying for his healing, so he welcomed their visit.

Mr. Hopkins, the head deacon, took the lead and said, "Reverend Hawkins, we greatly appreciate your years of service to our church, but we feel you're too ill to continue under your heavy load. We see the pain you're in most of the time, and it's affected your ability to pastor. We've offered the pastoral job to the Reverend Smothers for six months while you concentrate on getting well."

Jay William turned red in the face. "You did this behind my back!" he shouted. "You want to fire me as your pastor just because of my health. I'm trying hard to improve it."

"No, you don't understand," Mr. Hopkins said. "We just want to give you a chance to get well, and then you can resume your job. We plan to pay your salary for the six months. You and your family will continue to live in the parsonage. I believe we're being very fair to you."

"You say you're being fair when you hire another pastor? I believe you're telling me I'm not doing my job. Do you think I'm too old to manage my duties? I've poured all my energy into my church. I'm only thirty-nine years old, and I'm not as old-fashioned as some have said! Go get Smothers. I'll resign on my own accord," Jay William told them.

The deacons became nervous and shook their heads. "No, Reverend Hawkins, we will not accept the answer you've given us tonight. Pray about this and talk with your wife before you make such a quick decision," Mr. Hopkins said.

But Jay William would not change his mind even when Nancy tried to reason with him. A week later, he handed the deacons a letter of resignation.

CHAPTER 42

J AY WILLIAM HAD made a poor choice. He still had six children
to support. (John was now serving in the military.) He was
unable to work because the headaches remained so frequent. The
congregation had now voted to hire the Reverend Smothers as the
new pastor.

When he was asked to move out of the parsonage so the new
pastor and his family could move in, the reality of his predicament
hit Jay William hard. He was embarrassed and avoided being
seen in the community. He left for his beloved Tennessee to visit
Wilma's niece, Wendy, who was married to a pastor. There he
poured out his heart, expressing pain and regret. He could not
figure out his next step or how to support his family.

Wendy and her husband listened and prayed with him for
hours. They were surprised to see Jay William in such bad shape.
He was spiritually drained and regretted his decision to resign.
He realized he had done this without praying, without knowing
God's will in the matter. For a week Jay William was unable to
sleep for longer than an hour at a time. Then he slept for three
days straight, waking only for a little food before going to sleep
again. He thanked Wendy and her husband for their help and left
to visit Catherine. But after two days with her, he decided he had
better go home to see his family after leaving so abruptly.

Returning to Silverton, he discovered Nancy had moved the
family into a house given to her at no cost. It was in a low-income

neighborhood and it was in bad shape. There was a hole in the kitchen floor, and the outhouse was in poor condition. Nancy and the girls did their best they to make the house livable. They found a piece of plywood in a back bedroom and placed it over the hole in the floor.

Veronica and Heather quickly learned to do the laundry and took babysitting jobs to bring in extra money. Nancy was now a Stanley home distributor, and many ladies from the church purchased products from her. Nancy also sewed for others to earn additional income.

When Jay William learned the family had moved out of the parsonage during his absence, he felt like a failure. He became depressed and withdrawn. A few days following his return, the bank repossessed his car because he had defaulted on the loan. Without transportation, Nancy had to cancel two Stanley home parties.

A gentleman to whom Jay William had given spiritual encouragement heard about the situation and gave him a car to drive. It was an older car with a rumble seat. The children struggled to hide their embarrassment when their daddy took them to school in it.

When he returned from the school, Nancy told him she needed to finish her sewing and asked him to go to the store to buy food for the little boys at home. He reluctantly did as she asked. When Jay William returned, the boys were playing in the back room, and Nancy asked him if they could talk. They sat on the couch and she said, "Honey, you have got to pull yourself together. Let's figure this thing out. I'm willing to keep on sewing and selling Stanley products, but we can't live like this forever. This house is okay for a short while, but it's not what we want long term for the family."

"I can't think straight now," Jay William said. "My head is killing me and I'm out of medicine."

"Okay, let me fix an ice bag and you lie down here," Nancy

said. "I'll turn off the light, and I'll take the boys with me to Dr. Wilson's office to see if he can give you something for the pain."

She returned with medicine and left to pick up the kids at school. They babysat for the boys as she prepared for a Stanley home demonstration that evening. The girls were used to keeping the boys quiet when their dad was sick. They went to the house across the street to watch their brothers play with the neighbor boys. At dusk they brought the boys inside to feed them and to put them to bed.

When Jay William awoke the house was dark and quiet. It took him a while to remember where he was. He heard laughter and voices near the back of the house and walked closer to listen.

Veronica was talking and laughing at the same time. "My goodness, weren't you embarrassed when we got out of that old car at school?" she asked.

"I was hoping no one was watching, but leave it to Billy Moore to see us and tell his friends," Heather said.

Veronica stopped laughing. "Oh no! What did you say?" she asked.

"I fooled him," Heather said. "I held my head up high and walked right past him without saying a word."

"I'm proud of you, sister," Veronica said. "We better go to sleep before we wake someone and get in trouble."

Jay William felt ashamed that he had let his girls down. *I know the community is laughing at my failure*, he thought, *but to hear my girls say they are embarrassed and laugh at me makes me sick all over.* He did not call on God for help, but in desperation, he thought of a way he could escape his pain and embarrassment.

Nancy would take the kids to school in the morning. He would make sure the boys went with her, saying he needed more sleep. When they left the house, he would get John's hunting gun, load it, and end his life. Jay William somehow thought he had solved his problem and he fell asleep.

The next morning he asked Nancy to pick up a newspaper

before coming home. He thought the extra stop would delay her return and give him more time to work his plan.

Once the house was finally empty, Jay William hurried to get the gun. Loading the shells, he sat on the couch, placed the gun to his head, and prepared to pull the trigger. The phone rang and would not stop ringing. Irritated by the interruption, he laid the gun at his side and picked up the phone. He didn't say a word but just listened.

"Brother, are you there?" the voice on the other end asked. "Brother Hawkins, can you hear me? I want you to know God told me to call you. I could have no peace until I made this call. We've missed you at to the pastors' meetings. Are you ill?"

Nancy returned home and saw the gun at Jay William's side. She quietly she picked it up. Removing the shells and dropping them into her dress pocket, she hurried out the door with the boys. She asked a neighbor to watch the kids so she could take care of an urgent need.

Nancy ran home and found Jay William still sitting with the phone in his hand. Taking the phone from him, she said, "This is Mrs. Hawkins."

"Is everything okay there?" asked Pastor Waters, a dear friend from the next town.

"No. I urgently need your help," Nancy said. "I found my husband with a loaded gun, and I think your phone call stopped him just in time."

"I'm in town and I'll be there quickly," Pastor Waters said. "I'll begin praying for God's help and direction so I can help Jay William."

Nancy made breakfast for her husband and told him to eat because he needed the nourishment. He was eating when Pastor Waters knocked on the door.

When he entered the house, Pastor Waters immediately told Jay William, "Brother, it's time for you to get out of the pit and to place your faith in God. He has work for you to do, and the devil is trying to make you give it up. I want you to get off that chair and clean up. We need to talk. I'll stay here until you're ready to go with me."

Jay William slowly headed toward the bedroom with Nancy on his heels. She helped him bathe and get dressed, and they made their way back to the living room. Pastor Waters was surprised to see Jay William in a white dress shirt and a tie with his hair combed into place.

The two men left. Nancy collapsed from the pressure and fell asleep. She was startled awake by a little voice at the door saying, "Momma, can we come home now; is Daddy okay?"

There was the neighbor tightly holding the boys' hands. Nancy looked up and said, "I am so sorry. I guess I fell asleep. I'm sorry I didn't get back over to pick them up. Thank you so much. Things are in God's hands now."

The neighbor gave Nancy a tender smile and said, "I fed the boys about an hour ago."

"Momma, where is Daddy?" Theodore asked.

"He left for a short while with Reverend Waters," Nancy said. "They'll be home later. It's time to pick up the others from school."

Nancy and the boys got into the car and headed for the school to fetch the other four children.

The children came running when they saw the old car enter the parking lot.

"How is Daddy?" Veronica asked.

"He's better and is with Reverend Waters," Nancy said.

"Daddy went with him? God must have heard me because I prayed for Daddy," Veronica said.

"Me, too. I prayed!" the others shouted. They did not want Nancy to think it was only Veronica's prayers that did the job. Nancy laughed at them.

"What's really wrong with Daddy?" Heather asked. "Do his headaches make him that way?"

"What way?" Nancy asked.

"They make him angry," Veronica said. "That scares me and I cry."

"You and Heather cry too easily," Nancy said. "You have to learn not to take everything so personally."

"I don't cry like they do," Martha said. "Do I, Momma?"

"No, you don't cry as much as the other two girls," Nancy said.

Heather looked at Veronica, and they smirked at their little sister's remark.

It was nearly six o clock and Jay William was still not home. Nancy made a quick meal of macaroni with tomatoes and bacon. After they had eaten, Nancy said, "Everyone has their homework done, so we can listen to the radio once the girls finish the dishes."

At 7 p.m., the door opened and in walked Jay William. He was standing tall and his frightened look had vanished. He smiled and said, "The bars are gone and I've escaped the prison of despair. Once again I have hope."

"Tell us what you mean," Nancy said. "What did you do while you were gone?"

"We prayed for God's guidance, and then we took action. Reverend Waters helped me send out six résumés to churches that needed a pastor. He's our sectional director, and he also wrote a letter of reference for me to use. And I have more good news. We're taking a vacation to the Assemblies of God family camp in three weeks. It's in the Ozarks, and there's a lake where we can swim."

Everyone clapped. "We can get our own cabin free. All we have to do is arrive two weeks ahead of the others and help get the camp ready for the summer events. We'll paint and do whatever else needs to be done. I know my children and they don't mind a little work, especially if fun follows."

"That's right, Daddy," Veronica said. "That's because we're the Hawkinses and we work hard."

CHAPTER 43

IN THE FALL of 1953, the Hawkins family was living in Bucoda, Missouri. The little rural town had a church and an elementary school. Jay William had become the pastor of the church, which had been locked for lack of a pastor. The family lived in the small parsonage next door to the church. Located in the southwest tip of Missouri, Bucoda was in the Cotton Belt. Almost everyone living there was involved in the cotton industry, either owning cotton fields or working as sharecroppers.

Unfortunately, a record rainfall that year prevented people from getting the cotton out of the fields. With the crop loss, there was no money to pay the pastor. To keep the church open for the community, Jay William preached revivals out of the area. Some were in Tennessee, and others were in Missouri churches outside of the Cotton Belt.

The money Jay William sent to Nancy was not enough to pay the parsonage's utility bills, but she managed to pay for the church's electricity. The electricity to the parsonage was turned off, and with the no funds to refill it, eventually the butane gas tank became empty.

Nancy cooked the meager meals in a large cast iron kettle and washed clothes in the same kettle. The school board discovered the home situation and the lack of good meals for the children, and officials paid Nancy a visit. They told her the children could not learn easily without good meals. They said a low-income family like hers would qualify for government assistance. The officials gave her the address of a place where help could be found; it was an hour away, and they provided directions.

The following day, Nancy reluctantly drove to the federal building in the next town and applied for food aid. The paperwork was lengthy and she needed more than an hour to complete it. Her application was approved, and then she had to stand in line for an hour and a half to receive food. It was a humbling experience but necessary so the Hawkins children could have nutritious meals.

A nice couple saw Nancy struggling to get the food to the car and offered to help.

The young man said to his wife, "You stay here with her, and I'll be right back with the kid's wagon." He quickly returned with the wagon and a boy.

"Ma'am, I just wanted my son, Ralph, to understand the joy of helping other people. He'll help fill the wagon and we'll follow you to your car."

"I appreciate your help," Nancy told the boy. "You resemble Peter, my seven-year-old son. He likes to be helpful. You have such kind parents. Always appreciate them."

"Yes, ma'am, I will," Ralph said, smiling as he helped put the food in the car.

As Nancy drove home, she thanked God for the food and for the young couple who helped her.

She was overjoyed when she got home. She was tired after a busy day but anxious to see her children. As Nancy neared the front door she heard the children arguing loudly and something go crash. She opened the door and saw her only table lamp broken on the floor. Her joy immediately gave way to anger.

"Just who did this?" she demanded.

They all pointed to one another. Then Veronica, the oldest, said, "I'm not sure. We were bored and started playing tag in here. Someone hit the table and it fell."

"Don't cry, Momma," little Jerome said. "I think I did it, but

I didn't mean to. I tripped when Theodore or Peter tagged me. I don't know which one did it, because I don't have eyes in the back of my head like you."

They all laughed. Nancy hugged him and said, "I have big surprises for everyone when you get this room straightened out."

The children hurried to clean up the mess.

"Okay, get your coats on and follow me to the car," Nancy said. No one could imagine what this was about, but they were all eager to get out of the house.

To their surprise, Nancy had brought more food than they had seen in a long time—cans of beef with gravy, American cheese, rice, dried beans, butter, peanut butter, dried cereal, and oatmeal.

"No more poke salad for breakfast," Theodore said.

This gave all of them a good laugh. The family had a big meal that night and then listened to gospel music from Del Rio, Texas, on the radio.

Jay William returned home about two weeks before Christmas Sunday and discovered the church planned to present a Christmas program under Nancy's direction. The church was decorated with greenery found in the area. The older children had placed fruit jars in the windows for decorations. Inside each jar was a candle made from melted crayons. The candles were very pretty when lit. The children were dressed as angels, shepherds, wise men, and, of course, Mary and Joseph. Jesus (a large baby doll) lay in a crude manger. The church was filled with homemade stars.

The Christmas program provided the most excitement the little town had seen in years. The children sang Christmas songs they had practiced for weeks. Peter's voice was loud and clear, especially during the singing of "Silent Night." At the top of his lungs, he sang, "Solid Night, Solid Night!" Peter's version of the old carol brought hearty laughter to the little church.

Each lady brought her own special Christmas dessert, and there was more than enough food to feed everyone. The children preferred the special treats in the bags that the Hawkins children had assembled. Each bag contained an apple, an orange, and a candy bar shaped like a Christmas tree. Their daddy had surprised them by bringing these items home from his last trip.

A few days before Christmas Eve, the Hawkins family pulled cotton bolls for half a day to have money for Christmas gifts for the younger boys. It was very hard work in the cold weather, but their spirits were high because after that they were going to visit Catherine and Johnny Maddox, always a treat for the girls.

They got lots of hugs and kisses at Aunt Catherine's house. More than anything, the children looked forward to her Christmas table, which was loaded with all kinds of yummy food. They especially liked the blackberry jam cake she had learned to make as a girl at Aunt Sophie's. It was the best dessert ever.

Veronica and Heather loved to see the gifts Aunt Catherine received from her neighbors. The ones they liked most were the pretty homemade dish towels. Many had crochet on the edges. Some were pretty prints made from flour sacks, but others were store bought. Aunt Catherine also had some in a drawer for her neighbors. A neighbor lady would come over to wish her a merry Christmas and would give her a dish towel. Then Catherine would let the girls find one in the drawer to give to the lady. Her home provided a humble but joyful Christmas setting that the Hawkins children treasured into adulthood.

Christmas vacation was over much too quickly. Spring came and Heather was the eighth-grade valedictorian. At the commencement she gave her first speech to a large group and did well. She knew she had made her daddy proud, because he gave her a rare compliment.

The family spent two years in Parma, Missouri, and then moved to Gray Ridge, Missouri. The kids felt instantly at home in the schools there. Jay William became the pastor of a little country church in Birds Corner. The town had a store and the Assembly of God church. Pastor Hawkins built a three-bedroom ranch-style parsonage there.

Heather, now a junior, liked Gray Ridge High School. Martha was in the seventh grade, Peter in fifth grade, Theodore in the third grade, and Jerome in the first grade. Veronica did not finish high school. She had fallen in love with a military man and was more interested in becoming a good wife and mother than in being a good student.

Martha played a flute in the band. Peter was popular among his peers. Theodore was a handsome little guy. Heather's best friend once said to him, "Teddy, you are so cute."

"Yes, I know!" he replied.

Heather was embarrassed and said, "Teddy, it's not nice to say that; just say thank you."

"But Heather," he said, "that's what everyone says to me."

By 1958 John was married to Lillie, and they had a four-year-old daughter, Patricia. Veronica was married to Ronald, and Cassandra was their newborn daughter. Heather had graduated from high school and had received a four-year scholarship to South East Missouri University. She also was hired as a resident assistant in her dormitory. Jay William was proud of all his children and of their accomplishments.

Jay William was called to be the pastor of the First Assembly of God Church in Bonne Terre, Missouri, in 1959. He and Nancy packed up their belongings once again and left with their three youngest sons and a daughter for the next place in God's plan.

CHAPTER 44

A T THE END of the school year in 1960, the Hawkins family was not happy in Bonne Terre, Missouri. The family had been there a little more than a year, but the place didn't seem right for any of them.

One afternoon Nancy asked Jay William, "Do you ever get homesick for Tennessee? Don't you think it would be nice to see our kinfolk more often at this stage of our lives? I think of my sister, Freddie Mae. She's been widowed for five years, and all her children are married and moved away. She was only fifteen years old when she ran off and married. My dad wouldn't let her visit until after she had children. I want to spend time with her. Can we go down and visit for a while? Perhaps we'll find out that's where God wants you to pastor."

"I could spend some time with Ernest, Catherine's only child," Jay William said. "He's now preaching the gospel himself. Yes, Nancy, I think you have a great idea. Let's pray about it. Perhaps God will open a door for us there. Let's talk to our children and get their take on this."

That night over a chicken and dumpling dinner, Jay William brought up Nancy's proposal. "Hey Martha, how would you like to live in Tennessee?" he asked. "Your mother and I were talking about checking out our possibilities down there."

"I'd like that very much," Martha said. "I find the people there friendlier and more forgiving than up here."

"What do you mean by that?" Jay William asked.

"Whenever I have one of my sick spells, people here make fun of me," she said, referring to her seizures. "It makes me feel bad. I can't help that I have those."

"I don't care for the schools here," Peter said.

Theodore laughed and said, "You can get along with anyone, Peter. Me, I tend to be shy."

"It makes no difference to me," young Jerome said. "As long as I have my brothers, I'm okay anywhere."

That weekend the family visited Sue and Jerome, Jay William's older brother, to see what they knew about housing and employment in the Covington area.

Jerome laughed loudly as he usually did. "Jay William, Sue and I were just talking last week about you. I told her that when you left in 1943, you were pastoring Detroit Assembly of God Church and working at the cotton mill. Both positions are available. I believe it's the night shift at the mill. There is a little house for sale on the street where you once lived. It's further up on Douglas Street than the one you and Wilma owned. It's across from the national guard armory.

"Betty's Grocery Store is about a half-block from the armory and is also for sale. Nancy and the boys could run it while you remodel and add on to that house. It's on a big lot right next door to John Smith's place. His house is beautifully kept."

"Why don't we take a trip into town to check out the house on Douglas?" Jay William said.

"Wait a minute," Nancy said. "I want to look at that grocery store."

Nancy got into the truck with Jay William and Jerome. She was excited about the possibility of having a store and making money.

The next month the Hawkins family moved into the house on Douglas Street, and the little neighborhood store became the Hawkins Grocery Store. Nancy loved the store and did a good business. Jay William decided not to return as pastor of the church and instead began a radio ministry. He also got a job as a contractor and built houses in low-income communities for the government.

Nancy was so friendly and personable that many customers who came into the store to purchase a sandwich and a soda wound up staying to discuss their problems with her. She eventually put a table and chairs on the concrete patio so people could sit and eat during those conversations. Schoolchildren also stopped by to chat with her, hoping for a free snack.

Ron Smith was the same age as Peter Hawkins and they became fast friends. Ron was a football star, but Peter didn't have time for sports; he helped his dad with construction cleanup after school.

Theodore was probably the most easygoing of the Hawkins children. He could do just about any job and do it well and seldom complained. Nancy and Jay William often counted on his help. He could do plumbing and mechanical work. He was also an electrician and was popular with the senior population for those reasons.

Peter graduated from high school in 1964 and went to work for McDonnell Douglas in St. Louis, Missouri. He loved his job, but the Vietnam War was raging and he went on active duty as a lieutenant following his graduation from officer school. He married Janice and had a son, Samuel.

The war was rough on him; he received a Purple Heart after surviving combat with the enemy, but he lost twenty of his men. Peter was hospitalized following the battle. He called on God for strength and God answered his plea.

Ron Smith lost his life in the first combat he saw. His father, John, came over to talk with Jay William.

"Tell me, Reverend Hawkins," he said. "Why did God allow my son to be killed while Peter lived? You have four sons while I had only one. You're a preacher, so tell me. Is God fair?"

"I can't speak for God," Jay William said, "but I know his

ways are higher than ours. I don't understand why this happened, but I know God is good. I don't understand how a loving God could have allowed his only Son to die for our sins, but he did. He wanted to make a way for us to go to heaven. I'm so sorry about Ron's death, and I pray God will comfort you and give you peace. Think about what an outstanding man Ron was and about his many friends. He made a mark in this town; that's for sure."

Mr. Smith never was able to cope with his son's death, and shortly after this conversation he died of a heart attack. Mrs. Smith remained good friends with Jay William and Nancy.

Jay William had twelve grandchildren by 1986. He enjoyed each one of them and made them feel loved. Most called him granddaddy. He enjoyed teaching them to count money and to make change. He taught them the importance of honesty and forgiveness and stressed seeing the best in people. "Praise, not flattery, is a good way to help friends," he always told them.

The grandchildren loved to hear Jay William deliver a sermon, and they seemed to understand his simple style of preaching the Word.

They found him to be a valuable source of wisdom and knowledge. During the early 1970s, grandson Ron wore his hair long, and he asked his granddaddy what he thought about that. "You always keep it clean and shiny," Jay William replied. "I know your generation likes long hair, and that's not a problem for me."

Nancy's health failed, and she was forced to sell her beloved store following open heart surgery. Jay William was concerned that the neighbors would not be able to buy fresh fruits and vegetables. He started two large vegetable gardens to accommodate their need.

He also put a refrigerator in a carport and kept canned soda there, charging ten cents per can. The neighbors placed their money in a jar. It was safe there, and the neighbors were grateful for the convenience.

CHAPTER 45

JAY WILLIAM NOTICED a peculiar smell coming from the area around a new plant that manufactured batteries. A green haze hung in the air, making it difficult to breathe. He called the plant and asked to speak to the manager. He told the manager about the strange odor coming from the plant. The manager asked him where he lived and why this bothered him.

"The odor is awful," Jay William said, "and I think the green haze is particularly dangerous to the elderly with lung disorders. My neighbor, Mr. Wilson, has COPD and is confined indoors because of the heavy air."

"Mr. Hawkins, you and all your friends on Douglas Street need to find something else to occupy your time besides calling the plant with complaints," Mr. Lowry, the manager, said before hanging up the phone.

The heavy, malodorous air was a problem almost every day. Jay William began to note the times and the dates of the occurrences. After hearing of a third death on his street, he decided to find out what had caused the deaths. All three people had died of respiratory failure.

Mrs. Grimes told him her husband's disease became worse after the plant opened.

Mr. Segar pointed to the plant and said, "That plant is ruining our quality of life. My wife would still be alive if not for the plant and its pollution."

Jay William felt compassion for his neighbors and prayed for wisdom in talking to Mr. Lowry about the deaths. He told him the plant had to find a way to make batteries without creating a foul odor in the neighborhood.

Mr. Lowry again responded rudely, saying, "Mr. Hawkins, stop stirring up trouble and get a life."

Jay William decided to talk to the people affected by the pollution. He wrote a petition:

> To the Environmental Protection Agency:
>
> We the people who have signed below wish to inform you that the Anderson Battery Company of Covington, Tennessee, has allowed pollution from its plant to cause dangerous respiratory problems in our neighborhood. We ask you to please intervene on our behalf.

Jay William walked to twenty-five houses, introducing himself by saying, "I'm Jay William Hawkins. I'm here is to find out if you've been affected in any way by the smell and the haze coming from the new battery plant. If you have, I ask you to sign this petition to the EPA. This is a government agency that forces manufacturers and other companies to control pollution to prevent harm to people's health. The battery manufacturing company is polluting our neighborhood with the terrible odor and the green haze from its plant. I can't make any promises, but I believe if enough of us sign this petition, we may convince the EPA to check on this plant and to make the company fix the problem. This is the only way I know to get the EPA's attention."

Every person Jay William contacted signed the petition. When he called to tell Mr. Lowry he had forty names on a petition to the EPA, the plant manager said, "Oh, you've been busy, but I'm not concerned."

"Sir, I'm just trying to protect my neighbors from harm to

their health," Jay William said. "I care about their quality of life. This is my reason for calling you. Perhaps you could contact them yourself and get their help in finding the source of the problem. I'll send this petition to Mr. Wessington, our congressman, in five days if you don't call me back."

Within two weeks the EPA was at the plant. The problem originated with the burning of waste products from the battery assembly line. The agency was able to help the company perform this operation more safely, preventing the pollution.

For several months following the EPA's visit to the plant, Mr. Lowry would call Jay William saying, "We've just destroyed the waste materials. Have you noticed any odor or haze coming from the plant? I know you'll tell me if you do." Jay William was happy to tell him there was no problem.

Later Mr. Lowry called to thank Jay William for his interest in helping the neighborhood. He told him the new method was saving the company money. Jay William became a friend to him.

The extra step Jay William took to help his friends and neighbors was a good thing for his community.

CHAPTER 46

AT SEVENTY-THREE, JAY William felt strongly that God was calling him to build a church in the countryside. This was a big task and would be done in two stages. First, a simple rectangular building would be constructed to use as the worship center.

The sanctuary, a much larger building, would be erected when the church grew. The worship center would then become a multipurpose building to be used for church events such as congregational meals, wedding receptions, and dinners after funerals.

Because of Jay William's advanced age, his children were very concerned about him undertaking such a major project. However, he was determined to move forward with this plan. "This is God's plan and I must follow God," he told them. Jay William purchased the land, applied for and got a building permit, and put up the worship center. He chose the name Westfield Assembly.

Only twenty-five or so people attended the first Sunday service. The church did not grow as quickly as Jay William had hoped. Some of the original members left, and the church could not meet all of its expenses. One deacon was greatly troubled about the situation.

Jay William's health began to decline, but he sincerely believed this was a church he had been led to begin, so he continued to preach to the few who still attended. He had one stroke and then another, and the church was closed temporarily.

Deacon McQueen came to his home and offered to purchase the deed to the church, promising to keep it open until Jay William's health improved. The pastor trusted the deacon would be honest enough to abide by this agreement.

When Jay William recovered and checked the status of the church, he was devastated to find the building had been converted into two apartments and was ready for tenants.

"This is God's house and you can't turn it into an apartment building," Jay William told Deacon McQueen.

"I did just that," the deacon said. "I paid you for the deed. If you want it back, you must pay me what I paid for it plus an additional $4,000. I put that much equity into it. But you don't have the money to cover that."

"If I get the money, will you sell it back to me?" Jay William asked. "After all, this place was built for the glory of God."

Deacon McQueen agreed, and Jay William mortgaged his home to make the deal.

The church was reopened, and with a new pastor it began to grow. Jay William died before the sanctuary was built. Today it is an active church and a great place to worship.

When Jay William's children attended a ten-year homecoming, they were surprised to see the church in its present state. It was beautiful and was filled with a sweet spirit of unity. Hope in God is never in vain.

EPILOGUE

THE REV. JAY William Hawkins had passed away five years earlier. Nancy and Heather were at his side when he died in his sleep. Suddenly he looked twenty years younger. The last prison bars were broken and he no longer suffered pain. The room suddenly became like holy ground and was alive with the presence of God. Nancy and Heather described the experience as awesome. Jay William had clung to his faith with the hope of glory, and he was ushered into heaven.

Jay William, who had lived his early years feeling unwanted and unloved, was now safely home. He had hope when hope seemed impossible. His faith in God was stronger than any challenges he encountered throughout his lifetime. He will be remembered by many as a man who lived his faith to the end. Jay William persevered in "hope to the end for the grace that is brought at the revelation of Jesus Christ" (1 Peter 1:13).

Three of his children attended the ten-year homecoming at the Westfield Assembly. As they drove into the church's parking lot, they were amazed at the lovely church with a majestic cross on it new steeple. "Isn't this beautiful?" Heather said to the others. "And to think God used our daddy to get it started."

"They used the blueprints Daddy made to build the second portion of the building," Theodore replied.

"Look at the number of people here," Jerome said. "Oh, Daddy would have been so happy to see the result of his obedience to God in building this church."

They walked into the church and saw in the entrance area a picture of their daddy with an engraved plaque under it saying, "Reverend Jay William Hawkins, Founder."

Joining the others, they were surprised to see long tables laden with beautifully arranged food, but they were too excited to eat. They just wanted to walk around and enjoy the atmosphere. Pastor Smith approached them and introduced himself. After learning they were children of Jay William, he thanked them for coming to the celebration.

"Thank you for completing the church," Heather replied. "It's so pretty. I wish my daddy were able to see it as it is today. He would be so happy."

The pastor said their daddy's life was one of tragedy and triumph. God is the same today as he was during Jay William's life. His love, mercy, and grace are available to you. "Trust in the Lord with all your heart and lean not to your own understanding. In all your ways acknowledge him; he will make your paths straight" (Proverbs 3:5–6).

Printed in the United States
By Bookmasters